S0-BZK-203

"I was right all along, wasn't I?" Abby asked.

"What do you mean?" Derek countered.

"Life is all dollars and cents to you." She looked at him.

His eyes glinted dangerously and he grabbed her shoulders. "You accuse me of seeing life only in dollars and cents. But you . . . you run away from life. You chase after lost causes that keep you from facing yourself, your loneliness. You look for things you can escape into."

She struggled against his hold, tears in her eyes. He gripped her tighter. "Sometimes, Abby, there is no escape."

Dear Reader,

Welcome to the Silhouette **Special Edition** experience! With your search for consistently satisfying reading in mind, every month the authors and editors of Silhouette **Special Edition** aim to offer you a stimulating blend of deep emotions and high romance.

The name Silhouette **Special Edition** and the distinctive arch on the cover represent a commitment—a commitment to bring you six sensitive, substantial novels each month. In the pages of a Silhouette **Special Edition**, compelling true-to-life characters face riveting emotional issues—and come out winners. All the authors in the series strive for depth, vividness and warmth in writing these stories of living and loving in today's world.

The result, we hope, is romance you can believe in. Deeply emotional, richly romantic, infinitely rewarding—that's the Silhouette **Special Edition** experience. Come share it with us—six times a month!

From all the authors and editors of Silhouette **Special Edition**,

Best wishes.

MAGGI CHARLES
Shadows on the Sand

Silhouette Special Edition

Published by Silhouette Books New York

America's Publisher of Contemporary Romance

To the windmills of America . . .
and the people who love them.

SILHOUETTE BOOKS
300 East 42nd St., New York, N.Y. 10017

SHADOWS ON THE SAND

Copyright © 1991 by Koehler Associates Ltd.

All rights reserved. Except for use in any review,
the reproduction or utilization of this work in
whole or in part in any form by any electronic,
mechanical or other means, now known or
hereafter invented, including xerography,
photocopying and recording, or in any information
storage or retrieval system, is forbidden without
the permission of Silhouette Books, 300 E. 42nd St.,
New York, N.Y. 10017

ISBN: 0-373-09647-X

First Silhouette Books printing January 1991

All the characters in this book are fictitious. Any
resemblance to actual persons, living or dead, is
purely coincidental.

®: Trademark used under license and
registered in the United States Patent and
Trademark Office and in other countries.

Printed in the U.S.A.

Books by Maggi Charles

Silhouette Special Edition

Love's Golden Shadow # 23
Love's Tender Trial # 45
The Mirror Image #158
That Special Sunday #258
Autumn Reckoning #269
Focus on Love #305
Yesterday's Tomorrow #336
Shadow on the Sun #362
The Star Seeker #381
Army Daughter #429
A Different Drummer #459
It Must be Magic #479
Diamond Moods #497
A Man of Mystery #520
The Snow Image #546
The Love Expert #575
Strictly for Hire #599
Shadows on the Sand #647

Silhouette Romance

Magic Crescendo #134

Silhouette Intimate Moments

Love's Other Language #90

MAGGI CHARLES

wrote her first novel when she was eight and sold her first short story when she was fifteen. Fiction has been her true love ever since. She has written forty-plus romance and mystery novels and many short stories. The former newspaper reporter has also published dozens of articles, many having to do with her favorite avocations, which include travel, music, antiques and gourmet cooking. Maggi was born and raised in New York City. Now she and her writer husband live in a sprawling old house on Cape Cod. They have two sons and two grandchildren.

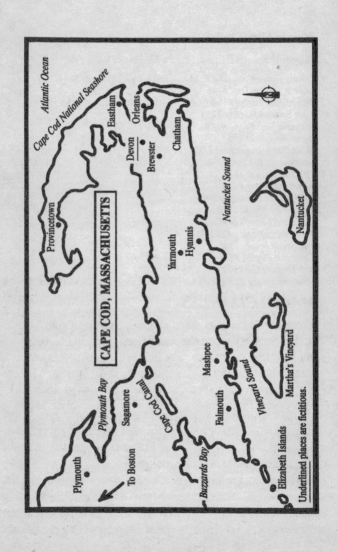

CAPE COD, MASSACHUSETTS

Atlantic Ocean

Cape Cod National Seashore

Eastham

Orleans

Devon

Brewster

Chatham

Provincetown

Nantucket Sound

Nantucket

Yarmouth

Hyannis

Plymouth Bay

Sagamore

Cape Cod Canal

Mashpee

Vineyard Sound

Martha's Vineyard

Falmouth

To Boston

Buzzards Bay

Plymouth

Elizabeth Islands

Underlined places are fictitious.

Chapter One

The yellow walls of the town hall lobby were covered with photo blowups of Devon's historic windmill. Banners blazed the message Save Our Mill. Long wooden tables heaped with bumper stickers, buttons and brochures flanked the wide oak staircase leading to the big auditorium on the second floor. The meeting was scheduled for eight o'clock. It was only a quarter past seven, but already people were streaming through the doors of the classic Victorian building.

Abigail Eldredge, watching the scene, experienced a mix of elation and apprehension. She was thrilled by this heartening response. She was also a little nervous at the thought of the speech she'd soon be making.

Tonight was her big chance, and it was so important that she put her message across. Many of the people heading upstairs to the auditorium were her staunch supporters, but others might feel differently about her advocating the town's purchase and preservation of the old mill. Those were the people she'd have to convince.

She glanced at her watch. The hands had inched to 7:19—still too early to go upstairs. She didn't want to enter the auditorium until the last minute. It would make her much too jittery to sit on the stage and face the audience while she waited for the meeting to begin.

Melanie Doane, handing out bumper stickers at one of the tables, caught Abby's eye and beckoned. Melanie, six months pregnant, looked like she needed help.

Abby crossed over to her. "What's up?"

There was a hint of desperation in Melanie's voice. "Could you take over for a minute?" She nodded in the direction of the rest rooms.

"Sure." Abby smiled.

She smoothed the skirt of her pink cotton dress, then took the chair Melanie had vacated. When Roscoe Chase approached, leaning heavily on his polished, silver-handled cane, Abby's smile widened and she felt a genuine flash of triumph. Roscoe was an authentic old Cape Codder, a vanishing breed. His family had lived on this narrow New England peninsula for more than two centuries. His making the effort to come out to a night meeting struck her as a good omen.

"Nice to see you, Mr. Chase," she greeted him. "How about a bumper sticker?"

Roscoe shook his head. "Don't do much driving these days, Abby," he said. "But I'll take one of those buttons there."

The buttons were bright blue, emblazoned with a white line drawing of the historic mill surrounded by the slogan Save Our Mill printed in red. Abby selected a button, then stood to lean over the table and pin it on Roscoe Chase's shirt pocket.

He patted her hand. "Keep up the good work, young lady," he encouraged her. He started to move along, then paused. "Almost forgot to tell you," he said. "Went out to the nursing home yesterday and had a talk with Clara Gould."

"Oh? How was she?"

Lately, Abby knew, Clara Gould—who owned the Devon Mill property—had been having bad days as well as good days. But then, Clara *was* ninety.

"Clara's failing," Roscoe reported regretfully. "But—" his tone brightened "—yesterday she was fine. We talked about this campaign of yours to have the town buy the mill. Clara says she knows she could sell the land to a developer for a mint more money then the town could pay. But she wants to see Devon Mill preserved as a memorial to Randolph."

"That's what she told me, too, Mr. Chase," Abby said with a nod. "You know how much the mill meant to her husband. To have it restored . . ."

Abby broke off as she became sharply aware of the man standing behind Roscoe—a tall, dark, strikingly handsome man whose forehead was creased in a frown. Obviously Roscoe was in his way.

Roscoe was chatting on about how long he'd known Clara and her late husband, about how they'd all gone to school together here in Devon, many decades ago. Abby didn't have the heart to hurry the old-timer, regardless of the impatient man towering practically on top of him.

The stranger, she realized, wasn't even listening to what Roscoe was saying. But he was having a disconcerting effect on Abby. As a woman, she couldn't help but react to him—he was unusually attractive. But as a civic activist in her hometown, she was instantly alarmed by his presence, to the point that imaginary warning bells began clanging in her head.

What was this man doing here?

One thing was certain. He seemed totally out of place. He looked like a man who'd just come from chairing a corporate board meeting and was on his way to another important rendezvous—an appointment that dealt with concerns way beyond anything that could come up at Devon Town Hall.

The mid-June evening was warm, and most people were dressed casually in cool, comfortable clothes. By contrast, this outsider was a fashion plate in a pale cream suit, a coffee-colored dress shirt and a bronze paisley tie. With his glinting gold-and-topaz cufflinks, polished brown Gucci shoes and stylishly coiffed dark hair, he looked like a model from the pages of an exclusive men's clothing catalogue. Except...he wasn't plastic. He gave the impression of power and command, attributes that would make him stand out even if he were not so good-looking.

Abby tried hard not to stare at him, but knew she wasn't succeeding. He reminded her of someone. A movie or TV star, maybe? No...she didn't think so. She tried to jog her memory, but drew a blank.

Roscoe said, "Guess I'm holding things up," and finally moved on.

The stranger came directly abreast of the table, and Abby actually flinched as she looked up into deep blue eyes that were as cold as the North Atlantic in December. She felt a chill sweep over her, plus an odd sense of impending disaster. She knew she was overreacting. Still, she could not repress the conviction that this handsome visitor's presence spelled trouble.

She forced a smile and made herself ask pleasantly, "Could I interest you in a brochure about our windmill? Or perhaps a button or bumper sticker?"

"A brochure," he replied coolly.

Abby proffered the pamphlet she had written about the mill, instinctively taking care to avoid hand contact with this disturbing man. His touch, she guessed, would be either fire or ice, and she didn't want to find out which.

He moved on, and it took all of Abby's willpower not to watch him climbing the stairs. It was a welcome diversion when Helen Rogers, the town librarian, stopped at the table to say that the library needed a new supply of brochures. "We only had a few left when we closed this afternoon," she told Abby.

"I'll bring a box over first thing in the morning."

Mrs. Rogers studied Abby closely. "Are you all right?" she asked. "You look as if something's upset you."

"I'm okay."

"You're not anxious about your speech, are you?"

"Not really." Abby straightened a stack of brochures and realized she'd nearly forgotten about the speech she would be making in just a few minutes. "I know exactly what I'm going to say, Helen."

"Then don't worry, dear. You'll do just fine."

Abby watched the librarian head up the steps, but her thoughts were still concentrated on the handsome stranger who'd loomed up on her scene like a storm front. She placed him in his late thirties, give or take a couple of years. And she imagined, involuntarily, a body that would match the attractiveness of his face and clothing. No doubt there'd be well-toned male muscles and a hard stomach concealed beneath those fine threads, plus all the other requisites for a sexy masculine physique.

Annoyed with herself, Abby blocked out that picture and concentrated, instead, on his negatives—the impatience he'd displayed standing behind gentle old Roscoe Chase, the aloof way he carried himself, the arrogant tone she'd heard when he'd agreed to take a brochure. Also, despite his good looks, his face was too stern, his expression uncompromising.

Melanie Doane came back and apologized, "Sorry I took so long. Seems like the bigger I get, the slower I get."

Abby smiled. "That's natural, isn't it?"

"I guess so. This is my third pregnancy, but they've all been different."

Abby relinquished the chair to Melanie, then glanced at her watch again. A quarter to eight. Fifteen minutes to go. She visited the rest room briefly, and was standing against the lobby's yellow wall going over her typewritten speech when she saw Greg Nickerson come in. Quickly she intercepted him. Right now, she needed her best friend's moral support. She noted, though, that Greg appeared tired. His thin face was strained, and his light brown hair looked like he'd been plowing it with his fingers.

"Hey, are you okay?" she asked.

"I'm fine," Greg said. "But Bobby was complaining of a stomachache when I left." Bobby, Greg's nine-year-old son, was like a nephew to Abby, just as Greg was like a brother.

"Think it's anything serious?"

"Frankly I think Bobby was faking. He doesn't like having Mrs. Baker as a sitter. Says all she does is doze off and snore when they're watching TV. I would have called Melanie," he added, waving a hello to Abby's volunteer, "but you snagged her first."

"The afternoons are working out okay?" Abby suggested, referring to the fact that Bobby spent daytimes at the Doane house playing with Melanie's two young sons.

"So far, so good." Greg gazed around the lobby, taking in the people crowding up the staircase. "Great turnout," he complimented her. "Looks like you're going to have standing room only. Way to go."

"Thanks," Abby said, then added, "look, Greg, maybe Bobby really is sick. Perhaps you should go home."

"And miss hearing you speak? Not a chance. Besides, Mrs. Baker has the number here if there's a problem. Which there won't be."

"You're sure?"

"I'm sure. Come on, Abby, let's go upstairs. It's about that time."

"Yes, I guess it is."

Greg gripped her hands. "You're not getting cold feet, are you?"

Her smile was weak. "My feet have felt warmer."

"Look, you'll do fine. Everyone's behind you."

"Everyone?"

"Okay, almost everyone."

"I hope so," Abby murmured. Her mind was suddenly swamped with the memory of the handsome, dark-haired man whose cold blue eyes and stern expression had struck her so adversely. "Greg?" she ventured.

"Yes?"

She hesitated, then shrugged. "Nothing."

She'd never been able to fool Greg, and she couldn't now. "Out with it," he commanded. "What's bugging you?"

"There's a man here . . . who doesn't belong here."

She couldn't blame Greg for looking puzzled as he asked, "Who doesn't belong here?"

"Someone I've never seen before. A stranger."

Greg chuckled. "These days, Devon is full of strangers. People who've retired here. Wealthy property owners who only show up for a couple of weeks a year. Absentee landlords. Not to mention the summer crowd that takes over Devon Heights." He shook his head. "Once, I knew practically everyone in town—"

"This man was . . . different," Abby cut in, then tried to describe the man whose disturbing image wouldn't go away. "Tall with dark hair, very handsome, very well dressed..." She finished lamely, "You'll spot him, Greg. He stands out."

Greg's eyes narrowed. "What should I do if I spot him?"

"Try to find out who he is."

"I'll do my best. Now come on, let's go."

Upstairs, Abby discovered the auditorium was full. As Greg had predicted, there was standing room only. The late arrivals were edging down the side aisles to take up positions against the walls. The seats in the balcony were occupied, too.

Abby said, "You should have come ahead without me so you could have gotten a seat."

"My problem, not yours." He gave her a nudge toward the stage and urged, "Go on. You'll do great."

Abby squared her shoulders, started down the center aisle and felt like she was being carried along by a wave of goodwill, until she was almost to the stage. Then she faltered.

The tall stranger had taken a second-row aisle seat, and the brief, dark glance he accorded Abby as she walked by sent cold chills up her spine. It took nerve to keep moving forward, climb the steps to the stage and approach the folding metal seats that had been set up for Devon's town officials.

George Cobb, chairman of the board of selectmen, was fidgeting with the microphone on the lectern placed out in front of the chairs. He paused to grin at Abby, then gave her his stamp of approval, saying quietly, "You really got 'em to turn out for this. When I come up for reelection, how about handling my campaign?"

That forced a laugh out of her. "You'd trust me with your political future, George?"

"Are you kidding? I wish we could get turnouts like this at town meetings."

"Well," Abby said soberly, "I only hope everyone's on my side. I know you are, George...."

"And the other selectmen. And the finance committee."

"Even so, the issue's not cut-and-dried. The feedback I get tonight will be a barometer of how the vote will go when the article comes up at the special town meeting. Maybe..."

The rest of what she'd been going to say froze in her throat as, glancing out over the audience, Abby inadvertently zeroed in on the handsome stranger. He was looking right at her, his gaze steady, void of expression.

If only he'd smile, Abby thought to herself.

"Who's that man in the second row?" she asked George Cobb, her voice low.

The selectman didn't look up, didn't need a further description to know whom Abby was referring to. "I wondered the moment I saw him," he admitted. "Kind of stands out, doesn't he? I've never seen him around town before."

"Neither have I, which makes me wonder why he's here."

"A reporter, maybe, for one of the Boston papers?"

"He doesn't look like a reporter, George."

"No, I guess he doesn't."

There was no chance to pursue the subject further. Other town officials were coming up on stage and taking seats, and Abby joined them. With everyone accounted for, George Cobb glanced at his watch, saw it was five minutes past eight and called the meeting to order.

First, he welcomed the audience and complimented them for a "fine showing of public spirit." Always the politician, George. Next, he made a few pleasant quips, then got down to business by presenting Abigail Eldredge.

"Abby is a native of Devon," he began. "She's lived here all her life, not counting four years she spent at the University of Massachusetts in Amherst. I'd say Abby's about as dedicated to this town's welfare as anyone could possibly be. She's president of the historical society, chairman of the conservation commission, and a third-grade teacher at Devon Elementary School."

George Cobb paused, then went on, "Abby's seen the great changes that have taken place on Cape Cod over the past twenty-five years. She's witnessed the transformation of sleepy, oceanside villages into thriving, populated communities. She's watched the farmhouses and fields give way to shopping malls, parking lots and condos.

"Like most of us, Abby has applauded some of the changes, but deplored others. She's hated seeing rustic old homes, many dating back before the American Revolution, razed and replaced by homes more geared to suburbia. She's hated seeing acre upon acre of precious woodland and marshland bulldozed and developed, solely for profit. She's hated seeing historic structures like Devon Mill wiped off the shrinking Cape Cod landscape.

"You could say Abby has a special interest in Devon Mill, because the land on which it stands once belonged to her ancestors. But suppose I let her tell you about that herself. Ladies and gentlemen . . . it's my pleasure to present Abigail Eldredge."

Abby stood to move toward the podium, but was halted by an ovation she'd not expected. Here and there, people actually got to their feet to applaud her, their tribute an ego boost she badly needed. The handsome stranger, she noted, sat perfectly still. Watching her, waiting.

It took a minute for the big auditorium to quiet down, and Abby used that breathing space to take the podium and focus her attention on the first lines of her speech. She prepared herself to speak clearly, confidently and with conviction—despite the unnerving presence of the man in the second row.

In a strong, steady voice, she began, "The use of wind as a means of harnessing power goes back into history's more obscure reaches. In the early days, from the pre-Revolutionary period to the end of the last century, windmills were not merely scenic structures set against the horizon as a backdrop for souvenir snapshots. They were vital parts of everyday life."

Gathering momentum, she continued, "Here on Cape Cod, windmills often did quadruple duty. They were used as gristmills, as sawmills, to pump water and to aid in the processing of salt. Devon Mill, built high on a bluff overlooking Cape Cod Bay, played a major role in the history of our town. To give just one example of its importance—during the Civil War, the mill was constantly busy grinding local grain that was transported to Boston by ship and sold to the government. That grain became a staple in the Union army's diet."

Abby paused for breath and tried to avoid the steady gaze of the dark-haired stranger. The way he was looking at her was making her come close to forgetting what she wanted to say. Briefly she glanced at her text.

"In the eighteenth and nineteenth centuries, there were dozens of mills on the Cape," she said. "A few have survived, but the vast majority have disappeared. Of the survivors, most have been moved from their original locations. Devon Mill is probably the only Cape Cod windmill that remains on the spot where it was originally constructed. And there's a very special significance to that.

"But for Devon Mill, the British might have captured our town in the War of 1812. The miller, at that time, was hard at work one day fixing the mill's cloth sails when, from his high vantage point, he saw enemy boats approaching. He immediately summoned his sons, who went forth to warn the townspeople not only here in Devon, but over in Orleans and up in Brewster, as well. As a result, one British landing party was repulsed at Snow Harbor here in Devon, and another at Rock Harbor in Orleans.

"Today, a handful of Cape Cod mills still operate on a part-time basis. The gristmills in Sandwich and Brewster and the windmill in Eastham are beautifully preserved, working examples of our history. Visitors can observe grain being ground and purchase packets of what I like to call delicious nostalgia.

"As Mr. Cobb said in his introductory remarks," she told her audience, "too much of what once made Cape Cod so unique, so charming, has been lost in the name of progress. Progress is inevitable. We all know that. But bulldozing history into oblivion is something else entirely, and that's what will surely happen to Devon Mill, unless we act to prevent it."

Abby drew a deep breath. "Until about ten years ago, Randolph Gould worked the mill every summer day, whenever the wind was right. It is my great hope," she concluded, "that next summer we'll start that custom again. It is my hope, and the hope of all of us who have worked on the Save Our Mill campaign, that the citizens of Devon will vote favorably at the upcoming special town meeting on July 2 to acquire Clara Gould's twelve-acre property. I urge all of you to attend the meeting, to vote yes on the acquisition of the mill site, and thus take the first step toward preserving an irreplacable piece of our history.''

When Derek Van Heusen heard Abby Eldredge talk about "bulldozing history into oblivion," he had the distinct feeling she was addressing her remarks directly at him.

Impossible, of course. She had no idea who he was ... so far. Before much longer, in a matter of days at most, she would find out his identity, as well as his reason for being in Devon. That reason would undermine everything she was trying to do, and incur her bitter fury.

He'd had no idea who she was when he had sauntered up to her table in the lobby downstairs. So when she'd stepped up on the stage to be introduced as Abigail Eldredge, it had surprised the hell out of him.

In place of the little old lady he'd expected to hear spouting off about a silly, sentimental cause, he was viewing an extremely attractive young woman who was making history come alive for her captivated audience as she gave an impassioned yet thoroughly professional presentation.

Abigail Eldredge's pretty pink dress emphasized her graceful feminine curves in just the right way. Her rich chestnut hair—which should have been at war with the color of her dress, but somehow wasn't—tumbled about her shoulders in thick waves, framing a piquant face that reminded Derek of Audrey Hepburn in *Breakfast at Tiffany's*. Her low-pitched, melodious voice was easy to listen to. And her body language, whether she realized it or not, was extremely sensuous.

Her appeal went beyond the physical, though. Her convictions were coming through to her audience and making a major impact. Derek didn't doubt that Ms. Eldredge believed in everything she was saying. Still, it astonished him to think that anyone could put such undiluted zeal into an attempt to preserve for posterity what amounted to little more than a heap of scrap lumber.

All right . . . admittedly, he'd never been a sentimentalist. An object was an object. A building was a building. Property was property. When he wanted something, he bought it. When he didn't want something, he sold it. Transactions, deals and takeovers were the stuff of which real life was made. He failed to understand how anyone could become so impassioned by a two-hundred-year-old dilapidated windmill.

True, he'd never given much thought to windmills. So he'd been skeptical when Tom Channing, his vice president in charge of the newly opened Boston office, had phoned him at the company's San Francisco headquarters to say that buying the mill property in Devon—a deal that was already in the works—might be a serious mistake. If word got out that the old mill would be destroyed to make room for a modern resort complex, they would be in for strong, potentially damaging, local opposition.

Derek's immediate reaction had been to scoff. In the twelve short years since he'd founded Van Heusen Inc., twenty Voyagers had been built—in California, Arizona, Colorado, the Caribbean and on Florida's Gulf Coast. None had been opposed, and all were successful. Now it was time to move into New England, to build four new Voyagers—the first of which was slated for Devon. That was Derek's scenario, and he seldom if ever deviated from a scenario once he'd mapped it out.

Abigail Eldredge had finished her speech with a confident ''Thank you'' and was returning to her seat when the applause started. In seconds, Derek felt like he was surrounded by a sea of clapping hands. A few enthusiasts actually whistled and cheered.

Reluctantly, to avoid standing out even more than he already did, Derek went through the gesture of slapping one hand against the other.

Was it his imagination? Derek wondered uneasily. Or was Abby Eldredge staring directly at him as he dutifully applauded? Suddenly he felt not only out of place, but uncomfortable.

Derek pushed those speculative thoughts from his mind, rose from his seat and strode up the aisle toward the exit without looking back.

Tomorrow would be time enough to deal with Abigail Eldredge. A chore that—now that he'd seen her—he didn't relish.

Chapter Two

Abby stepped down from the stage and was engulfed by well-wishers. Her hand was pumped so many times she felt like her wrist bones were dissolving. Also, she was limp all over. She'd put everything she had into her presentation. Not easy, when all the while she was distracted by the chilling presence of the man in the second row.

She'd found it impossible to keep her eyes from straying in his direction. And each time they did, she'd met a cool, impassive gaze that set imaginary moths fluttering around inside her. Regardless of his outward inscrutability, she knew this man was paying strict attention to what she was saying. His intensity and concentration came through, and puzzled her.

Now, as people continued to congratulate her, Abby peered over shoulders and tried to spot him, but to no avail. Evidently he'd already left the auditorium.

Finally the crowd thinned. Greg broke away from a group of friends and came over to ask, "Ready to leave?"

"More than ready."

Halfway up the aisle, Greg said, "Incidentally I spotted your stranger easily enough. And one of those guys I was just talking to recognized him."

Abby stopped short. "I kept thinking he looked familiar. Who was he?"

"Derek Van Heusen. You've heard of him?"

Derek Van Heusen.

Yes, she'd heard of him. A hotel mogul, if her memory served her correctly. Yes, that was it. Derek Van Heusen owned the Voyager Resorts. Abby recalled seeing his picture in *People* magazine awhile back, above a blurb naming him one of "American's most mysterious—and most eligible—young entrepreneurs." There was mention of his resort complexes on the West Coast, in the Caribbean and elsewhere, and mention of the fortune he'd accumulated while still in his early thirties. Other than that, the story about Van Heusen Inc.'s founder and CEO hadn't been too informative. Evidently he kept a very low profile.

Abby's warning bells started clanging again. Derek Van Heusen would have only one reason for making an appearance in Devon. Obviously he was checking out a location for a Cape Cod Voyager. His presence at the meeting meant his target might very well be Devon Mill—or more precisely, the twelve bluff-top acres the windmill was centered upon.

"Thank God Clara Gould cares more about a memorial to her husband than she does about money."

Abby didn't realize she'd mumbled her thoughts aloud until Greg asked, "What was that you said?"

"It doesn't matter, Greg. Look, I'm bushed. Let's get out of here, okay?"

"Sure."

They were at the bottom of the stairs when Abby groaned. "I should pack up the promotion stuff," she said. "The posters can stay on the walls, but I can't leave all these brochures and buttons lying around."

"I'll handle it," Greg told her. "Go home and get some rest. I'll drop everything off at your place tomorrow."

"No, I'll help. Just give me a minute to unwind."

Abby walked across the lobby and took a peek outside. The last glow of sunset was coloring the evening sky, and people were still clustered in groups, talking animatedly. But it was two men in the parking lot who caught her attention—Derek Van Heusen and Gordon Ryder, Clara Gould's nephew.

"Greg!" she urged. "Come here."

In seconds, he was at her side, following her gaze.

"Well, well," he muttered. "Strange bedfellows, wouldn't you say?"

"Too strange," Abby decided, and immediately started to worry. "I don't trust Gordon. I've never liked him. Not even when we were in high school."

"No one liked Gordon back in high school," Greg reminded her. "But that was a long time ago. People change."

"Do they? Sometimes I wonder. Gordon's probably just as greedy now as he was then. He always wanted everything for nothing."

"Those are pretty harsh words, Miss Eldredge," Greg protested. "Innocent until proven guilty, remember?"

"Maybe," Abby conceded. "But...this bothers me. I wonder how much influence Gordon has on Clara?"

"What does that have to do with anything?"

"Are you kidding? It has everything to do with *everything*."

"Meaning?"

"Meaning, I spoke with Roscoe Chase before the meeting tonight. He visited Clara at Devon Manor yesterday, and they talked about the mill. She knows a developer would pay her many times what the town could pay for her property."

"So?"

Abby sighed. "When Clara dies, Greg, Gordon will inherit her estate. He's her only relative."

"So what if he is?" Greg reasoned. "Clara fully endorses the idea of the town buying her place, right? Wasn't she the first person to sign your petition to have the mill article included in the special town meeting warrant?"

"You were the first. Clara was second."

"Then what are you worried about? Clara's not the type to change her mind. I'd bank on that."

"I hope you're right."

Abby began packing up the Save Our Mill campaign materials, haunted by the prospect of running into Derek Van Heusen or Gordon Ryder in the parking lot. She was thankful there was no sign of either man when she and Greg headed outside.

With the last of the cartons stashed in her bright yellow Volkswagen, she and Greg lingered, catching their breaths.

Leaning against the fender of his pickup truck, Greg said, "Abby, stop worrying about Van Heusen. Maybe he's just thinking about buying a summer home on the Cape."

"Somehow, I don't think so."

"Whatever, the town's on your side."

"I hope so." Despite the reception she'd received, doubt still nudged. "Taxpayers can get nervous when they're asked to spend half a million dollars, Greg. God, I wish the vote had been tonight instead of two weeks from now."

"The time'll pass before you know it."

"That reminds me. I need an estimate from you."

"An estimate? For what?"

"For restoring the mill."

"Me? Restore the mill?"

Abby laughed at Greg's surprise and teased, "You *are* a custom carpenter, aren't you?"

"Yes, but..."

Sobering, Abby explained, "Phase one, Greg, is buying the mill site. Phase two is the actual restoration of the mill, plus creating a park around it. People will want to know what the restoration's going to cost, and where that money's going to come from."

"You're planning fund-raising events to handle the restoration, right?"

Abby nodded. "I want to assure the taxpayers they'll only be liable for the money needed to acquire the property. Do you suppose you could get away from work for a while tomorrow and meet me out at the mill? Look it over and give me an estimate?"

"Sure," Greg said. "What time?"

"Whatever's best for you."

"Nine o'clock. That too early?"

"Of course not."

Greg gave Abby an affectionate pat on the shoulder and hoisted himself up into the pickup's cab.

"Thanks for doing my detective work for me. About Derek Van Heusen, that is," Abby said.

"Just don't lose any sleep over him, okay?"

"I'll sleep like a rock."

Abby watched Greg drive off and realized anew how much he meant to her. They were like brother and sister— that close and that special. They'd been through a lot together, weathered intense, personal storms. The result was a deep, caring friendship bound to last forever.

She drove along Main Street, then headed onto Beach Road toward East Devon, where she lived. All the while, she reviewed everything that had happened tonight and tried to come to a sensible conclusion.

Maybe Greg was right. Maybe Derek Van Heusen wasn't a threat. Maybe his presence at the meeting had been a strange coincidence. He could be a man on vacation looking for something to do. Or a prospective summer home buyer, checking things out.

She made a face at the moon.

Who was she kidding?

Derek noticed the sandy-haired man in the blue suit standing near the bottom of the stairs in the town hall lobby, but paid no attention to him. He brushed by him, headed outside and was halfway to the parking lot when he heard his name called.

"Mr. Van Heusen?"

Jolted, he stopped. Only Tom Channing, his top man in Boston, and Andy Bennett, the field rep who'd found the mill tract, knew he was in Devon. Bennett was supposed to have attended the meeting tonight. At the last minute, Derek had decided to take over. He wanted to see both the Gould property and Abigail Eldredge firsthand.

Now he was glad he'd made the trip to Devon—and annoyed as well, because Bennett had certainly missed the boat in his preliminary investigation of Abby Eldredge. The "little old lady" was a beautiful young woman. The sentimental cause was a helluva lot more than that. If the twelve prime waterfront acres Bennett had found for the Cape Voyager were less than ideal, he was going to back off from a potential can of worms.

Derek turned, as the man in the blue suit repeated his name. "Mr. Van Heusen?"

"Yes."

"My name's Gordon Ryder."

Derek's eyes narrowed. So this was Ryder, the man who'd been refusing Van Heusen Inc.'s three-million-dollar offer for the Devon Mill property, and was holding out for a million more. Derek appraised Ryder, guessed his height at an even six feet, three inches shorter than himself. He was thin, not bad-looking. But he presented the kind of deferential manner that automatically grated on Derek.

"I expected to see Mr. Bennett here," Ryder said.

"Bennett's in Boston. I decided to attend the meeting myself."

Derek caught the uneasiness in Ryder's light eyes. The man seemed unsure of himself. Strange for someone who, according to the Boston office, had been unwilling to budge a financial inch.

"What can I do for you, Mr. Ryder?" he asked.

Ryder cleared his throat, sidestepped an answer. "Could I interest you in a drink?" he suggested. "There's a lounge just up the street."

"Not tonight, thank you."

"You're staying over in Devon?"

Derek hesitated. That was really none of Ryder's business. Grudgingly he admitted, "Yes."

"I think it would be to our mutual advantage to talk, Mr. Van Heusen. Perhaps we could meet for lunch tomorrow?"

So, Gordon Ryder wanted to negotiate. Derek found that interesting. Abigail Eldredge's speech evidently had Ryder, who'd been so confident of getting the price he wanted, thinking second thoughts, beginning to run scared.

Maybe I owe Abby Eldredge a thank you. The idea was amusing. *Maybe she just saved me a million bucks.*

"Could we meet for lunch?" Ryder suggested again.

Derek showed no trace of a smile. He started toward the blue Thunderbird he'd rented, then turned back. "I'm at the

Oceanside Motel," he said. "Give me a call in the morning, early. I'll let you know then if that's possible."

Abby's Volkswagen bumped down the sandy lane that led to her house, a winterized summer cottage nestled in a grove of pines. As she pulled to a stop, her black Lab streaked around the corner of the house, barking excitedly.

"Hello there, Captain," she greeted him, bending to rub his silky ears. "Bet you're hungry, right?"

The dog communicated his answer with frantic tail wagging as he galloped toward the moonlight-splashed front door of the cottage. Inside, Abby made for the kitchen, found a box of dog biscuits and gave Captain his treat. Then, as he crunched away, she almost started to tell him about Derek Van Heusen, but brought herself up short.

It was one thing to talk to Captain. It was something else to hold long conversations with him, complete with questions and conjectures. Such was a peril of living alone. No one to talk to.

She'd been living by herself for six years—since Ken, her husband, had run off with Greg's wife, Sally. It had caused quite a stir in Devon, led to rumors about Greg and herself that were totally untrue. Time, thank God, had smoothed things out. Yet Abby still wasn't entirely comfortable with solitude. Sometimes the house seemed so empty. Especially in summer, when she didn't have the daily diversion of settling in behind a desk and teaching a classroom full of capricious, lovable third-graders.

Funny...by the time June rolled around she couldn't wait to get out of school. She'd be champing at the bit for her vacation, loaded with ideas for summer projects. But soon the lonely void the kids unwittingly filled would start to creep in. It always happened that way, and this summer would probably be the same.

She would have asked Greg back for coffee or a beer if Bobby hadn't been sick. Then she could have fully vented her fears about Derek Van Heusen's presence in Devon and convinced Greg that she had real cause to be worried.

As it was, Derek Van Heusen had made a strong impact on her. During their brief encounter in the town hall lobby, Abby had felt an instant sexual chemistry flow between them. Her imagination? No, there'd been an undercurrent running beneath Van Heusen's cool exterior and her politeness—an unsettling undercurrent that flowed stronger every time she looked his way while she spoke, an attraction that came close to pushing aside her apprehensions. But having learned who he was, she knew how right those initial warning bells had been.

Abby brewed herself a cup of herbal tea and glanced through the Cape's daily paper. There was an item about tonight's meeting buried on an inside page. The Devon Mill issue wasn't that big a deal except in Devon itself, which made her wonder how Derek Van Heusen had found out about the meeting.

Probably, she decided, from Gordon Ryder.

Had Gordon changed?

He'd been a real jerk as a teenager, subjecting literally every girl in school to his unwanted passes and riding around Devon in his aunt's convertible like he owned the town. He had been equally unpopular with the boys. He'd been cocky, Abby recalled, conceited with nothing to be conceited about.

Gordon had left Devon after high school, done a stint in the army, then had started a real estate business in Falmouth up at the other end of the Cape. Nowadays he made the forty-mile drive to Devon only to check on his ailing aunt. But that, according to Clara, wasn't too often.

"Gordon," she'd proudly explained to Abby one day, "is a very busy man."

He'd made the drive tonight, though.

The urge to talk to someone about all of this was so strong that Abby nearly reached for the phone and dialed Greg. At the last second, she resisted. It was a quarter past ten. Greg was a classic early-to-bed, early-to-rise person. He was probably already asleep.

She thought about how much she and Greg had been through together, about how much she depended on Greg's friendship, about the project she'd taken on. It would be so great if the whole thing went through, if the town bought Clara Gould's twelve acres and Greg restored the mill.

But then Derek Van Heusen's stern, handsome face popped into her mind, like a large stop sign at the edge of a cliff.

Derek drove from the town hall directly to the Oceanside Motel where Tom Channing had booked a room for him. He got a glass from the bathroom, splashed some Scotch over ice, then reached for the phone and dialed Channing's home number.

He had interviewed Channing for the Boston job six months ago at the San Francisco headquarters. At that time, he was favorably impressed, and his initial impression still stood after spending Sunday evening, most of Monday, and most of today, in the man's company.

Channing had done his homework. He was well-prepared for his boss's visit east. He'd invited Derek to stay with his wife and himself in their Westwood home, but Derek preferred the privacy of a Boston hotel, so Channing had reserved accommodations for him at the Four Seasons.

Their subsequent meetings at Van Heusen Inc.'s New England headquarters—an impressive suite of offices in a new skyscraper overlooking Boston Harbor—were productive. The four field representatives who'd been scouting New England for proposed Voyager complexes gave detailed reports. Sheila Casey, who headed the Boston architectural firm Channing highly recommended, was also present. She was an attractive, thirtyish blonde, but it was her portfolio that had grabbed Derek's attention. That, and the preliminary renderings she'd done for each of the proposed Voyager projects.

"The Cape, the Berkshires, northern New Hampshire and coastal Maine," she'd told Derek. "Four different areas, four different concepts for you to consider."

All in all, Tom Channing had done well, Derek conceded, listening as the phone rang at the other end of the line. But he'd failed in one respect—rather, his man Bennett had failed.

Channing's wife answered.

"Louise? Derek Van Heusen. Put Tom on, will you please?"

A moment later, Derek asked, "Tom? What can you tell me about Abigail Eldredge? Is there something you haven't given me?"

"I went by Bennett's report, Mr. Van Heusen. Obviously her plans for the mill tract are entirely counter to ours. Unfortunately for her, they're not about to become reality."

"Maybe they are, Tom. At the meeting tonight, Miss Eldredge came across as an activist with considerable clout. She's young, she's forceful, she sold her audience. If the people at the town hall represented a majority of Devon taxpayers, I'd say she convinced them their old windmill is worth saving."

The coolness of Derek's tone would have intimidated many of his employees. But one thing he liked about his Boston VP—the man didn't back down easily.

"I can't buy that, Mr. Van Heusen," Channing said crisply. "Andy Bennett is a good man. If he'd felt Abigail Eldredge was a real threat to the project, he'd have said so immediately."

"I was there," Derek replied. "I heard her speak, and I'm concerned. I personally think Bennett underestimated this woman. I want background on her, everything there is to know. As fast as possible."

"I'll get on it first thing in the morning," Channing promised. "But . . . I'll admit I'm puzzled. There's nothing this Eldredge woman could do to block the sale unless Mr. Ryder gets a better offer from the town of Devon. And that won't happen."

"That's another thing," Derek said. "Ryder was at the meeting tonight. He approached me afterward. Says he wants to talk, suggested lunch tomorrow. I stalled."

"Maybe he's ready to bend."

"That would expedite matters considerably. Three million was our highest offer to date, right?"

"A quarter million per acre, fair market value."

"It'll certainly make Ryder rich overnight."

"Yes, which is why I've wondered why he's held out. The real estate market has been slow for a long time. Mr. Ryder certainly knows that, being in the business."

"True," Derek agreed. "Okay, I'll see what he has to say. My gut feeling is he'll come down in his price."

"He's been adamant."

"I know that. But tonight he acted like a man who's suddenly discovered he's standing on shaky ground. I can see why. If he doesn't consummate a deal with us before the second of July, he stands to lose a helluva lot of money."

"The date of Devon's special town meeting?"

"That's right. People will be asked to appropriate five-hundred-thousand to purchase the Gould property . . . with the idea of restoring the mill and turning the grounds into a park.''

Derek frowned. "Are you sure Ryder has a bona fide power of attorney for his aunt?''

"Absolutely. I had our legal staff check that out as soon as Mr. Ryder approached us with his offer.''

"Why did the old lady gave him her power of attorney?''

"Because she's ninety, living in a nursing home and apparently isn't up to handling her affairs.''

"She's mentally incompetent?''

"Not incompetent, no,'' Channing said. "She's just old, that's all. Bennett visited her at the nursing home, and she fell asleep while he was talking with her.''

"He didn't discuss Ryder and the power of attorney with her, did he?''

"No, definitely not. We didn't think that would be wise. He invented a pretext for his visit. Told Mrs. Gould he was looking for a rest home for his mother, who used to summer in Devon. Said Mrs. Gould's name had been given to him as a possible reference for Devon Manor. As far as she knew, Andy was just a young man concerned about his mother.''

"Sounds reasonable.''

Derek considered the situation, came to a decision. "Get Bennett and the other field reps together tomorrow and hose them down a bit. Have them do their reports over, check out each community we're interested in as thoroughly as possible. If any more Abigail Eldredges surface, I want complete investigations. No more surprises.''

"Will do.''

"That's about it, Tom. After I've talked to Ryder and found out what he's got up his sleeve, I'll get in touch. In the morning, I'm going to head over to the mill site, check it out myself. I want to be certain it's everything Bennett says it is. If that proves out, there shouldn't be any problems.''

"What about Miss Eldredge?"

"Well, if Ryder becomes reasonable about price, I may approach her myself and defuse any potential negative repercussions. Get me her background ASAP. We need to know what's in this for her.''

As he signed off, Derek visualized Abigail Eldredge giving her presentation in front of the packed auditorium. Was she really as unselfishly civic-minded as she appeared? Did she picture herself as a small-town heroine, a late-twentieth-century Joan of Arc? Was public adulation, of which she'd received a great deal tonight, all she was looking for? Or were her motives more complex?

Profit was the motive Derek knew best. But unless there was something here he was completely blind to, profit could hardly be the motive behind Abby Eldredge's crusade.

He finished the melted-down Scotch and poured himself another drink. It was a long time since he'd been personally involved in one of the Voyager projects at a local level. But moving into New England was a big step, and it had to go right.

He stretched, and realized this on-the-scene type of action felt good. It was a welcome change from being the man at the top. High up in a plush cocoon of an office overlooking San Francisco Bay, he was far removed from the details, the pros and cons, of a project.

Glass in hand, he strolled outside onto the balcony of his second-floor room. The motel was built on a grassy hill that sloped down to Devon's prime ocean beach. Illuminated by the nearly full moon were undulating dunes, and beyond, the dark Atlantic sparkled with moon motes.

Too bad this property and a few adjacent acres weren't for sale, he reflected. But, even if they were, it would do him no good where building a Voyager was concerned. This stretch of Devon's oceanside was within the borders of the Cape Cod National Seashore. Thus, further construction was prohibited. The government owned much of the best land on the Outer Cape, and the Department of Interior—which governed the Seashore—frowned on development even more than Abigail Eldredge did.

Abigail Eldredge. Derek could see how she'd swept people to her side, convinced them that her thinking was right. She was an attractive woman—a very sexy, desirable woman. When she'd given him that brochure about the mill, an initial, sensual thrust had propelled itself between them.

Miss Eldredge had shown no visible reaction to that...force. Yet, thinking about the way she'd looked at him, remembering how her eyes had singled him out several times during her speech, Derek was willing to swear she'd been as inwardly swayed as he'd been.

Too bad he couldn't get her on his side, make her see that building a Voyager Resort in Devon would be the best thing that had happened to the town in a long, long time. But that wasn't about to happen.

Abigail Eldredge had a cause. And, having seen her in action tonight, Derek was sure she'd hang tough till the bitter end.

Chapter Three

Abby drove along Mill Bluff Road and turned onto Mill Lane, the private road that bisected Clara Gould's twelve acres and ended in a sandy circular loop. She passed the crumbling stone steps that climbed the bluff on the windmill side of the loop and, out of habit, pulled into the driveway of the Gould homestead.

Memories swept over her, gentle memories edged with sadness. As a child, she'd come here many times with her grandmother to have tea with Clara Gould. In recent years, she'd often visited Clara by herself, listening while Clara reminisced about growing up in Devon, marrying Randolph and settling into his family's old home. Clara's recollections spanned the better part of a century. To Abby, she was not only a wonderful person, she was an invaluable source of information about Devon's history.

Abby slid out of her car and glanced fondly at Clara's gray-shingled home, a classic Cape Cod "double house" dating back to 1788. Then she started along the hard-packed sand path to the mill, the route by which, in an earlier era, the miller had walked from home to work.

Several years ago, conservationists, in an effort to prevent erosion, had obtained Clara Gould's permission to plant the bluff with a type of grass hearty enough to withstand the Cape's strong winds, the heat of summer and the icy cold of winter. The grass had grown high and in some places had crept across the path, nearly obliterating it.

Devon Mill was five hundred feet north of the homestead. The morning sun highlighted the back of the eight-sided structure, while the front, facing Cape Cod Bay, was shadowed. The contrasts of light and shade were beautiful. Now, Abby thought, would be the perfect time to photograph the windmill.

Pink-and-red wild roses grew in profusion along the weathered, split-rail fence that surrounded the mill yard, itself a tangle of weeds and brambles. As she neared the fence, Abby saw that many of the rails were broken or missing. The entrance gate was hanging loose from its hinges. She pushed it open, fearing it would break away entirely and fall down.

A feeling of sadness filled her as she waded through the tall grass and prickly weeds that blocked her path to the mill. Since Randolph Gould's death a decade ago, little had been done to maintain the mill and its immediate environs. Abby was well aware of that. Still, the effects of the neglect were painful.

She reached the door and gripped the latch. Rust stained her fingers as she pried it loose, and the door creaked as it reluctantly inched open, giving Abby the crazy illusion that it was in physical pain. She stepped inside the mill's musty interior, then squinted to adjust her eyes from the brightness of the June morning to the gloomy darkness.

The mill's small, square windows were opaque with grime. Without a flashlight, there was no point in trying to explore. Hopefully Greg would bring one with him. Thinking that, Abby heard the door creak again, and turned to see that it had swung closed by itself. As she groped in the darkness to unfasten the latch, cobwebs brushed across her hand. Involuntarily she shuddered. As much as she loved Randolph Gould's old windmill, she had to admit that, at the moment, the atmosphere was creepy, crawly, and she wanted out.

To make matters worse, the door seemed to be stuck. Abby gave a strong tug, and was still hanging on to the latch when she found herself face-to-face with Derek Van Heusen.

Their shock was mutual. Both instinctively recoiled—Abby back into the mill, Derek out into the sunshine.

After an awkward second or two, he advanced and peered inside. The figure he saw was partly obscured by shadows, and he had to wonder if Abigail Eldredge had a younger sister. This person looked more like a college coed than the mature woman he'd watched on the town hall stage last night. Maybe, he conceded, it was the way she was dressed. She was waring faded blue jeans and a yellow T-shirt, and her wavy chestnut hair was tied in a ponytail with a ribbon that matched the shirt.

"Miss Eldredge?" he asked uncertainly.

Abby emerged from the shadows, her pulse thumping. Her fears about this man's presence in Devon were quickly resurfacing. So were some entirely different reactions she tried hard to suppress. At the worst possible moment, her body was playing tricks on her. Every nerve tingled, and her skin felt as hot as if she'd been lying out on the beach all day.

"You *are* Abigail Eldredge, aren't you?" Derek persisted.

Abby nodded. Started to speak, but her voice stuck in her throat. Those dark blue eyes were raking her from head to foot just as coldly as they had last night. And that handsome face was just as tight, the expression just as stern.

"Sorry I startled you." His apology sounded perfunctory. "I didn't realize there was anyone inside."

"I didn't realize there was anyone outside," Abby retorted. She glanced toward the loop at the end of Mill Lane and saw a blue car that hadn't been there earlier. "What are you doing here?"

He *had* to be after the mill property. The idea of that turned Abby's heart to stone. Would Derek Van Heusen, she wondered, have the gall to visit Clara Gould at Devon Manor and lay out a proposition? Would he make her an offer that no doubt would be many times what the town of Devon could pay?

Clara might not care about the money—but Gordon would.

A mental picture flashed…a picture of Van Heusen, with Gordon Ryder in tow, visiting the nursing home and making his pitch. The vision nearly made Abby sick. If that visit were to occur, pray God it would be on one of Clara's good days, at a time when she would see right through the motives of two men who didn't give a damn about the windmill.

She stared at Derek Van Heusen more closely. To merely say he was tall, dark and handsome was an understatement. But so far, she'd seen little evidence of charm. She'd noticed only an outward inscrutability, aloofness and arrogance. Even so, she guessed he could light up a chandelier with charisma, turn up the wattage in a flash—if it were to his advantage to do so.

Derek broke the silence between them. "I heard you speak last night," he said. "You motivated me to come out here and take a look at the mill for myself."

Abby's eyebrows arched, and she was sure her skepticism was showing. She was tempted to let it out verbally, to challenge "I'll just bet I did." But if Derek Van Heusen wanted to play games, fine. She'd tag along, for the moment.

"It *is* impressive, isn't it?" she observed innocently. "Needs a little work, of course...."

"It needs *a lot* of work," Derek corrected her. "What's it like inside?"

Abby was blocking the door, unconsciously protecting her treasure. Without waiting for her answer, Derek advanced. In her effort to get out of his way, Abby felt something sharp snag her leg, a nail, maybe, or a protruding piece of wood. Whatever it was, it stung. She flinched and muttered, "Ouch!"

"It's too dark to see very much," she managed. "But go ahead and take a look, if you like."

He peered around briefly. "Pretty bad." Stepping back into the light, he added, "You're bleeding."

"What?"

"Your ankle is bleeding."

Abby looked down, saw the trickle of blood, then felt a handkerchief being pressed into her hand. This time, her fingers meshed with Derek Van Heusen's, and the effect was electric. She wondered whether his touch would be fire or ice. Now she knew. It was pure fire.

Inside, was he as hot as his manner was cold? Was that aloofness, that austerity, that hint of arrogance she disliked, all veneer?

Abby bent over, halted her bleeding with Derek's hand-kerchief, and noticed the monogram DVH stitched in gold. "This is going to get stained," she mumbled.

When there was no answer, she looked up. Derek didn't appear to be listening to her. He'd turned to face Cape Cod Bay and seemed absorbed by the tranquil sapphire water, the sea gulls flying in lazy circles, the fishing boats dotting the distant horizon. His profile—strong, masculine, deter-mined—nearly took her breath away.

Abby smelled the perfume of the wild roses, felt the sun's warm rays caressing her cheeks, noticed a bee drone by, took in the beach that stretched beneath the bluff. But the flowers, the bee's buzzing, the sand, the sun, the wa-ter...all were like parts of a huge Impressionist painting dominated by the very real man in her foreground.

He was not entirely perfect, she saw. There was a slight bump in his nose, an interesting cleft in his chin. And his hair, so in place last night, was a little unruly in the morn-ing breeze. Abby fought the impulse to reach up and smooth the dark tendrils that had strayed across his forehead.

He was wearing a blue polo shirt open at the throat, stone-washed gray jeans and brown deck shoes without socks—casual clothes, completely unlike what he'd been wearing last night. Abby saw more tendrils of dark hair curling in the hollow of his neck and noted the way the shirt fabric molded his broad shoulders, emphasized his arm muscles, the way the jeans hugged his rear end, the way his belt cinched his narrow waist.

It came upon her quickly—a sensual ache starting deep down inside, spreading upward and suffusing her with sweet yearning. This surge of feeling both shocked and trans-fixed Abby. Desire had been a stranger for so long. But God, she desired this man right now, insane though that was.

She was startled when Derek said, "The view is spectacular." His voice was low, husky, faraway. It was as if he were speaking to himself. Regardless, Abby heard him all too clearly, and his words were like a quick catharsis, a plunge into cold water.

She'd been in danger of forgetting that this man was her enemy, of forgetting his intentions.

"I know who you are, Mr. Van Heusen."

Derek swung around, saw the hostility in Abigail Eldredge's beautiful green eyes, and was taken aback. He had deliberately kept a low profile. Always had, always would. The last thing he wanted was exposure as a successful entrepreneur, as good as that might be for business.

He stared at Abby for only a moment, then looked back at the bay. It had to be that article in *People,* he realized, and chided himself, for perhaps the thousandth time, for ever having given the interview. Either that, or someone in Devon had recognized him, as Ryder had, and relayed their discovery.

"I should have introduced myself," he said, turning to face Abby. Automatically he probed a rear pocket for his wallet, extracted a business card and thrust it at her. For a moment, he thought she wasn't going to take the card. And when she did accept it, she used only the very tips of her fingers, as if the stiff, smooth paper might poison her.

She was beautiful. Beautiful . . . and also angry. Her animosity showed not just in her extraordinary eyes, but in the expression on her piquant face and in every curve of her body. She'd drawn herself up straight, shoulders squared defiantly, causing the fabric of her T-shirt to stretch across her breasts. Derek saw her taut nipples straining through the fabric, and felt a sudden jab of heat in his loins.

Desire rose within him, and he tried to rationalize it. Maybe he was finding his opponent so desirable because she *was* his opponent. And because this was the first time a woman had ever really challenged him.

Abby looked at the business card, then handed it back to Derek. "I know your name," she added. "I really don't need your address or phone number."

Derek was amused, despite himself. His lips curved into the slightest of smiles. "No," he agreed, "I suppose you don't."

Abby saw the smile and wished he would let it become full-fledged. Maybe a real smile would bring with it a personality transformation. She was about to ask, "What brings you to Devon?" when she heard a truck motor. Looking past Derek, she saw Greg in his pickup, coming to a stop behind Derek's blue car.

"Excuse me," she muttered. "I'm meeting someone, and I see he's just arrived."

Abby hoped Derek would take that as a cue to leave and started to move around him. Instead, he asked, "Refresh my memory, will you? How old did you say this mill is?"

She stopped short. "Both the mill and the Gould homestead were built in 1788. In fact, the land was given to the miller as an incentive for him to live and work in Devon."

"Interesting."

"Necessary. Milling was a highly respected and highly specialized profession. Millers were much in demand."

Abby started to move on, but was again stopped, this time by, "And this mill was used commercially until a few years ago?"

His persistence nettled her. Certainly she hadn't intimated anything like that during her talk. "This mill hasn't been used commercially for decades," she said. "Randolph Gould came from a family of millers, but he wasn't a miller himself. He inherited the mill and took up milling as a hobby when he retired from the telephone company."

"I see." Derek's tone was a shade too mild.

Abby glared at him suspiciously. Why Derek Van Heusen would ask her questions about the mill's operation was a puzzle. Whatever he was, he wasn't a history buff, she'd swear to that. In fact, she could imagine the speed with which both the mill and the homestead would be cast into oblivion if he ever got his hands on this property.

She might have pursued that line of thought, but Greg was climbing the crumbling stone steps up the bluff, heading their way. It occurred to her that Derek Van Heusen had deliberately ignored her cue. Probably he wanted to see whom she was meeting and what she was up to, intending to stall her plans.

Greg stepped into the yard, then turned and gave the gate an experimental push to and fro. Abby knew him so well she could read his mind. No doubt Greg was saying to himself, *This'll have to be replaced.*

He crossed the tangled yard, giving no indication that he might be shocked to see Abby's "stranger" on the scene.

Concealing her irritation, Abby said, "Greg, this is Derek Van Heusen. Mr. Van Heusen, Greg Nickerson, a local carpenter and a very good friend of mine."

Derek thrust out his hand, a strong, square hand with blunt-edged fingernails. His hand surprised Abby. It belied her picture of him as a man who spent his time sitting in a cushioned swivel chair behind an enormous executive desk, barking orders to subordinates.

"My pleasure," Derek said.

"Likewise," Greg returned. He added, to Abby, "I'm afraid I don't have much time. We had a little disaster on the house I'm restoring. Burst water pipe."

"This won't take much time," Abby promised. "Did you bring a flashlight? The windows in the mill are so dirty you can't see a thing."

"Hold on a minute," Greg said. "I've got a flashlight in the truck."

Abby watched him head back to the steps and wished Derek Van Heusen would follow. He didn't.

"What are you planning to do to the mill?" he inquired politely.

He really had nerve. Hadn't he listened to her speech? Was he so impervious to the vibes she was sending out that he didn't realize he wasn't wanted here?

"Greg is an expert on renovations," she said stiffly. "He's going to work up an estimate on the cost of restoring the mill."

"Restoring it?" Derek walked around the windmill, stopping to view it from several angles.

Watching him, Abby groaned. This inspection of his was a charade. It didn't take an expert to see that one of the four arms was broken off entirely, the others were missing cross spars, the shingles were rotted, and the foundation was crumbling.

He came back, stood beside her, but kept his eyes on the mill. "I'd say it's in pretty bad condition, Miss Eldredge," he opined. "Probably the exterior deterioration is nothing compared to the dry rot and water damage you're likely to find inside."

She didn't attempt to keep the frost out of her voice. "Restoration of a two-hundred-year-old windmill, Mr. Van Heusen, takes time, research and skill."

"It would also take a fair bit of money."

"I'm well aware of that. In any event, restoring the mill is phase two of our campaign. Phase one is purchasing the land and buildings from Mrs. Gould. I believe I made that clear when I was speaking last night."

Yes, she had, Derek admitted silently. He'd been concentrating so much on *her*, especially toward the end of her speech, he may have overlooked a couple of points. Or, her talk of restoration could have slipped by him simply because there was no chance it would happen. It was June now. By September, if all went according to plan, the Devon Mill and the old Gould homestead would be memories. Only Gordon Ryder could hold up the sale. And that wouldn't happen, either. Not after he talked with Ryder at lunch.

Suddenly it seemed wrong not to tell Abby Eldredge what was going on under her nose. Wrong to let her go on spinning a dream web while she worked so hard for a lost cause. Derek almost said something, when he heard Greg Nickerson approaching again.

"Care to join us and take a look inside the mill, Mr. Van Heusen?" Greg invited.

Abby could have throttled him. Whose side was he on?

"Maybe another time," Derek said. "Right now, I'll be getting along." He shook Greg's hand again, then offered his hand to Abby.

Reluctantly she took it. This time, it was cold.

She watched Derek manipulate the sagging gate and cautiously descend the steps. Then she moaned, "Dammit, I knew this was going to happen."

"What's going to happen?" Greg demanded. "Why was Van Heusen here? Did you know he was going to be here?"

"One question at a time," Abby said wearily. "No, of course I didn't know he would be here. He showed up just a few minutes after I did. As to why he was here, he said my talk motivated him to take a look at the mill himself. Can you believe that?"

The mere idea angered her. She wished she'd spoken up while she'd had the chance—to tell Derek Van Heusen that he would get nowhere in Devon, that he might as well start looking elsewhere, if building another Voyager Resort was what he had in mind.

"You were a big help," she scolded Greg. "Inviting him to check out the mill with us. I couldn't believe my ears."

"Back up, will you? What happened between you and Van Heusen?"

Abby shook her head despairingly. "He commented on the beauty of the view, then told me the mill was in pretty bad shape."

"Right on both counts. What else?"

"I don't know. We were only together a few minutes."

Together. The word choice was unfortunate. Abby remembered her fingers touching Derek's when he gave her his handkerchief, remembered the desire that flared inside her when she'd studied his profile, unwillingly checking him out. She felt the wadded-up handkerchief in her pocket and flushed.

"Come on, Greg," she said quickly. "Let's take a look inside."

Their inspection, for Abby at least, proved disappointing. Greg tested the steps that led to the upper levels and found several spots where the wood broke right through with only a little pressure.

"You stay down here," he commanded. "I don't want you to break your neck."

Abby did as he asked, listening as the floor creaked above her. Now and then, she glimpsed the flashlight beam coursing through the darkness. When Greg finally rejoined her, he said thoughtfully, "A lot of work, Abby. A lot of work to get this mill back into shape."

"But it could be done, right? It's not too far gone?"

"Not by any means," Greg told her. "Probably the whole mill would have to come apart piece by piece. You'd have to inspect each piece for damage, fashion new parts where necessary, then put it back together again. It's been done before right here on the Cape, many times. In fact, I can't imagine a more fascinating project. It would be a real challenge.''

Greg held the door for her. Outside, he said, ''That water pipe problem shouldn't take all day. Suppose I come back here later on and take a closer look? I'll make a few notations.''

''I take it an estimate's out of the question?''

''Until I've had a chance to really look things over, yes. You can't go fast on something like this, Abby.''

''How about working up an estimate in time for the special town meeting?'' She was feeling more anxious and depressed each second.

Greg looked up at the mill and shook his head. ''I don't mean to be discouraging, but facts are facts. Let's say you hired me and another guy. Six months' work is just a guess, but probably not that far off, assuming we worked six days a week, full-time. Even at a reduced rate, that would come to thirty, thirty-five thousand dollars for labor alone. The materials could easily run that much, possibly more.''

''So we're talking seventy, eighty grand. Is that what you're telling me?''

''Let me work up an estimate, okay?''

''I can raise the money, Greg. I know I can.''

He smiled. Brushed a cobweb out of his hair. ''If anyone can do it, Abby, you can. Right now, I've got to go. Talk to you later.''

Instead of following Greg, Abby walked across to the edge of the bluff and looked down. She loved Mill Beach. It was a perfect place to swim in summer, when the shallow bay water was as much as twenty degrees warmer than the frigid Atlantic on the other side of town.

She walked carefully along the bluff, trying not to trample the beach grass, and headed toward the long flight of wooden steps behind the Gould homestead that led down to the sand. She hadn't used them in a long time. Now, after Greg's discovery inside the mill, she wondered if they were dangerous, too.

She didn't have to find out. As she reached the top of the steps, she saw Derek Van Heusen coming up. It was a shock. She'd assumed he'd taken off earlier, but hadn't thought to check the loop for his car.

"Hello, again," he greeted her.

"Hello."

Derek negotiated the last step. "Rickety, to say the least," he commented.

Abby was instantly defensive. "No one uses this approach to the beach, Mr. Van Heusen. At least, they're not supposed to. It's private property."

Was she inferring he was trespassing? Maybe he was, Derek conceded. But he's wanted to get down to the beach, wanted to walk around to get the feel of the site. And he was excited. He had to commend Bennett, after all. This location was definitely right for a Voyager Resort. He thought of Sheila Casey's preliminary rendering and envisioned how the complex she'd sketched would fit into this marvelous waterfront environment.

If he'd seen this place sooner, he might even have gone for Gordon Ryder's four million dollar price tag. As it was, Derek was damned if he'd give Ryder the satisfaction of winning out, especially as it didn't appear he'd have to. Unless he was much mistaken, Ryder—thanks to Abby Eldredge's success last night—knew the cards were stacked against him.

Thinking about that, Derek watched Abby Eldredge turn away from him and carefully pick her way back toward the path that led to the homestead. She tossed her next words over her shoulder. "Be careful where you walk, Mr. Van Heusen. It takes this grass a while to catch on."

She could not have sounded more disapproving. Derek stared at her stiff back, and his resentment toward her flared. He had no illusions about his representing a threat to her. No illusions about their opposed views on development. But that didn't give her license to be so damned self-righteous.

They reached the path and were closer at this point to the house than they were to the windmill. Derek saw the yellow Volks parked near a shed. Hers, he guessed. He could picture Abby scooting along in the little car, windows down and radio on, her chestnut hair whipping back in the breeze.

Stopping beside her car, Abby swung around and frowned at Derek as if he were walking on hallowed ground. She refused to be intimidated by his impressive height, well-muscled physique and stern good looks.

"The homestead isn't open for inspection, Mr. Van Heusen, if that's what you were thinking," she informed him.

His resentment rekindled—until he saw the expression of pride as well as challenge, in her eyes. Her body language epitomized pride, too. But at the same time, she looked vulnerable. Derek sensed that something had happened at the mill, something to do with Greg Nickerson, something that had discouraged her.

"I wasn't thinking that," he replied evenly.

Abby looked away. "Will you be staying in Devon?" She might as well have come right out and suggested that he get out of town as fast as possible.

"No," Derek said. He waited to see her relief, waited for her to relax a little, but she didn't budge. "I'm driving back to Boston this afternoon," he volunteered. "Flying back to California tonight." He would have stopped there, but an unusual need pressed. He wanted to be out in the open with this woman, to warn her against having false hopes.

He chose his words carefully. "I plan to come back."

Did he plan to return to Devon? Did he really need to? Negotiations, finalizing the sales agreement and all the contract work could be handled by Channing and his staff. That was the way Voyager projects were usually done, by design, not by accident.

This time, though, was different. All because of a beautiful, green-eyed witch Derek didn't know nearly enough about. He had to make sure, damned sure, she wouldn't prove to be an insurmountable obstacle. He'd never underestimated a potential enemy, and he wasn't about to now.

Also . . . he wanted to see her again.

Abby got in her car without a word and started the motor. At the last moment, she said, "I trust you'll respect this place if I leave?"

That comment should have infuriated him, except . . . he couldn't blame her. She was within her rights. For now.

"I'll be right behind you," he stated.

Abby met his eyes and couldn't help swallowing hard. Derek, against all logic, was the sexiest man she'd ever seen. It frightened the hell out of her to think how easy it could be to give in to him. If he wasn't who he was . . .

She shut off the next vision as though she was slamming a door. Damn the sexual chemistry between them! It was making her think like a fool, making her mind wander completely off course. Making her body betray her.

"Well, then, Mr. Van Heusen," she said, summoning every ounce of control. "Perhaps we'll meet again."

"I'll guarantee that," Derek promised.

Chapter Four

There were two messages from Gordon Ryder waiting for Derek at the Oceanside Motel. Both gave the phone number of Ryder's Falmouth office.

Derek glanced at his watch. It was ten-thirty. If he checked out of the motel now, met with Ryder for an hour, he could be in Boston by two o'clock at the latest. That would give him time to touch base with Tom Channing and still catch a flight back to California.

The San Francisco headquarters of Van Heusen Inc. was currently considering the purchase of the American assets of a Japanese firm that had overextended itself. The negotiations were tricky. Derek frowned. He'd sent two of his best men to the bargaining table, but knew he'd feel most comfortable if he took charge at this point.

Yes, he had to leave Devon.

He opened his briefcase and extracted the report Andy Bennett had furnished on Ryder. Ryder, thirty-three, was a native Cape Codder. He'd grown up in Devon, was a graduate of Devon High School. He probably knew Abigail Eldredge personally.

Derek dialed Ryder's number, and Ryder himself answered on the second ring. It took thirty seconds to set up a lunch meeting.

"I'm heading off the Cape," he told Ryder. "Can I meet you on the way?"

"The Whaler Lounge in Barnstable village,' Ryder suggested, and gave Derek directions.

The conversation with Ryder concluded, Derek contemplated calling Tom Channing. He glanced at his watch again. 10:35. Too soon to expect Tom to have come up with a detailed report on Abby Eldredge, he supposed, and started to dial San Francisco to get an update on the situation with the Japanese company. Midway through the familiar number, he remembered it was three hours earlier on the West Coast. Only a quarter to seven.

What the hell's the matter with me?

Derek put the phone down in disgust, knowing he wasn't thinking straight. The Devon Mill deal was important, but not to the point that it should be affecting his concentration, throwing his thought processes completely out of sync.

A mental picture of a pretty, chestnut-haired woman swam before his eyes. A sexy young woman with gorgeous green eyes that sparkled even when she was angry. A woman who was espousing a hopeless, ridiculous cause that could be a real thorn in his side.

Impatient, restless, needing action, Derek thought about going for a quick run, just a mile or two. But he quickly discarded the idea, deciding he could make more productive use of his time by preparing for his meeting with Ryder.

But how? he suddenly wondered. By reviewing negotiating tactics he already knew like the back of his hand?

"Damn Abby Eldredge!" Derek exploded. He should have leveled with her when he'd had the chance. He would have, if Greg Nickerson hadn't arrived on the scene. Later, when he had her alone again, he couldn't think of what to say.

"Damn," he repeated, and knew he couldn't leave Cape Cod without seeing Abby again—just to set the basic facts straight, he assured himself.

"Helen, I need help."

Abby stood in the door of the librarian's office, having failed to find what she wanted in the card catalog.

Helen Rogers smiled. "That's what I'm here for. Incidentally, thanks for the brochures. The way people are taking them, we may need another carton. Now... what's the problem?"

"I want to look somebody up."

"You want to *look somebody up*?" Helen's curiosity showed.

"Find out some facts on someone."

"About whom are you talking, Abby?"

"Derek Van Heusen. The entrepreneur."

Helen bustled around the end of her desk. "Is it true he's in town?"

Abby hedged. "Where did you hear that?"

"Abby, you know this town. Rumors blow around like the breeze. Several people mentioned this morning that they heard Derek Van Heusen was at your meeting, but I didn't put too much stock in what they were saying. From what I've read about him, I wouldn't think he's the kind of man who attends small-town meetings."

"You're right, Helen. Nevertheless, he *was* at the town hall last night."

"What do you suppose he's doing in Devon?"

Abby wouldn't have expressed her fears to most people. She didn't want to give her supporters the impression she was running scared. But she trusted Helen to keep this bit of news to herself.

"I'm afraid he's after Clara Gould's property," she confessed.

"You've no worry on that score," Helen assured her. "I take reading material out to Clara from time to time. There's no doubt about her stand on the windmill. She wants the town to have it. And the land, too."

"Yes," Abby said. "Yes, I know."

To her relief, the librarian didn't pursue the subject. Instead, she said, "Let's use Infotrac and see what magazine articles have been published about Van Heusen."

"Infotrac?"

"An information source we have access to through the computer," Helen explained. "Perfect for checking book and magazine references on just about any subject you can think of."

A short while later, Abby was seated at a table in the library's reading room with copies of *Forbes* and *Business Week*, plus the *People* article, which she'd decided she should read again.

Unfortunately none of the stories told enough about Van Heusen to fully satisfy her curiosity. He was a native Californian, had attended the University of California at Berkeley, then obtained his master's degree in business administration from Stanford. He'd begun his career with Faulkner Enterprises, the conglomerate founded by the late Hugh Faulkner, a classic tycoon in the mold of J. Paul Getty and Howard Hughes.

A dozen years ago, Derek had branched off on his own, opening his first Voyager Resort in Monterey, south of San Francisco. The rest was business legend. In short order, the number of Voyagers increased, and all were marvelously successful.

Frustrated because she couldn't find anything personal about Derek's life, Abby returned the magazines to the checkout desk. It was almost noon. She needed to stop by the Conservation Commission's office and pick up revised plans from a builder who seemed determined to fill in some marshland, regardless of state and federal laws. Then at two o'clock, she had a meeting at the Historical Society to coordinate the construction of the windmill float she'd planned for the Fourth of July parade.

After that, Abby pledged, she'd pick up a few essentials at the market and head straight home. She would permit herself the indulgence of a long, relaxing bath before taking a much-needed nap.

Derek Van Heusen had her in a turmoil. She had to get him out of her system, make herself stop thinking about him. Abby couldn't recall when she'd ever felt so edgy because of one man. Was it his money and power that bothered her? Not really. Money and power, she'd taken on before. No, it was *him*.

She remembered his dark blue eyes, his stern, handsome face, his dark hair, and tight male muscles concealed beneath a polo shirt and stone-washed jeans. She remembered his mouth—cold one minute, inviting the next—and her body reacted.

She felt a wave of self-consciousness as she hurried out of the library. By now, thank God, Derek Van Heusen must be on his way to Boston. From there, he'd be flying to California.

The problem was, he'd be returning to Devon. Abby recalled his words: "I plan to come back." She felt a funny kind of pain, like she was emotionally being torn in two. She wanted him out of Devon, out of her life...yet she couldn't wait to see him again.

The Whaler Lounge was built on a dock that jutted into Barnstable Harbor. Gordon Ryder was waiting inside the entrance when Derek arrived. The redheaded hostess took one look at Derek, smiled appreciatively, then led the two men to a choice corner table on a big open deck.

Ryder ordered a Bloody Mary and a lobster roll.

Derek shrugged and said, "Make mine the same."

He intended this to be a short lunch. One drink, a sandwich, and as much information as he could glean from Ryder.

Ryder tried to break the conversational ice by detailing some local history about Barnstable village and its environs. Derek felt as if he'd been plunged up to his ears in local history ever since setting foot on the Cape. He cut into Ryder's dialogue as soon as he could without being blatantly rude.

He came to the point with, "I wasn't aware that Devon was interested in buying your aunt's property. Not until I heard Abigail Eldredge's speech, that is."

Ryder toyed with the long red drink stirrer with a plastic lobster at the end. "The town wasn't interested until Abby Eldredge came up with this farfetched notion of preserving the mill as a memorial to my uncle."

The bitterness in Ryder's tone wasn't wasted on Derek, and he pursued what might be an advantage. "What about Miss Eldredge? She seems to have quite a following."

Ryder put the stirrer down. "If it isn't one cause with Abby, it's another," he said. "She's a combination history-conservation freak. She gets people behind her with her good looks and enthusiasm. You know that, you heard her. But she doesn't always win."

"For example?"

"A few years back, she did her damnedest to stop construction of the Devon Mall. Said the mall would create pollution problems, insisted waste would be carried into Mayo Creek, an inlet from Cape Cod Bay."

"What happened?"

"She lost, but not before the developers altered their plans considerably. They made a number of changes to get by her objections."

"But ultimately the mall was built?"

Ryder nodded.

"It must have cost a bundle to make the changes."

"Guess there's no denying that."

"Then in a sense, Abigail Eldredge won."

"I don't think she'd agree with you, Mr. Van Heusen. She wanted to stop the mall from being built. Just like she'll want to stop your plans for a resort."

"I'll worry about that if or when the time comes, Mr. Ryder," Derek stated. He paused to test his Bloody Mary, and decided he liked the strong flavor of the horseradish.

Ryder was scowling. Derek waited, sure the man wanted to vent more of his hostility toward Abby Eldredge. He wasn't disappointed.

"I'm not much for activists," Ryder admitted. "Especially female activists. Even back when we were in high school, Abby was always into some cause, something that would purify the environment, or make the town better, or stop someone from making an honest buck. But she's a helluva lot worse now than she used to be. Compensation, I guess."

"Compensation? For what?"

"Her husband ran off with another woman. One of Abby's best friends, matter of fact. Sally Nickerson. Married to Greg Nickerson. Maybe you saw him with Abby last night?"

"No," Derek said, which was the truth.

"Well, Abby was married to Ken Howes. She took back her maiden name after she was divorced. The four of them—Abby, Ken, Greg and Sally—were all in the same class with me at Devon High." He shook his head, adding, "When Sally and Ken ran off together, it was the scandal of the year."

This was the last kind of story Derek had expected to hear. He thought about beautiful Abby Eldredge and couldn't imagine why any man in his right mind would want to leave her.

"When was this?" he asked Ryder.

"Oh, five or six years ago, I'd say. I'd left Devon long before it happened. After high school, I did four years in the army. After that, I got into real estate. My only reason for going back to Devon these days is to see my aunt and help her with her affairs."

Derek waited, watched Ryder pick up his plastic stirrer again. "After Sally and Ken split, Greg and Abby took to consoling each other," he said. "There were lots of rumors, but who knows what's true? I'll only say that it wouldn't surprise me if Abby and Greg wound up together someday."

Suddenly Derek had heard enough. He could see that Ryder was enjoying the potentially sordid overtones of the story he was telling, and he cut him off.

"You said it would be to our mutual advantage to meet," he said tersely. "I don't imagine you were thinking of Abigail Eldredge when you said that."

Ryder blinked. "No...except where her campaign might affect the sale of my aunt's property."

"In other words, it's true your aunt would be willing to sell to the town for half a million dollars?"

"My aunt doesn't know what the hell she's doing. Most of the time, she's out of it. There's no way I could let a sale to the town go through. The price involved is a joke. It would have been a joke twenty years ago."

Derek ignored that. "You've been unwilling to compromise, Mr. Ryder, which has forced us to seek an alternative location on the Cape."

Ryder froze. "What's that supposed to mean?"

"It means you'd better make a decision, soon. Get in touch with Tom Channing in Boston and let him know what you want to do. Frankly, my company can't wait any longer to start something on the Cape. It's dollars and cents, Mr. Ryder. Simple as that."

"Rather than let the property go to the town for a pittance, I'd be willing to make a price adjustment."

"Then I'd suggest you contact Tom Channing as soon as possible. Maybe the two of you can still work something out."

The hostess loomed up. "Is everything all right?" She directed the question to Derek.

"Everything's fine," he said. "Just bring me the check."

"Right away, sir."

Ryder didn't object to Derek picking up the tab. On the way out of the restaurant, Derek wanted to use the phone in the lobby, to alert Channing to an upcoming call from Ryder. He also wanted to check the status of the report on Abby Eldredge. But Ryder stuck to him like glue all the way to the parking lot, where they separated at last.

Frustrated, Derek took a left turn out of the lot instead of a right, and soon discovered the road dead-ended at a town beach. He reversed direction and headed back toward Devon. Plans, he decided, had changed.

He followed Route 6A along the north side of the Cape and didn't fail to notice how relatively undeveloped this side of the Cape still was. Many original homes had been meticulously restored, and most of the newer homes and businesses conformed to a colonial-style look. Attractive, Derek thought, but not entirely practical.

After a while he switched on the radio, heard the Rolling Stones doing an updated concert version of a song that brought back memories. It had been a hit his first year in high school. Abby Eldredge, at that time, would have been in the second or third grade, if he was calculating correctly. He was thirty-nine. Gordon Ryder was thirty-three. That would be Abby's age, too.

She was a young-looking thirty-three, he decided.

Were she and Greg Nickerson lovers?

What the hell difference did it make?

Derek tried to blot Abby Eldredge out of his mind. It didn't help when he passed a handsomely restored windmill in West Brewster. Or when Mick Jagger sang the refrain, "You'll come running back ... to me."

Abby checked in at the Conservation Commission's office on the first floor of the town hall, then headed over to the house on Cove Road where the Devon Historical Society was quartered. It was a vintage sea captain's house complete with widow's walk, bequeathed to the society by a longtime, wealthy summer resident.

The seven members of the float committee, four women and three men, were already there when Abby arrived. She was immediately congratulated on last night's speech, and then peppered with questions about Derek Van Heusen's presence in Devon.

Helen Rogers was right. Rumors in Devon blew as freely as the Cape Cod breezes. Abby flinched when she remembered how those rumors had once centered on Greg and herself. There would always be gossip, she supposed. Thankfully most of Devon's residents had long gone on to talk of other things.

Abby let the committee members speculate on Derek Van Heusen for a few minutes, then steered them into the reason for their holding a meeting. She told them Greg was almost finished with the replica of the mill he was building in his shop, and a lively discussion followed about the final features that should be included on the parade float.

By the time she left the Historical Society it was four o'clock, and Abby wanted nothing so much as a little peace and quiet. But when she stopped at the market, she ran into more people who wanted to discuss either the Save Our Mill campaign, or Derek Van Heusen, or both.

Once home, she fed Captain, put him back outside, then unplugged her telephone. She wanted no further interruptions as she tested her bath water and began soaking. Soon, the warm, scented water was doing its job. She felt relaxed, downright lethargic, as she got out of the tub, toweled herself dry, and then slipped on her oversized terry robe.

She was about to crawl into bed and yield to the luxury of an afternoon snooze, when the doorbell rang. She groaned and would have ignored the summons, but she remembered Greg had said he'd get back to her with preliminary findings about the windmill.

Abby tugged her robe's rope belt tightly around her waist, ran a hand through her hair, still damp from the steamy bath, and pattered, barefoot, across her living room to the front door. The bell rang a second time before she got there. As she opened the door, she started to say, "Hey, what's your hurry, Greg?" But she never got the words out.

Derek Van Heusen was standing on her doorstep.

His eyes swept over her, and Abby knew he wasn't missing a single, miserable detail of her appearance, from the damp hair to the chipped pink polish on her toenails.

"Sorry to barge in like this," he said. "I tried calling first, but your line's been busy."

"Busy?"

"Yes. Busy."

Abby scowled. "Then something's wrong with the phone."

"How so?"

"I had it unplugged. It should have rung, I think."

"Maybe you should call a repairman."

"Maybe." Suddenly Abby was fully cognizant of whom she was talking to.

"Come in, if you like," she invited uneasily. Suddenly Captain dashed out of the pine woods in back of the house and raced through the doorway.

His normally sleek black coat was a mess, covered with a mixture of sand, dried leaves and pine needles. If Abby was reading his canine mind correctly, he was annoyed at himself for not having heralded the arrival of this stranger with loud barking. As a result, he blocked the doorway and growled menacingly.

"Move, Captain," Abby ordered. But the Lab only kept growling and staring balefully at Derek Van Heusen.

"Move!" she repeated loudly.

At that, Captain reluctantly turned away from Derek, but stayed close to Abby as she led her unexpected visitor into her living room. She motioned Derek to a chair and asked politely, "Would you care for coffee? Or a beer?"

"Not just now, thanks."

Abby paused to plug the phone back in and listened to the dial tone. It sounded okay. Then she sat down in an armchair not far from Derek, painfully aware of her terry robe, which had seen much better days, her shiny face, devoid of even a trace of makeup, and her messy hair.

"I thought you'd be back in Boston by now," she said.

"I thought so, too. But I wanted to see you first."

"Me?" she asked, surprised.

Derek nodded, trying to keep his eyes off the opening that started at Abby's neck and continued down between her breasts, revealing an expanse of creamy white flesh. Obviously she didn't have a thing on under the robe.

Suddenly his throat felt bone dry. "Maybe I will have a beer," he decided. "If it's no trouble."

"No trouble at all."

While Abby went to the fridge to get the beer, Derek put his thoughts together. He said, "Look, Miss Eldredge...there's no point in our being other than frank with each other. I got the impression this morning that you knew I was interested in the Gould property. Am I correct?"

Abby stared at him. She'd *suspected* he was interested in Clara's land. What he'd just said was a confirmation of her direst fears.

"Well, am I?" he persisted.

She cleared her throat. "It goes without saying that a lot of developers would like to get their hands on the land Devon Mill occupies."

"I don't consider myself a developer, Miss Eldredge. But that doesn't matter. The thing is . . . it's only fair, under the circumstances, to tell you I'm going to buy Devon Mill."

Abby forced a skeptical smile. "You can't do that."

"Why not?"

"Because Clara Gould would never sell to anyone like you."

To anyone like you.

The words stung, and Derek felt himself going on the defensive, a position he never took. He fought back anger. Abby Eldredge had no right to be so condemnatory.

"The Gould property was offered to my firm several months ago," he informed her.

Abby shook her head. "That's impossible."

"On the contrary, the only impossible thing was the price Mrs. Gould's representative was asking."

"Mrs. Gould's representative? You wouldn't be talking about Gordon Ryder, would you?"

"That's exactly who I'm talking about."

Abby laughed and couldn't resist the thrust, "Yes, I saw him talking with you last night."

"Is something funny?"

"You might as well know, Mr. Van Heusen, that Gordon Ryder definitely does *not* represent Clara Gould. If you're dealing with him, you're wasting your time."

"Am I?" he challenged, then met Abby's eyes and felt like he was being bombarded by green sparks.

"That's my opinion. Of course, you're free to solicit others." She shifted, and the robe slipped a bit.

The tension vibrating between him and Abby made Derek want to do ridiculous things—like span the distance to Abby's chair, grab her in his arms and kiss her until she was breathless.

Was he losing his mind?

As if able to read that mind, Captain growled.

Abby bent to pat his head. "Easy, boy," she said softly, glad of the momentary respite.

Facing Derek Van Heusen's clear blue gaze was tilting her emotional equilibrium to a dangerous slant. She'd known several extremely handsome men over the years, but none who'd affected her the way he did. Often, very handsome men were either plastic, personality-wise, or had more than their share of conceit.

Derek Van Heusen, regardless of his aloofness, his hint of arrogance, his stern facade, did not seem conceited in the least. Also, right now he looked tired and perplexed, which was exactly the way she felt.

Abruptly Derek said, "Don't underestimate Ryder, Miss Eldredge. He may have more influence with his aunt than you think."

Abby was trying to decide how to answer him when the phone rang. She picked up the receiver and heard Greg Nickerson say, "It's about time! I've been trying to get you for ages. Either there was no answer, or the line was busy."

"I know," she said, glancing toward Derek.

"I just wanted to tell you I never got a chance to get back to the mill."

Her voice was low. "No problem, Greg. Can you get to it in the next day or two?"

"Absolutely. Meanwhile, how about coming over and charbroiling the flounder Bobby caught today?"

"Thanks, but give me a rain check, will you?"

"Got other plans?"

She managed a chuckle. "Not really. It's just one of those nights when I need to curl up early with a good book."

There was a pause before Greg said, "You sound funny. Are you okay?"

"I'm fine."

"Talk to you tomorrow then."

"Right." She hung up, turned to face Derek and saw that he was standing. "Going so soon?" she asked. "You haven't even finished your beer."

Derek was thinking their conversation had gone far enough. It might be to his disadvantage to say anything more about Gordon Ryder. He'd thought of telling Abby that Ryder had Clara Gould's power of attorney, which legally empowered him to act for the old lady. But powers of attorney could be revoked.

As it was, he'd been up front with Abby Eldredge about his intentions. He'd told her he was out to buy the land on which the mill stood. When the purchase became a reality, the shock to her would be lessened. That was about the best he could do, all things considered.

He moved toward her front door, saying, "I have some things to do. Again, I didn't mean to barge in."

Abby tagged along. "Are you going back to Boston tonight?"

"No, not until tomorrow."

She stood on the threshold, just a breath away from him. "Have a good trip back to California," she said.

"Thank you."

Involuntarily Derek swayed slightly in Abby's direction, smelled the delicate scent of soap and the fragrance of her hair. The effect was incredibly erotic. Quickly he thrust his hands into his pockets. He needed to get away from this woman!

He almost made it. And would have . . . but for the large black dog that dashed past him and leaped into the front seat the moment he opened the door to his car.

Chapter Five

Abby muttered a few colorful adjectives, drew the belt on her terry robe a shade tighter and stalked out to the blue Thunderbird. Derek was standing in front of the open driver's door, urging, "Come on, fella. Out!"

Captain's reply was a low growl.

"Why do I have the feeling he'll take my hand off if I try to haul him out of there?" Derek asked over his shoulder.

Abby didn't bother to explain that Captain's bark—like that of most dogs—was considerably worse than his bite. Instead, she moved around to the passenger side of the car, intent on hauling Captain out by herself. The door was locked.

Scowling at Derek, she snapped, "Open this, will you?"

He came to her, looking as exasperated as she felt, and bent close by her side to insert the car key in the lock. Inadvertently his hand brushed the soft curve of her breast.

"Sorry," he mumbled.

Abby flinched as if she'd been stung. If Derek had deliberately chosen a sensitive target to get her attention, he'd found it. She watched him, hoping he wasn't aware of her reaction—a magnified reaction, way out of proportion to the actual incident, she chided herself. To her relief, he was focused on fumbling for the right key to the door.

"Give me a little more room, will you?" he requested.

Abby took a step backward, but she was still too close for comfort. Irate at himself for letting Abby Eldredge get to him like this, Derek fumbled even more and dropped the keys on the ground. He quickly bent over to retrieve them— and so did Abby.

Their heads bumped hard.

Derek stood, touched his forehead and winced. Abby rubbed her temple, glared at him with accusing eyes, then bent down and picked up the keys. She knew she was just as guilty of the impact as he was, yet she stubbornly felt it was his fault.

Without glancing at Derek again, she moved to unlock the door. It was time to show Captain in no uncertain terms who was master in this situation.

A deep chuckle stopped her. Startled, Abby looked up at Derek, and saw that he was smiling—a rather rueful smile, but one that totally transformed his face. Suddenly he looked younger, and not nearly as stern or uncompromising. His dark blue eyes had lost their glacial coldness, and his mouth, relaxed, was full and tempting. Again, his striking looks stole her breath away.

Still smiling, he observed wryly, "You have a very hard head, Miss Eldredge."

That was enough to snap her back to action.

"Yours isn't exactly soft," she retorted, gingerly touching her temple. "In fact . . ." She broke off, seeing the purple lump forming over Derek's right eye. There was no denying he'd gotten the worst of the deal.

"You'd better come back inside," she told him.

"Why?"

"Have a look in the mirror, then ask that question."

His smile faded. "It's nothing. If you'll give me my car keys, I'll be on my way."

"With a purple egg on your forehead? Seriously, Mr. Van Heusen, maybe ice will reduce the swelling, if we act now."

To her surprise, Derek shrugged. "If you insist."

They started for the house. Captain, no longer the center of attention, scampered out of the car and pushed his way between them.

"Loyal, isn't he?" Derek observed.

"Very."

Abby led the way to her kitchen, then paused to survey Derek's injury. He was so tall there was no way she could deal with the bruise if he was standing up. She steered him to a straight-backed wooden chair. "Sit," she said.

Captain obeyed instantly, and Derek laughed. "Loyal *and* obedient. I like that in a dog."

Abby wondered if he liked that in people, too, but wasn't about to ask. She went to the fridge and tried to brake her increasing nervousness as she got a tray of ice, then wrapped several cubes in a wad of paper towel.

Derek watched her, mildly amused. She was putting on a great show of efficiency.

His amusement did not last long. The moment Abby came near him, chemistry started taking over. Bad, considering the circumstances. He needed to shake this effect she had on him.

He tensed as she pressed the ice against the bruise. She wasn't kidding—a purple egg probably was forming. It hurt like hell, and was beginning to throb.

Abby was so close he could feel her warmth and soft-ness, and he knew he should have left when he'd had the chance. He should have broken away outside and tended to the bruise himself back at the motel.

The problem, Derek soon discovered, was that he didn't want to break away. He hadn't anticipated the feelings of pleasure that crept over him as Abby held the cold pack gently against his forehead. The ice didn't feel all that great. But having Abby bending over him so solicitously was terrific.

The terry robe was gaping open at the neck again. This time Derek could easily see down her front, and his eyes lingered on the creamy swell of her breasts. He moistened his lips, and again caught the scent of her soap, a pure, clean scent, nothing exotic. Why was it so much more provoca-tive than the aroma of expensive perfume?

Derek wanted to bury his face in the hollow of Abby's throat, wanted to taste her skin, caress her neck with his lips. Fortunately he was distracted by a sudden cold sensation in the region of his chest.

He identified the problem, and managed a husky, "Abby?" hardly realizing he'd used her first name.

Abby continued to hold her ice pack against his wound.

"You're dripping water down my shirt front."

She sprang back, clutching the wet wad of paper and melting ice. Her cheeks turned scarlet. "Sorry," she mut-tered. "Stay put. I'll get a towel."

Derek watched her leave the kitchen and wished he'd let her go on soaking his shirt front. The heightened color in her cheeks made her look especially beautiful. Her un-brushed chestnut hair, falling in a wild mass around her shoulders, was beckoning to be touched. And her oversized terry robe was incredibly sexy. She was irresistibly attrac-tive . . . and also more than a little vulnerable.

Derek sensed that vulnerability and came to the conclusion that Abby Eldredge was far more complex than he'd suspected. On the stage last night, and this morning out at the mill, she'd been so determined, so seemingly one-tracked, not unlike the majority of women he encountered in business, women who rarely attracted him for more than a moment.

Careers stereotyped people, and eventually made them dull. Hell, the same could be said of him. He had started up the ladder with the single goal of making it to the top. Problem was, he'd achieved that goal by the time he was thirty. Success followed success to the point where the excitement, the uncertainty, was lost. Spontaneity, humor, romance . . . something was cast aside on each step up the ladder, shelved for the sake of "making it."

It was no joke, the saying, "It's lonely at the top."

Hugh Faulkner had boosted Derek up to the first rung of a corporate ladder that half the businessmen in America would have loved to just touch. Later, the climb had been made easier by the inheritance Faulkner had left him. But he would have made it, anyway. He knew that without conceit. The reason was simple. He'd cut everything out of his life, except the goal of making money.

Along the way, there'd been little time for reflection. Action had been paramount. Moving forward, not looking back. So he'd never really missed what he'd never had. He'd substituted tangible assets for intangibles . . . like love.

A home? A wife? A family?

He'd made his choice early on, deciding that devoting himself to a wife and kids and effectively manipulating Van Heusen Inc.'s complex reins were incompatible goals. Only in the last year or two had he really started to delegate authority, to trust other people to do things right.

He looked around Abby Eldredge's kitchen. He could see through into her living room. Everything was simple, comfortable, with a lived-in look, reflecting some aspect of her life, her personality. Quite the opposite of his personal world, what little of that there was.

He tried to equate his motivations, his life choices, with the kind of forces that drove Abby Eldredge, and barely got to first base before she returned.

She pressed a towel to his chest, but after only a few seconds, muttered, "That isn't going to work. Why don't you take off your shirt and I'll toss it in the dryer? I should have done that in the first place."

As she spoke, Abby visualized Derek taking off his shirt, imagined his body, exposed from the waist up, saw those curly tendrils of dark hair she'd seen earlier, at the mill. She wondered what it would be like to press her face against Derek's chest, to hear his heartbeat.

"I'll be fine," he said. Getting up, he added, "The Oceanside's just a few minutes drive from here. Car keys, please?"

Captain, close behind Abby, whimpered.

"He knows the word 'car,'" she explained to Derek. "I think he blames himself for your lump."

"You're telling me your dog has a guilt complex?"

She laughed. "No. Captain's never that hard on himself. When it comes to guilt, he has a short memory."

"Dogs have all the luck." Derek hesitated, then ventured, "Why do you think he jumped in my car? I had the distinct impression he wasn't especially fond of me."

"He loves cars," Abby said, smiling. "He loves to go for rides. I guess his loyalty wore a little thin when he saw you about to drive away. He was hoping for an adventure."

"And he got a show instead." Derek chuckled. "Captain's been watching your ministrations with intense interest."

"Yes, and I think I'd better hold his collar this time when you go. Otherwise, history might repeat itself."

They were moving toward her front door, Captain pattering at their heels. Derek looked down at the dog and said, "You may be right."

"I know I'm right. Hold on just a second. In the interest of peace, I'll give Captain a couple of dog biscuits and close him up in the kitchen."

"Won't he object to that?"

Abby shook her head. "Captain takes life a step at a time," she informed Derek. "He'll go for the biscuits first, then worry about getting out of the kitchen later."

Captain takes life a step at a time.

Derek thought about that as Abby tended to her dog. Perhaps that was the way everyone was supposed to handle life. It was a formula he'd never tried. He tried it now, as he stood on Abby Eldredge's threshold.

"A while back, when you were on the phone, I couldn't help hearing you say you didn't have any plans for tonight," he confessed.

Abby didn't answer.

"Tom Channing, who heads my Boston office, was telling me about a great Portuguese restaurant out in Provincetown. La Chama—something."

"La Chamarita?"

"That sounds right."

"I've been there three or four times," Abby admitted. "It's named after an old Portuguese dance."

"Tom said Provincetown's an interesting place. Fishing boats, artists, lots of tourists this time of year."

"That's true."

Derek felt surprisingly awkward as he took the next step. "Abby, would you have dinner at La Chamarita with me tonight?"

"I...don't know."

He advanced another symbolical step. "I'll make a pact with you."

"What kind of pact?"

"I won't bring up the subject of Devon Mill or the Gould property, if you won't."

Abby's mind was spinning. She knew the last thing she should do was accept a dinner invitation from Derek Van Heusen. But even if she did, the last place they should go together was La Chamarita. The restaurant was on the waterfront overlooking Provincetown Harbor. If the moon were anything tonight like it had been last night, the ambience would be impossibly romantic.

Abby's hand shot out as if propelled by a force over which she had absolutely no control. "Truce," she offered.

"Truce," Derek Van Heusen agreed, as his fingers closed over hers.

Provincetown was colorful and pulsing with activity. The quaint streets teemed with a fantastic cross section of people, and the unique, vibrant atmosphere was contagious.

Abby, seated across from Derek at a narrow table in La Chamarita, knew she'd have to bracket her time spent with him tonight, keeping it separate from those times she anticipated spending with him—or his representatives—in the future. Those times might be anything but pleasant.

She'd make a memory bundle out of tonight, then store it in the deepest recesses of her mind...and heart. Maybe someday, when she was old, she'd dare open the bundle, she decided whimsically. At the thought, her lips curved into a smile.

"Share," Derek suggested.

"I was just thinking what a lovely place this is," she evaded.

Derek lifted his wineglass to her. "That it is."

They were drinking Portuguese rosé, and the pink wine was as mellow as Abby's mood. Flickering candles lit the room, moonlight streamed over Provincetown Harbor, soft Portuguese music drifted in the background. A woman was singing, her plaintive voice accompanied by strumming guitars. The song sounded sad and nostalgic. A plea, maybe a prayer, to a lost love.

Abby's eyes misted.

"What's the matter?" Derek asked.

"The music."

"Do you know the song?"

She nodded. "It's a *fado*, a Portuguese folk song. They all tell stories." She smiled ruefully. "Mostly sad stories."

"Do you know the story of this one?"

"The *fadista* is singing about a man she loved. A fisherman who left her. He went to sea, and she doesn't know whether he drowned or whether one day he'll come back to her. Each night she goes to the shore and watches for his boat. She watches night after night, but he doesn't return. Yet, she still can't bring herself to admit he's gone forever."

Derek watched Abby and was spellbound by her words. There was sadness in her eyes, and her voice was soft and compelling, as if this story she was relating was personally familiar. Was she thinking about the husband who had left her for another woman?

A bolt of jealousy shot through Derek. Did Abby still love her ex-husband? Did she miss him? Want him back?

What a fool the man must have been!

Abby was wearing a mauve dress with a low, scooped neckline. A tiny gold heart nestled in the hollow of her throat. Derek wondered who had given her the heart. Her husband? Did she still wear it to remind her of him?

She'd put her hair up tonight, arranged it in a coil on top of her head. Her gold and amethyst earrings—antique, he guessed—swung delicately against her slender neck whenever she moved. She was leaning toward him.

"What is it?" she asked, echoing his question of a moment ago.

Derek couldn't take his eyes away from her. He tried to concentrate on something other than her full, generous mouth and that enticing hollow in her throat where the gold heart rested.

"Are all *fados* so sad?" he asked huskily.

"A lot of them are, yes."

Abby tried hard not to think about the story she'd just told Derek, reminding herself that this man would one day fly out of her life, go back to California, his home. He would leave the Cape forever, just as the Portuguese fisherman in the song had gone off in his boat, never to return.

On that score, Abby had no illusions, nor was she going to let herself have any. If she built a castle of dreams—a castle where Derek Van Heusen was her knight, her king—it would most certainly dissolve. And that would be much too painful to endure.

She'd been badly hurt by Ken. But years ago, she'd faced up to the truth about the hurt caused by Ken's desertion. A lot of the pain had been due to loss of pride, not loss of love. Almost from the beginning of their marriage, she'd known she and Ken weren't right for each other.

Losing Derek would be entirely different. This was not a case where "'Tis better to have loved and lost, than never to have loved at all" applied. For the sake of her sanity, for the sake of knowing anything akin to peace for the rest of her life, it would be far better never to love Derek Van Heusen, than to take the chance—and lose him.

Abby fought to keep her emotions under careful control as they worked their way through three courses of delicious Portuguese food. Then the waiter persuaded them to try a pastry dessert that was one of La Chamarita's specialities and to finish with demitasse cups of sweetened, strong black coffee.

Driving along the Mid-Cape Highway, heading back toward Devon, Abby couldn't repress the feeling that she and Derek had just taken a step out of one dimension and passed into another. They had crossed from fantasy into reality, and she wished they could push the real world away a little longer.

She was quiet, huddled on her side of the car.

After a time, Derek said, his voice very low, "Abby?"

"Yes."

"I wondered if you'd dozed off."

"No."

"Abby, La Chamarita was great." When she didn't reply, he added, "Thanks for going with me tonight."

"Thank you for taking me."

Their conversation was disintegrating into flat words, nothing more. Derek glanced across at her, saw she was staring at her hands. She seemed so subdued. He thought back to the *fado*. She'd been far away, absorbed, ever since she'd told him the song's story.

He tried to think of something to say, something that might shake her out of her mood, and it shocked him when he couldn't conjure up a subject. He didn't want to talk about himself. He certainly didn't want to talk about business.

No. This was a moment when he should take Abby in his arms and make love to her. Impossible, he thought to himself. Totally, hopelessly, impossible.

As they neared Devon, Abby suddenly spoke. "Would you be in the mood for a walk?"

Derek was startled. He'd been getting the impression from her silence that she wanted him to take her home, bring this evening to a close. All because of the *fado,* and the memories it must have engendered.

He rallied. "Sure."

"It's such a beautiful night." There was a wistful quality to Abby's voice. "Why don't we ride over to Snow Harbor?"

He slanted another glance at her, and saw that she was gazing at the moon. "Just tell me the way."

They turned off the highway at the Devon exit, and Abby gave directions to the bay side of town. At Snow Harbor, they parked by the docks. Commercial and party fishing boats rocked gently in the moonlight-splashed water. The night harbor scene appeared coated with a mystical, celestial silver paint.

At the end of the dock area, Abby stepped down into the soft sand and slipped off her shoes. "It's easier walking barefoot," she said. "We can leave our shoes here. They'll be perfectly safe."

Derek hesitated briefly, but then removed his shoes and lined them up next to hers. A moment later, they started off along the sand, side by side.

It was natural, instinctive, that Derek reach down and take Abby's hand in his, entwining his fingers with hers, without a word. They walked on in silence, caught up in the beauty of the night, the moon, the stars, the sound of the water lapping gently against the shore—and caught up in each other.

Then, suddenly, Abby stopped short.

Why had she chosen this particular beach for a stroll, when they could have stopped at any number of other beaches between Provincetown and Devon? Snow Beach became Mill Beach past a bend beneath the bluffs just ahead. Once they rounded that bend, Devon Mill would be visible on its perch above the bay.

Abby tried to think of a reason for turning back, but her mind was a blank. They'd only been walking for a few minutes and hadn't gone that far. Suggesting they should return to the marina would sound strange, awkward. Yet in another minute, their journey would take on a new significance. The truce they'd made would be broken.

She felt miserable as they started around the curve of the beach. The moon, which had been hiding behind a cloud, emerged right on cue. It draped the view with a dramatic silver mantle, casting shadows of the mill's giant arms across the sand at their feet.

Abby heard the sharp intake of Derek's breath. This time, it was he who stopped in his tracks.

"Is this why you brought me here?" he asked coldly. "To see how impressive your mill can be at night?"

Abby shook her head, took her hand from his and tried to speak.

"Is that why you agreed to have dinner with me?" Derek persisted. "So we could wind up here?"

"No," she choked. "It's not like that at all."

"We made a truce, remember? At least, I thought we did. Evidently promises don't mean much to you."

"That isn't so." Hot tears stung her eyes. "You can believe this or not, but I'd forgotten all about the mill when I suggested a beach walk. I just wanted . . ."

He waited, then demanded roughly, "You just wanted *what*?"

"I just wanted to walk with you in the moonlight."

Abby turned away from him, fighting back tears she didn't want him to see. How she hated losing control!

She felt Derek's strong hands on her shoulders, felt herself being swung around, forced to face him. She expected a torrent of protests to be unleashed from Derek's mouth as she looked up into the most eloquent eyes she'd ever seen.

Derek started to speak, but the words died in his throat when he saw the misery etched on Abby's face, saw her tears. Compassion overrode his anger. Instead of despising her for what she had done, he wanted her more than ever.

He drew Abby to him, held her close against his chest and buried his face in the mass of hair coiled on top of her head. He felt a rush of desire that threatened to spin out of bounds. It didn't help when she pulled back and stared up at him. It was as if something had suddenly ignited, an irresistible force too strong for either of them to push away.

Abby knew if she had any sense, she'd turn and run. But...she did what she wanted to do. She raised a hand and tentatively touched Derek's dark hair. Then her fingers lingered, stroking his hair back from his forehead, gently touching the spot that was still swollen.

Derek groaned, captured her hand, and held it to his mouth. And Abby shivered, she wanted him so much. Heedless of what might happen, she flung her arms around his neck and pressed her breasts against his chest, inviting him to claim her mouth.

He did.

Their kiss, at first, was slow-paced, deep, intense, probing. But then the tempo picked up, and the probing became searching. Claims were staked, relinquished, then staked again. Abby plunged her fingers into Derek's shoulders, felt his hands rove over her hips, cup her buttocks. She felt his heat rising as he pressed against her until suddenly something splashed their feet.

Water, cool water, lapping over their toes, snaked around their ankles.

Abby drew back and shakily said, "The tide's coming in." She fought back an impulse to laugh, because the laugh would have been laced with hysteria. "We'd better go back."

It was over just like that. Passion, extinguished, became impotent, like a defused bomb. But only for the moment. They couldn't always count on an incoming tide to stem the flow of desire.

They both knew that as they retraced their steps to Snow Harbor, retrieved their shoes and walked beside the boats to Derek's car.

Chapter Six

Derek read until two in the morning, then fixed himself a Scotch on the rocks and took the drink out on the balcony. Beyond the dunes, the dark, silver-coated Atlantic stretched to the horizon, stretched all the way to Portugal. He listened to the waves breaking on the beach, stared at the moon. And knew that every time he saw a full moon, or even a sprinkling of silver moonlight, he would think of Abby Eldredge.

He hadn't handled their evening's finale very well. They didn't say much on the drive back from Snow Harbor. At Abby's house, Captain rushed out to greet them with enthusiastic barks, no growls this time. Captain, in fact, acted as if he expected Derek to follow Abby inside. Maybe he would have, if he'd been invited.

Their parting had been stiff, awkward. They'd mumbled good-nights. They made no moves toward a good-night kiss, as if mutually realizing the kiss would either be anticlimactic, or would start things up all over again—with dangerous results.

If Abby were another woman, Derek thought now, he'd follow his usual procedure. He'd send her a dozen long-stemmed roses and blot her out of his life.

But . . . Abby wasn't another woman. She was very, very special, like no one he'd ever met before. It wasn't only her natural beauty, her sexiness. There were intangibles about her, things he couldn't define. Certainly he'd never touched a woman who aroused him the way she did. Last evening had been only a sample, only a hint of what could be—but never *would* be.

When Abby realized that her precious windmill belonged to Van Heusen Inc., when she came to grips with its imminent destruction, whatever she felt toward him would die. Derek knew she would hate his guts, and there was nothing he could do about it.

"Amen," he murmured bitterly, and went to bed.

Sleep was elusive, a frustrating sequence of hour-long dozes mixed with periods of restless wakefulness. Derek tossed, turned and tried to lose himself listening to the rhythmic pounding of the surf. But images of Abby, images of Devon Mill, made deep sleep impossible.

He woke up late, at almost nine o'clock, feeling like he had a giant hangover—tired, lethargic, depressed and headachy—though he'd actually had very little to drink. A good breakfast would help. But first he wanted to work the kinks out of his system, to force himself back on track with fresh air and exercise.

He put on gym shorts, a sweatshirt and a scuffed pair of running shoes, and stretched for five minutes. Then he started forth, jogged away from the beach with no particular destination in mind.

Soon he was running along Beach Road, then Main Street, heading toward Devon Center. There were a lot of cars with out-of-state license plates. Tourists, or summer residents, Derek supposed. Also, there were any number of pickup trucks and service vehicles—builders, plumbers, electricians and landscapers out on jobs.

Derek branched off onto a side road, seeking less traffic, and was rewarded by discovering a sparsely settled residential area where the homes were far apart, separated by open stretches of woodland. Not every acre of the Cape was developed. At least, this part of Devon was still intact.

The road meandered over hills, went by a church, past a good-sized lake. Derek smelled pine forest, honeysuckle and wild roses, then the tang of sea air as he came to a saltwater landing. Cars with empty boat trailers in tow lined both sides of the road. Derek spotted a concrete boat ramp and a long narrow dock jutting out into the water.

There was a floating platform at the end of the dock. Derek slowed, then came to an abrupt halt, seeing the boy fishing off the platform. It could have been him, almost thirty years ago. He felt a knot form in his chest...and time went into reverse.

On a hot California June morning, a dark-haired boy walked out on the deserted pier at Jacaranda Beach. Jacaranda was a desolate little coastal town halfway between Laguna and La Jolla. There were abandoned shacks, boarded-up storefronts, not many people. But the boy loved the pier, felt as though it was his own. Now that school was out for the summer, he vowed to go there every day.

It was a shock, on the third morning of vacation, to find someone else already sitting at his spot—an elderly man hunkered over a fishing reel, untangling his line. The man wore baggy brown pants, a plain tan pullover and a battered straw hat. He looked up as the boy approached and indicated the tangled line.

"I've made a mess of this," he said.

"Maybe I could help," the boy offered. "My fingers are smaller than yours."

"So they are," the man concurred. "Maybe you *could* help. What's your name?"

"Derek."

"Well, Derek . . . go ahead and give it a try."

Derek worked on the reel, conscious that the man was watching him closely. But his confidence kept him steady—he knew he was good with his hands. Whenever he managed to save a little money, he'd buy a Revell model. He would carefully assemble a plastic plane or car, then paint it in exacting detail. It kept his mind busy and gave him a way to make money by selling the finished models to other boys, or to the hobby shop for their display. But mostly, it gave him something to do while his father was sleeping off a drunk.

"There," he said, and handed the pole back to the man. "Line's okay."

"So it is," the man observed. "Thanks." He glanced at Derek's dented blue tackle box. "What are you using for bait?"

"Worms."

"Worms, eh? I've been using shrimp. Shrimp work well."

Derek spotted the red-and-white cooler and wondered if there were fish inside. "Had any luck?"

The man cast before he answered. His line whizzed out, then plopped into the greenish sea below the pier. "Sure have."

"What have you been catching?"

"Sea bass. Yellowtail."

"Can I look?" Derek asked, going over to the cooler.

"Oh, they're not in there, son," the man said.

Derek met hazel eyes deep-set beneath thick, salt-and-pepper brows. He heard the words, "I throw 'em back."

"You do?" he sputtered, trying hard to conceal his shock. Fish were valuable, something Mario said he could trade for enchiladas or chili. Mario owned the cantina over which he and his father rented a room. They ate a lot of Mario's food. Not great, but not bad.

The man invited, "Want to try a shrimp, Derek?"

"Sure," Derek said eagerly. He wasn't about to admit that the worms hadn't worked, but added, "This is only my third time fishing."

"Third time, eh? You untangled my line like an expert."

"Just lucky," Derek told him.

The man didn't comment. Instead, he took a shrimp from his bait box. "Give me your hook, son. You put 'em on like this . . . see how I'm doing it?"

Soon after, Derek felt a sharp tug, and his pole bent nearly in half. At once, the man was by his side, encouraging him, instructing him.

"You got yourself a mackerel, Derek. Pretty good one, too."

Derek was grinning from ear to ear. It was the first fish he'd ever caught. "I brought newspaper," he said excitedly. "I can wrap him up in newspaper, right?"

"Sure. Just keep him in the shade, that's all. Stash him under the bench here so the pelicans don't swipe him."

Derek did exactly that. He liked the man, so he didn't mind that his spot had been discovered by someone else. The man obviously knew how to fish. He hooked something every four of five minutes—yellowtail, sea bass, another mackerel. Problem was, he still threw them back.

Derek soon decided his first catch was luck. He got bites almost every time he put his line out. But he just couldn't snag anything, and kept reeling in empty hooks.

"I'm wasting your shrimp," he finally said.

"No, you're not, Derek. Keep trying."

He did, but with no luck at all. Suddenly he felt the focus of the man's sharp hazel gaze. He'd just pulled in another large yellowtail.

"You want this one, Derek?"

"Yeah...that is, I wouldn't mind."

"You live near here, son?"

Derek gestured over his shoulder. "Back in town."

"Guess your folks must like fish."

"My mother's dead," Derek said, and tried to shrug off the bleakness that always came over him when he had to say that. "I live with my father."

"How old are you?"

"Ten, going on eleven."

The man chuckled. "When will you be eleven?"

"October."

The man opened the red-and-white cooler, took out a thermos and two sugar-crusted doughnuts. He held out the doughnuts. "Could I interest you in one of these?"

"Sure," Derek said quickly. "Thanks." He put down his pole, munched the doughnut...and knew he'd found a real friend.

"What's your name, mister?" he asked, his mouth full.

The man looked out at the sea before he answered. "You can call me Faulk, Derek," he said.

"Just...Faulk?" Derek repeated curiously.

"Just Faulk."

The summer passed, and Faulk came to the pier three, sometimes four times a week. Derek fished with him and got pretty good at it. He listened when Faulk spoke, which wasn't all that much. Still, he liked Faulk a lot, liked his easy companionship.

Bit by bit, Derek began telling Faulk things about himself—things he never told anyone. Faulk didn't ask many questions. Rather, he had a way of drawing things out by making a chance remark, or by just waiting.

"How old were you when your mother died?" he asked one day.

"Six," Derek said. "She had cancer. I guess she had it a long time before she died. She ... well, she always seemed sick, but I guess she was pretty brave. She smiled, even on bad days. I used to have dreams about her after she died. She was always smiling like she was telling me not to worry, things would be okay."

"Do you still dream about her?"

"Not so much anymore."

"No brothers or sisters, right?"

Derek shook his head. "Just Dad and me. We've been in Jacaranda since December. That's the longest time we've spent anywhere since I can remember."

"What does your father do, Derek?"

What did his father do?

Derek hedged on that one. Sam Van Heusen did odd jobs, field work, pumped gas, most recently had worked in a hardware store until they fired him. Most of the time, he drank beer. When he didn't drink, he slept. Trying to sober up, maybe. Or trying to get away from his problems.

What little money Sam managed to make went for case after case of bargain beer. Beer was bought before the rent got paid, and it was gone before the rent got paid, too. That was one reason Derek and Sam had to move so often.

Sam, Derek knew, wasn't a bad person and he wasn't mean. He was just ... lost. He wasn't much of a father, but that was the way it was.

Most of the time, Derek made his own life. He had his late afternoon paper route—Sam let him keep the tips. He had his models, and his fishing. He had his meals from Mario's—tortillas and eggs for breakfast, chili and enchiladas for supper. He had Faulk for a friend, and their private pier on the Pacific. And he had the treats Faulk always brought for lunch.

He didn't intend to tell Faulk about Sam, about the beer, the lost jobs. But gradually it came out, until Faulk knew everything there was to know.

Faulk didn't say much. He never said anything critical about Sam. He only commented, once, "He must have loved her very much. Your mother, I mean."

"He carries her picture around all the time," Derek said. "In his pocket. It's gotten kind of crumpled."

"You still miss her, don't you?"

"Uh-huh."

The summer passed, and Derek realized that he knew very little about Faulk. He didn't know where he lived, or if he was married, or if he had any kids or grandchildren. Faulk didn't volunteer information. He was always in a good mood, yet not receptive to questions. The only things Derek knew for sure were that Faulk was a good fisherman, and Faulk was never very hungry. He barely ate the treats he brought for lunch, while Derek was always ravenous.

Time went by…and Derek knew he was beginning to love Faulk like the father he really didn't have. Maybe it was a hell of an admission to make…but back when he was ten going on eleven, if he'd had to choose between Sam Van Heusen and Faulk, he would have taken Faulk.

And what a mistake that would have been.

Faulk—Hugh Faulkner, who eventually became the most influential person in his life—had taught him a bitter lesson one day, a lesson he would never forget. Faulk had stripped him of illusions, made him face the hard truth of reality—that money, not dreams, makes the world go round.

For a time, he'd hated Faulk for teaching him that lesson, despised him for the way he'd taught it. Later, the hatred faded and was gradually replaced by respect and admiration. But never again had Derek loved Faulk. Nor had he loved anyone else.

Now Derek drew a deep, rasping breath, staring at the boy fishing from the end of a Cape Cod dock. He saw the pole jerk, watched the boy reel in furiously only to find a sinker and an empty hook glinting in the sunlight. His slight shoulders sagged in disappointment. Derek knew the feeling, but it had been a long time since he'd experienced it.

In recent years, the only fishing he'd done was the deep-sea variety off the California coast. More often than not, it was pleasure connected with business, an excursion via a chartered fishing boat—complete with special touches like chilled Dom Perignon champagne, Beluga caviar, and maybe a couple of attractive women to add a little spice and color for the sake of the important business contacts he was hosting.

The fishing he'd done long ago off the pier at Jacaranda Beach had been a helluva lot more fun, he thought, as he watched the kid scrounge in his tackle box for bait.

Just then, the boy looked up at him, and waved.

Derek had intended to walk away from this scene and jog back to the motel. But something inside, maybe a voice from the past, pushed him forward. The planks on the dock creaked under his feet. The sun was warm, but the breeze was cool. The air smelled salty and wet.

He stood on the floating platform and looked at the boats on their moorings. Then he watched the boy bait his hook, slowly, deliberately... and cast. With the line successfully back out in the water, the kid glanced up.

"Hi," he said.

"Hi," Derek returned. Then he found himself asking, just like Hugh Faulkner had, "What're you using for bait?"

"Worms," the boy said.

Derek fought a second episode of déjà vu. He hadn't thought of the Jacaranda pier in ages, and he didn't want to think about it now. The memory would always be painful.

"Been catching anything?" he asked the boy.

"Not yet. But I got three flounder yesterday."

"What else do you get here?"

"Snapper blues, sometimes. Once in a while, an eel." The kid grinned. "I don't like eels. They look too much like snakes. But some people say they're good to eat."

The pole jerked, but as soon as the boy started reeling, there was nothing. "Darn," he said, seeing the empty hook.

Derek moved closer, couldn't resist observing, "That's a pretty heavy sinker you're using."

"You think so?"

"Well, was that a bite you got, or did your line just snag on something?"

"I'm not sure," the boy admitted. "But the flounder are on the bottom. I have to use a sinker."

"Try a lighter one sometime."

"Maybe you're right."

Derek looked around and asked, "You come out here by yourself?" The boy seemed young to be fishing alone. Then again, he'd been young when he'd spent whole days by himself fishing, or just wandering around Jacaranda.

"I stay with Mrs. Doane while Dad works," the boy said. "She lives in that house there." He pointed, and Derek saw the gray-shingled house not a hundred feet from the dock.

"Anyway, Dad says it's okay if I fish by myself. I'm a good swimmer. I started taking lessons when I was five."

"How old are you now?" Derek asked.

Again, history seemed to repeat itself. "I'm nine, going on ten."

"What's your name?"

"Bobby." The boy returned the question. "What's *your* name?"

"Call me Derek." Derek heard a voice saying, *"You can call me Faulk."*

They both turned at the sound of a truck approaching. "Hey, there's Dad," the boy said, and waved.

The pickup stopped just short of the boat ramp, and a man climbed out of the cab and sauntered toward the dock.

Derek recognized him at once.

Greg Nickerson.

Derek spoke first. "Good morning, Mr. Nickerson. I didn't know this was your son I was talking to."

Bobby cut in before his father had a chance to speak. "Dad, Derek says maybe I should use a lighter sinker."

"We'll check on that when I get home tonight," Greg Nickerson promised. "Right now, plans have changed. Mrs. Doane has to go to Hyannis, so pack up your gear."

"Sure, Dad. Where are we going?"

"You'll see when we get there."

"Okay."

Derek was silent as Bobby Nickerson started reeling in his line. Greg, looking out across the inlet, observed, "Nice day."

"Yes, it is."

"You run, I take it."

"Not avidly. Just two or three times a week."

Greg nodded and said, "I used to do some running my-self. Now..." He smiled ruefully. "Let's just say there aren't enough hours in the day."

Derek smiled, too. On that, he and Greg Nickerson were in accord. He imagined the pace of his usual day was con-siderably different than that of a Cape Cod carpenter's but their complaint was the same.

"All set, Bobby?" Greg asked.

"Yep."

Greg turned to Derek. "Are you going to get a second wind, Mr. Van Heusen, or would you like a ride to wher-ever you're staying?"

Derek still needed the exercise, needed to work out both his physical and mental kinks. But he made a sudden deci-sion. This would be a chance to talk to Greg Nickerson.

"I'm at the Oceanside Motel," he said. "If it's not out of your way, I'll take you up on a ride."

"It's not out of the way at all."

Bobby stashed his fishing gear in the back of the pickup, then climbed into the cab. Again, memory washed over Derek when Bobby asked, "Got anything to eat, Dad?" He'd always been hungry when he was Bobby's age.

"No," Greg said. "But Abby'll have something."

Abby?

God . . . were they heading for Abby Eldredge's house?

They were, Derek discovered. After driving a few min-utes, Greg turned up the now-familiar lane, and Captain appeared on cue. This time he jumped up on Derek, ready to lick his face if he could get close enough. Derek was stroking the Lab's smooth head when Abby appeared at her front door.

"Catch anything, Bobby?" she called out, then froze when she spotted Derek.

"Nah, not today," Bobby answered, then ran off with Captain close behind him.

Abby forced her knees to stop wobbling and met Greg and Derek halfway between her house and the truck. "Hi, Greg," she said lightly. To Derek, she added, "Good morning."

"Good morning."

Greg handed her a manila folder. "I went over the mill for an hour this morning," he said. "Managed to jot down a few figures. Take a look when you have time, and we'll go over them later."

"Fine." Abby's eyes were still on Derek. "Listen," she said, "I just baked some corn muffins for Bobby. There are plenty if you haven't had a coffee break yet, Greg." She added hesitantly, "For you, too Derek."

"Unfortunately, Abby, I have to run," Greg said.

Derek was tempted, terribly tempted, to say he hadn't even had breakfast yet. But he refrained, saying instead, "I'm getting a ride back to the Oceanside."

He met Abby's eyes as he spoke. Was that regret or relief in their green depths? Last night aside, Abby Eldredge would probably be very happy if he left town.

Derek climbed back into the pickup and watched Greg say something to Abby in a low voice. Abby answered, and Greg reached out and patted her arm.

There was an easy familiarity between them, and Derek tried to identify what it meant. Were they lovers? They didn't come on like lovers. If he hadn't known otherwise, he would have guessed Greg Nickerson might be Abby's brother.

Abby went back into the house with a farewell wave. Greg got behind the wheel of the truck, and they jounced up the lane to the paved road.

Derek didn't want to be overtly inquisitive, but it was hard to hold back questions. He settled for, "I take it Abby watches Bobby some of the time when you're working?"

"She'd watch him all the time, if I let her," Greg answered. "But I'm not about to, because Abby needs her free time just like the rest of us."

"So Bobby stays with a woman who lives in that house by the landing?"

"Right. Most days, Bobby is at Melanie Doane's. She has two young boys he can play with. In fact, I'm surprised they weren't out there on the dock with him."

"Abby and Bobby are pretty close, I take it?"

"Very close. But then, Abby's a natural with kids. She's possibly the most popular third-grade teacher Devon Elementary School has ever had."

Derek chose his words carefully. "Judging from that meeting the other night, I'd say she's pretty popular with the adults in this town, too."

Greg slanted a glance at him. "Yes, she is."

Momentarily they were silent. Derek broke it with, "I wanted to ask you something, Mr. Nickerson."

"It's Greg," Greg replied easily. "What did you want to ask?"

"It's about the mill, Greg. I know Abby's interested in restoring it. I gather you're looking into what that would cost?"

"Yes, I am."

"I'd be interested in a cost estimate myself."

"You would?" Greg was taken aback. "Why?"

Derek decided he had nothing to lose by leveling with Greg Nickerson. The odds were heavily stacked in favor of Van Heusen Inc.'s acquiring Clara Gould's twelve acres. To have Greg on his side, or at least to have Greg hear the truth from the source, made good sense.

"My company's negotiating with Gordon Ryder for the purchase of the mill tract," he said.

Greg didn't answer.

"If we come to terms with Mr. Ryder, we'll be building a Voyager Resort on the site."

"I had an idea that's why you were in town," Greg admitted.

"You were right. And frankly, it's been my intention to demolish Devon Mill, and the Gould homestead, if we acquire the property."

"But?"

Derek took a deep breath. "But after hearing Abby's speech, I've been thinking about . . . alternatives."

"About not building a Voyager, you mean?"

"No, not that. I fully intend to build the Voyager. I just don't want to create problems when there might be ways around them. . . ." He broke off, seeing the Oceanside ahead, and wished this ride wasn't going to end so abruptly.

Greg turned into the motel parking lot, pulled into the space next to Derek's rented car and switched off the ignition. Leaning back, he said, "I'll be honest with you, Derek. There'd be a lot of opposition to a Voyager going up if it meant Devon Mill would be torn down. The windmill's an irreplaceable piece of history. The symbol of Devon's past. You know about Abby's campaign. . . ."

"That's why I'm interested in renovation costs." Derek let the idea form in his mind, rather than automatically discarding it as sentimental foolishness. "It occurs to me that perhaps the best way to handle Devon Mill would be to follow a custom that's not unusual on the Cape, from what Abby said the other night."

"You mean, move the mill to another site?"

Derek nodded.

"Well, there are several problems with that idea," Greg said slowly. "You saw for yourself that Devon Mill's in pretty bad condition. To be renovated, it would have to be completely dismantled, each piece inspected for damage, and so forth. All of that would best be accomplished at the site, without moving anything any distance."

"Okay, suppose you did that...restored the mill right where it now stands. *Then* it could be moved, couldn't it?"

"That's the real problem. It's true that most of the windmills that exist today on the Cape have been moved around. Some of them, many times. Building a mill was a specialized profession, just like running one was. Plus, there was a shortage of suitable timber on the Cape. It was cheaper to move a mill, rather than buy lumber and build a new one."

"I'm not sure I get your point."

"The point is...Devon Mill was built right where it now stands, on that bluff overlooking the bay. That's what makes it unique—it's never been moved. I think Abby mentioned that it's possibly the only windmill on the Cape that stands on its original site."

"Yes, I think she did."

Derek had been thinking that moving the mill to a new site—even if that meant purchasing the site himself—might be a way to compromise with Abby. In business, there often had to be compromises. And he was not unwilling to make one—when it served a purpose. But from what Greg Nickerson was telling him, moving Devon Mill would be out of the question, a solution Abby would never accept.

He smiled ruefully and said, "Well, thanks for the ride, Greg, and for the information. I'd still be interested in knowing what the renovation will cost."

"Abby will have a full estimate in a week or two," Greg said. "Maybe you could check with her then."

"Maybe I could."

But as he headed to his room, showered, and then packed for his trip to Boston, Derek knew there was little likelihood that he would.

Chapter Seven

Tom Channing said, "I've set up an appointment with Gordon Ryder for tomorrow afternoon at two. We've spoken on the phone twice...once yesterday after you called, then again this morning. I don't think there's any doubt he's willing to negotiate."

Derek rubbed the sore spot on his forehead—a tangible reminder of Abby Eldredge. The outside bruise would fade. The memory wouldn't.

He inquired wearily, "Just what do you mean by willing to negotiate? The site may be perfect, Tom, but I'm reluctant to go a dollar above our offer of three million. We don't have to."

"I know that," Channing agreed. "And I'd say Mr. Ryder knows it. He'll probably try to jack up the price a bit, say half a million. But when he sees we're firm, I'm certain he won't take any chances. Hell, he can't afford to. He mentioned you spoke about choosing another location for the Cape Cod Voyager. Just a ploy?''

"I ran the thought past him, yes." A throbbing headache was blending with the sore spot on Derek's forehead. He asked abruptly, "Everything set up for my trip back to the Coast?"

"You're booked on a five-thirty flight. The only problem might be the rush hour traffic. If you'd like, I'll drive you out to Logan and drop your rental car off myself. It might save you a few minutes."

"Don't worry about that now, Tom. If you feel sure you can close the deal with Ryder, have the legal people put the final touches on the contract."

"I took the liberty of doing that this morning."

"Fine," Derek approved. He liked employees who weren't afraid to take the initiative when it was warranted. "If Ryder agrees to sell for our price, give Sheila Casey a call. Tell her I'll be getting in touch with her from the Coast."

"Do you plan to commission her firm to design the Cape Voyager?"

"Yes, I do. But I'll want to talk to her first. Then, when I get back, I'll want to meet with her in Devon so we can go over the site together."

"Any idea when that will be?"

"No," Derek said. "It depends on a number of factors."

His return east did, of course, depend on a number of factors. He was positive of only one thing. If the deal with Ryder went through, he needed to be back in Devon before Tuesday, July 2. Maybe he didn't owe it to Abby to offer her a chance to withdraw her article from the warrant before the special town meeting. But he wanted her to have that opportunity, and he wanted to give it to her in person.

Channing said, "I have more reports back from the field investigators about potential locations in the Berkshires and in the White Mountains. There's a good tract of land available not far from Tanglewood, the concert center out in west Massachusetts...."

"Yes, I've heard of it."

"There's also a large estate going on the market near Franconia, in the resort region of New Hampshire."

"Good, Tom. I'll take the reports along with me and read them on the plane."

Abby was glad to have Bobby's company that Thursday. She didn't want time to brood about Derek Van Heusen, about Devon Mill, about where her life was going. Lately she had been feeling like she was stuck in a rut.

Having Bobby around was a guarantee against being introspective. His energy level was phenomenal, but more than that he was fun to be with, always bursting with ideas.

Last year, when Bobby had been in her class at Devon Elementary, Abby had noted he had a slight reading problem. This year, his fourth-grade teacher had suggested a summer course in remedial reading. Bobby, horrified at the thought of being cooped up in a classroom a couple of afternoons a week over the summer, had come to Abby for help. She'd promised to work with him on his reading, and intended to keep that promise. The problem was pinning Bobby down long enough for his attention to zero in on a book.

After they finished lunch at the picnic table in her backyard, Abby said sternly, "Work first, Bobby. Then we can do something fun."

"You mean reading, Abby?" Bobby asked. "Reading's fun when I do it with you."

Touched, Abby brought out a book, a story about a boy who had a dog like Captain and lived in the mountains.

They read for an hour, and Abby was satisfied Bobby was making progress. "How about going for ice cream?" she offered as a reward. "Then we'll take Captain for a romp on the beach."

Bobby needed no second invitation.

The rest of the afternoon passed quickly. Greg came for Bobby shortly after five, reminding him they had to hurry up with their supper because Bobby had a Cub Scout meeting that night.

"I would have fixed something for you if I'd known that," Abby told Greg.

"It's okay. I forgot about it myself," he said.

Abby watched them drive away, then straggled back inside her house feeling strangely disoriented. Here she was in the most familiar of environments, yet she felt like she'd been dislodged from the regular tenor of her life.

She'd built that life carefully these past six years alone, like building a house brick by brick. Okay, so maybe she'd also dug herself into a rut. But being in a rut was a lot more comfortable than feeling...empty.

Where was Derek right now?

The question sprang from her subconscious.

She was tempted to call the Oceanside to be sure he'd checked out. Then wondered what she'd do if he answered the phone in his room.

She told herself impatiently that *of course* he'd checked out. He'd driven up to Boston and was either still in the city right now or already on his way back to California. She imagined him sitting back in the jet, flying across the country as the stewardesses gave him extra attention. She tried to picture him in his San Francisco office....

Frustrated because she couldn't get Derek off her mind, Abby took the easiest escape route available. She switched on TV, found an old detective series rerun, and became halfway caught up in the zany plot. But only halfway.

Time crept along. Abby fed Captain, fixed herself a light supper, watched another rerun on TV. It was good, but not the total distraction she badly needed. By nine o'clock, she knew she either had to get out of the house or she'd start clawing the wallpaper.

"How about another beach run, Captain?" she suggested.

Captain had been curled up asleep, but he woke up quickly. Soon, Abby was driving across town to the bay side of the Cape, more and more aware that she was about to retrace the route she'd taken with Derek last night. It was an idiotic course of action, since she knew doing so would only torment her.

The torment was a kind of sweet agony, though. She parked alongside the boats at Snow Harbor, then sat for a while and let herself remember how it had been with Derek by her side, how it had been when they kissed.

What might have happened if the tide had been going out, instead of coming in? If cool saltwater lapping around their ankles hadn't put out the fire?

She glanced up at the moon. Maybe it was her imagination, but it looked a little bit lopsided tonight. The stars didn't seem quite as bright as they had last night, when their brilliance had dazzled her. Funny how the person you were with could affect your vision.

Suddenly she couldn't face a walk by herself along the beach. Each step in the soft sand would remind her too much of Derek, remind her of how they'd walked hand in hand by the bay in the moonlight. Of how, during the course of their evening together, she'd wanted him more and more.

The sight of Devon Mill had nearly ruined everything. In a strange way, it had brought them together—yet the windmill was an obstacle between them that seemed insurmountable. Even so...she felt a sudden need to see the mill again, now. She felt drawn by the mill, by its sad beauty, by its special, almost mystical force.

Was she impelled to view the mill to reaffirm her purpose? To underscore her views about preserving a piece of Devon's history—views which were so completely at variance with Derek Van Heusen's? Or was she deliberately trying to strengthen the barriers between Derek and herself? As if they weren't strong enough already.

Abby had no answers to those questions.

Captain whimpered when she put the Volks in reverse and started away from the beach. "Hang on, boy," she urged. "You can romp around by the mill. One dog won't ruin the grass."

She grove past the marina onto Mill Bluff Road, then swung into Mill Lane—and was startled to see lights on in the Gould homestead.

She slowed to a stop and stared at the house, disturbed. It had been unoccupied since Clara Gould had moved into Devon Manor eight months ago. Strange that lights should be on, especially at this time of night.

Abby drove around the loop at a snail's pace and pulled into Clara's driveway. Only then did she see the car parked just about where she'd parked yesterday...a gray Buick, unfamiliar to her. Clara, she rationalized, had probably asked someone at the nursing home to get something she wanted. What else?

Abby rapped on the solid old front door and listened for footsteps. When there was no answer, she rapped again. This time, she heard someone coming. But she was not prepared when the door swung open and she found herself confronting Gordon Ryder.

The moonlight was so bright he had no problem identifying her. "Abby Eldredge," he said. "Well, I'll be damned. Come in."

Captain growled.

"It's okay, boy," Abby told her dog. "Go take a run. I'll only be a few minutes."

She stepped inside, and Ryder closed the door behind her. In the living room, she stopped just past the threshold. This was a room she'd always loved—long and low-ceilinged, with a fireplace centering one wall. Beyond the fireplace, double windows looked out over the bay. There was oak wainscoting and cream wallpaper sprigged with little bouquets of yellow-and-white flowers.

Abby glanced at the spinning wheel next to the fireplace, the comfortable couches and chairs, the maple chest and side tables, the choice bric-a-brac, all antiques. She saw the marine painting, a Frederick Waugh original, hung over the fireplace. And the Tiffany lamp that her grandmother had especially loved. But she was shocked to see cartons piled everywhere, and a large stack of newspapers in the center of the floor.

What the hell was Gordon Ryder doing?

He was wearing dark blue slacks and a dress shirt rolled up at the sleeves. Abby saw his jacket tossed over an armchair and judged from his clothes that he'd come here directly from his office, evidently with the purpose of starting to pack up Clara's things.

"What brings you here, Abby," he asked.

It seemed stupid to answer, "I was just driving by." On the other hand, the lights in the house *would* be visible from Mill Bluff Road if she'd been looking in the right direction. As it happened, she'd been too wrapped up in memories of last night with Derek to do anything but concentrate on the road immediately ahead of her.

But she said, "I saw lights on in the house, Gordon. I thought I should check it out."

He smiled, a smile Abby didn't like any more now than she had when they were in high school. "You *are* the fearless one, aren't you?" he observed. "The way things are these days, the sensible thing would have been to call the police."

"Somehow, Gordon, I doubted it was an intruder. You've got the house lit up like a Christmas tree."

"So I have," he agreed. He removed cartons from an armchair and invited, "Here, have a seat. Can I get you a drink?" He pointed to a glass on an end table. "I'm having bourbon."

"No, thanks."

"Okay, then since you're here, we'll talk." He pulled out a gold-stenciled Hitchcock chair, straddled it and nodded at the cartons. "I made up my mind this afternoon I couldn't stall any longer."

"Couldn't stall any longer about what?"

"It's time to get this show on the road, Abby. Someone has to clean out this place. Looks like I'm elected. Aunt Clara wants a few things as keepsakes, so I'm packing them up for her. I haven't yet decided what to do with everything else. I'll probably just put most of this stuff in storage, think about it later. Maybe get in touch with an auctioneer."

"Why, Gordon?"

Ryder's pale blue eyes focused on her face briefly, then he looked away. "Why what?"

"Why are you doing this?" Abby demanded, feeling her anger begin to take over. "Can't you wait till Clara's dead before you start getting rid of her things? These things belong to her, not to you."

"You're missing the point, Abby. My aunt might live for years."

"She's *ninety*, for God's sake."

"Yes, she is. And she can't make the practical, daily decisions that go with owning a big old house that's full of antiques. She's getting the best of care at Devon Manor. She doesn't need to have extra worries. For instance, despite the No Trespassing signs posted around, how long will it be before someone breaks in?"

Abby couldn't answer him.

Ryder finished his drink and said, "Hang on a minute, will you, while I get myself a refresher. Sure you won't join me?"

"Positive."

With Gordon out of the room, Abby let her eyes roam freely. The collection of Sandwich Glass Christmas salts that had been displayed on window shelves was gone, as were the Heisey cruets Clara had positioned on the mantel. Other items were missing, too—the Rose Medallion vase that had always stood on top of the piano, the scrimshaw collection Clara kept on the maple chest.

Gordon had been busy.

Abby seethed with resentment as he came back and straddled the Hitchcock chair again. Greg had suggested that maybe Gordon had changed over the years. He hadn't changed. People didn't change. The thought brought Derek to mind. He would never change, either. They would never see eye to eye on certain critical issues, despite the attraction that flared between them.

Ryder said suddenly, "I'm not enjoying this job, Abby."

"No?" She'd spotted an antique price guide lying open on a couch. "Then what's that for?"

"Those books aren't accurate," Ryder said, flicking an indifferent hand toward the guide. "They give an indication of what things might be worth, that's all. Generally they price things too high."

"Nevertheless, you want to know, don't you?"

Ryder put his drink down and stood up. "Hell, yes, I want to know. I have to know. I don't want my aunt to be screwed by some shrewd antique dealer who'd jump at the chance to pull the wool over my eyes if I have to sell any of these things."

He added, "You might stop to realize, Abby, that Devon Manor is expensive. It's taking a bundle to keep Aunt Clara cared for and comfortable. She has one of the best rooms there, you know that. A large, private room. You also know she likes her privacy. She'd hate to have to live with a roommate."

Those things were true. Abby had to give Gordon that. Clara's room was spacious and attractive. The windows looked out onto a garden and, beyond the garden, to a lawn centered by a lily-covered pond.

She focused on something else. "Does Clara know what you're doing here?"

"You mean, am I going into details with her about all this?" Ryder asked. "No, I'm not. I told Clara to tell me what she wanted, and I'll take her those things as she mentions them."

"So she has no idea that you intend to get rid of everything else, things she might temporarily forget about?"

"For God's sake, Abby," Ryder protested, "it would be downright cruel to go to Clara with an itemized inventory of everything she owns, and say, 'What about this? What about that?' What purpose would that serve, except to bring back memories and depress her?"

Again, Abby couldn't answer Gordon. His point was well taken. If only it wasn't Gordon Ryder saying these things.

His greedy reputation still stuck after all these years. It was a factor Abby couldn't deny.

She quickly reviewed the last conversation she'd had with Clara. They had talked primarily about the mill, not too much about the house. Still, Clara was aware the town was being asked to buy the whole twelve-acre parcel. She had to realize the contents were something to deal with.

Then again, what was the rush?

Thinking about that, Abby said, "The town will give you plenty of time to get things cleared out, Gordon. Assuming the vote goes through, that is."

An odd expression flickered in Gordon Ryder's eyes, and Abby suddenly felt as if the warm June breeze had turned to an icy Arctic blast.

"There's not going to be a vote, Abby," he said.

She stared at him. "Come again?"

"I said, there's not going to be a vote. I'm selling this place to private developers. In fact, the deal's as good as done. I'm going to Boston to finalize it tomorrow afternoon."

Abby got to her feet, her fists clenched. "You can't do that." She heard her voice rise to a higher pitch, but couldn't control it. Heatedly she added, "You know damned well you can't do that."

"I can, and I intend to," Ryder said calmly.

"The hell you can! Everyone knows Clara wants the town to have this property, wants the mill to be restored as a memorial to Randolph. You don't give a damn about your aunt, do you, Gordon? Isn't it enough that one of these days you'll be inheriting everything she's got...including the half million dollars Devon's going to pay her? Isn't that enough?"

"No, it's not," Ryder said. He regarded Abby steadily and went on, "Clara will be getting three million from the company I'm selling to. I'd say that's a significant difference, wouldn't you?''

"Clara doesn't need three million dollars. You're the one who's going to reap *that* reward, aren't you, Gordon?'' Abby's eyes were twin pools of green fire.

Ryder laughed. "I see you haven't changed," he said. "You were a hothead back in high school, and you still are." His eyes roved over her body. "A beautiful hothead, I have to admit. I never could figure why Ken ran out on you, especially with Sally Nickerson. She was plain as a fence board."

Abby could feel her cheeks flush, but she held her tongue. She'd said more than enough to this man. And heard more than enough, too.

"I'll let myself out," she told him, not even trying to camouflage her contempt.

Ryder stood, clutching his drink. "Don't worry if you see lights on in the house again," he said. "I'll be here over the weekend, then I may take a few days off to finish up the job. There's just one more thing I'd like to say before you leave."

"What?"

"Clara has faith in me, Abby. That's why she gave me her power of attorney."

"She *what*?"

"She gave me her power of attorney when she went into the nursing home—the power to handle her affairs, make her decisions. She knows whatever I do will be in her best interest. If I were you, I wouldn't try to convince her otherwise."

Abby's jaw tightened. "Is that a threat, Gordon?"

"No, Abby," Ryder said, "it's not a threat. It's a fact. At this time in my aunt's life, a sudden shock could have very bad results. I intend to build this thing up to her gradually, so by the time she knows the whole story, she'll know it was the right way to go.''

The right way to go.

What a miserable specimen of a human being Gordon Ryder was, Abby thought angrily, closing the door of Clara Gould's house behind her. Captain loped over, and they got in the Volks. Abby, furious, nearly stripped the car's gears in her haste to get away.

She cooled down on the drive across town, but only slightly. She needed someone to talk to, and Greg was the best candidate. There was no one else to whom she could spill out her feelings, her fears and frustrations. Especially at this hour.

She turned off Main Street, drove along the road to Greg's house and was relieved to see there was still a light on in his living room. When he opened the door, though, she was sure she'd caught him dozing in front of the TV. He looked as exhausted as she felt.

"Abby, hey," he mumbled sleepily, but his face creased with delight at the sight of her. "Come on in. Quiet, Captain," he added, as Captain emitted a short bark. "Bobby's asleep and I don't want you to wake him up."

"Captain can stay outside," Abby said. In Greg's living room, she sank into a comfortable armchair and buried her face in her hands.

Greg stood over her and bent down to take a closer look. "Hey, what's the matter?" he asked.

"I've been out at the Gould homestead. Gordon Ryder's there. He's packing Clara's things in boxes. I . . . couldn't believe it." Her words came out in spurts.

"What are you talking about?" Greg held up his hand. "Wait a minute, something tells me you've got a story to tell. Let me get us a couple of beers before you begin."

Abby didn't usually care much for beer, but now the cold, tangy brew tasted good. She took a sip, leaned back in the chair and moaned, "I didn't mean to lay all this on you, Greg. But I've got to spill it out, or I won't be able to sleep."

"I'm listening," Greg said calmly.

Abby told him the story of encountering Gordon Ryder. When she'd finished, Greg asked, "Do you think Derek Van Heusen is the developer he was talking about?"

"Gordon didn't mention names, and I didn't ask. But it seems pretty obvious, doesn't it?"

"Yeah, I'd say so."

She remembered Derek's reaction when she called him a developer. Well, what else was he? Unless she could do something to stop him, he would transform twelve unspoiled acres—land replete with history and beauty—into a glitzy resort.

"To tell you the truth . . . Derek told me he intends to buy Clara's property," she told Greg.

"When did he tell you that?"

"He came over to my house yesterday afternoon."

"He was there when I phoned?" Greg asked.

"Yes."

"I thought you sounded strange. He could overhear your end of the conversation, I take it?"

"Yes."

Greg frowned. "I noticed today that the two of you were on a first-name basis."

Abby sidestepped that. She asked, instead, "What was Derek Van Heusen doing in your pickup truck, by the way?"

"He'd gone for a run and wound up at the dock on Wampum Cove where Bobby's been fishing. They got to talking."

"Derek and Bobby? About what?"

"Evidently he was giving Bobby advice about his choice of fishing tackle."

"Derek?"

"Is it that astonishing, Abby?"

"Well, it's hard to picture him in that kind of a role," she admitted.

Greg shrugged. "Hey, the guy's human. And Bobby, if I do say so, is a pretty engaging kid."

Abby leaned forward, made a decision. She hadn't intended to get into this, but now she confessed, "Greg, I had dinner with him last night."

"You, with Van Heusen?"

"We drove out to P-town, to La Chamarita. He...he's a very attractive man."

Greg's jaw actually dropped. "You're not telling me you're falling for him, are you?"

"No, no..."

"But you could?"

"I'm afraid so, yes."

Greg set down his beer mug with a thud and said bluntly, "That might be the biggest damn fool thing you've ever done. For God's sake, Abby, you'd be asking for it. No one wants you to find someone more than I do. But Derek Van Heusen?" He shook his head. "Sometimes I think you go looking for trouble. Though, never with a man before." He paused, obviously working through some thoughts.

Then, to Abby's surprise, he suddenly grinned. "Maybe the idea of you and Van Heusen isn't so bad after all," he speculated. "Differences can be...interesting. Bobby's certainly taken to him, and sometimes kids can be good judges of character."

"Shut up, Greg," Abby advised. She forced a weary smile as she added, "You were right in the first place. Falling for Derek would, indeed, be the biggest damned fool thing I've ever done. Believe me, I don't intend to deliberately walk into any punches."

"What do you intend to do, Abby?"

"Save Devon Mill. If it's true that Derek's company intends to buy Clara's land, I'll do my damnedest to stop the sale. The town meeting's a week from next Tuesday. That gives me twelve days. Tomorrow morning. I'm going to talk with Bert Mayo. There may be zoning ordinances prohibiting construction of any new buildings on Clara's property. Or conservation laws."

"Something tells me Van Heusen's people would already have checked those things out, so don't get your hopes too high."

"I won't. But Bert Mayo's been town counsel for years. He knows all the angles. There must be something he can do."

"Maybe, Abby. But he's not a miracle worker."

"Greg . . . I'm not sure I believe Gordon—about his having Clara's power of attorney, that is."

"Having her power of attorney would be the only way he could take legal action on the property without her knowledge. If Clara was considering selling to someone else, she'd have told you."

"There must be a reason. There must be something. . . ."

Abby knew she was floundering, clutching at straws. She also knew she couldn't give in on this, would never give in, regardless of the effect Derek Van Heusen had on her. No man had ever made her feel the way he'd made her feel when he kissed her last night. But for the tide, she might have wound up supine on the sand with him.

She pushed away a memory that burned like a torch she didn't want to carry, and got to her feet. "I need to sleep," she told Greg. "So do you. Thanks for letting me blow off steam."

"No problem, Abby. I only hope it helped. I don't suppose you looked over those figures I gave you about the mill?"

"I didn't get to it, Greg. I'm sorry. First thing tomorrow morning..."

"There's no hurry. Except, Van Heusen asked me for a similar estimate."

Hope flared. "Derek? Are you saying he might restore the mill instead of tearing it down? That doesn't make sense, Greg. The mill is situated practically in the center of the property. It would be smack in the way of anything he wanted to build."

"He was thinking in terms of moving the mill."

"I hope you told him that's out of the question!"

"Yes, that's pretty much what I told him."

"What did he say?"

"We dropped the subject at that point."

"Good," Abby said firmly. "Because Devon Mill's going to stay right where it is. Just you wait and see."

Chapter Eight

Derek's secretary advanced into his office and said, "Excuse me, Mr. Van Heusen...Mr. Yamasaki wonders if you'd have time to meet with him this afternoon?"

Derek, seated behind his massive mahogany desk, looked up from the report he'd been attempting to read. Behind him, a glass wall afforded an eagle's nest view of San Francisco and San Francisco Bay.

"I'm sorry, Grace...what did you say?"

Grace Duncan was a stunning silver-haired woman in her fifties. She was one of the most efficient persons Derek had ever known. She ran his schedule like clockwork, never brought anything or anyone to his attention unless it was justified, and she hoarded his hours as if they were her own. She'd been with him three years, and she suited him perfectly.

"Mr. Yamasaki, Mr. Van Heusen. He would like to see you this afternoon. He's returning to Tokyo tomorrow, now that your acquisition of his assets has been worked out. I think he just wants a farewell chat.''

"What else have I got this afternoon?"

"A meeting with Bill Engalls at four to discuss the reports you're reading now."

Bill Engalls was the company's executive vice president. First thing this morning, he'd delivered a file of documents and reports on a proposed takeover and had urged Derek to give it top priority. "If we can absorb Walthrop & Edwards," he'd waxed enthusiastically, "it'll put us up in the top twenty-five hotel systems in the country."

Derek had been ruffling through graphs, financial statements and the like for more than an hour. But his mind refused to focus on the benefits of a merger with Walthrop & Edwards, a holding company that listed a major highway motel chain among its assets.

"Mr. Van Heusen?"

Derek, lost in thought, snapped to. "Yes, Grace . . . oh, Mr. Yamasaki. Why don't you ask him to come in at two?"

"Very good."

Derek glanced at his desk clock. It was eleven-thirty, Pacific time. Two-thirty in Massachusetts. "Just a moment, Grace," he added, stopping her on her way out the door.

"Yes?"

"Get me Abigail Eldredge on the phone," he instructed. He drew out his wallet, extracted a crumpled slip of paper. "Here's her number."

Grace Duncan looked baffled. "Abigail Eldredge?"

"That's right, Grace."

As Grace closed the office door behind her, Derek returned to browsing over the file Bill Engalls had given him. But it was wasted effort. Right now he couldn't force interest in mergers, acquisitions or other routine business affairs, no matter how important they might be.

How many days had passed since he'd left Devon? He ticked them off on his fingers. He'd arrived back in San Francisco Thursday night. He'd met with Mr. Yamasaki and his representatives on Friday. Thanks to Derek's staff having done an excellent prep job, the sale terms for Yamasaki's American assets were quickly negotiated.

Saturday morning, he'd begun to feel as if the walls of his condo overlooking San Francisco Bay were closing in on him, so he'd driven up to his private retreat in the Sierras, not far from Yosemite National Park. The log cabin on a serene mountain lake was one of his favorite places in the world, his private oasis. Very few people knew of its existence.

All weekend, he'd thought about how much Abby would like it there. The cabin and its magnificent mountain surrounding would be her kind of a place, unless he were much mistaken. And now…it was Monday. He'd been away from Devon only four days. Four days that seemed like eternity.

The intercom on his desk buzzed.

"Yes?" he said.

"I have Miss Eldredge on the phone."

"Thank you, Grace."

Derek picked up the receiver. "Abby?"

"Yes."

Just the sound of her voice sent Derek's imagination swirling. He wondered if she was wearing her oversized terry robe. He wonder if she'd just gotten out of the tub or shower, if her hair was damp and her face shiny.

"Abby, how are you?"

There was a pause. And when Abby did speak, her tone was edgy. "Derek? What is this about?"

"What do you mean?"

"Why are you calling?"

He heard her apprehension, realized she must think he was calling her about Devon Mill. He smiled wryly, and at the same time felt frustration creeping in. Didn't it occur to her that he might have other reasons for calling?

He wished he could touch her, smell her, feel her warmth. He wished they could finish what they'd begun the other night at Mill Beach. His frustration increased.

His voice husky, he said, "I wanted to talk to you."

"Why?"

Derek paused.

"Why did you want to talk to me?" Abby persisted. She'd felt shaky all over the second she'd heard a woman say, "Miss Eldredge? I have a call for you from Mr. Derek Van Heusen." Now she clutched her phone, began pacing back and forth in her living room, going as far as the cord would allow. "Was that your *secretary* who placed this call?" she suddenly demanded.

"Yes, it was. Why?"

"You don't even make your own phone calls?" Just the idea of that made Abby freshly aware of the differences, the gaps, in their life-styles.

Derek said, "Why do I feel that's an accusation? Yes, I asked Grace to place the call for me. Call it force of habit."

That's what it had been. Force of habit. He couldn't remember when, during office hours, he'd last placed a phone call himself. But he could see how having his secretary get her on the phone must have seemed to Abby. Impersonal. A business summons.

"Abby..." he began, wondering what she'd come back with if he told her the truth. *I had to hear the sound of your voice....*

She interrupted before he could say anything. "Thursday night I was at Clara Gould's house. Gordon Ryder was there. He told me some very disturbing news."

"You spoke with Ryder?"

"I just said so. He told me he has Clara's power of attorney. I haven't been able to check that out yet, Derek. Maybe you could spare me the trouble. *Does* Gordon have Clara's power of attorney?"

God, he hated this!

"Yes," he admitted.

"That's why you were so sure of yourself when you said, right in the beginning, that you were buying Devon Mill. Is that it?"

"I knew Ryder had the power to act for his aunt, yes."

"Gordon told me he was going to meet with someone in your Boston office last Friday."

Derek didn't answer.

"Have you bought Clara Gould's land, Derek? Do you really own Devon Mill?"

The mellow dreams about Abby, intensified by a weekend spent alone in the Sierras, evaporated. Derek's lips tightened. He hadn't called her to get into this. Was that goddamned rundown windmill the only thing this woman could think about?

Frost crept into Derek's voice. "If you want to discuss Devon Mill, Abby, I'd suggest you call Tom Channing at my Boston office." He drew a long breath. "If there's nothing else, I guess I'll say goodbye."

Abby heard a click, then a dial tone, and stared at her phone. That was it? He'd politely hung up on her!

She angrily thrust the receiver into place, stalked over to the window and looked out at the pine woods that edged close to her house. It was raining, a steady downpour. The trunks of the pines were black and wet, and the sky was opaque. The bleak weather matched her mood.

Derek had called her... and she'd really botched things. She'd been put off by his secretary's cool, professional tone, and instantly decided that he had to be calling about the windmill. But she'd been wrong. Evidently Derek had meant the call to be personal.

Abby resisted the impulse to beat her fists against the windowpanes. There'd been just óne frustration after another, ever since Derek's return to California last Thursday.

First, when she'd called Bert Mayo's office on Friday, she had discovered the town counsel was off on a three-day holiday. Bert's secretary had given Abby a Monday morning appointment, but Monday seemed a long wait to find out if there might be legal grounds to block the sale of the windmill property. She had thought about talking to George Cobb or one of the other selectmen, then tabled that idea. She really needed to speak with Bert first.

Saturday, she'd driven to Hyannis and browsed around Cape Cod Mall. Sunday, it had been raining when she'd woken up. She'd tried to lounge in bed, but couldn't. She'd thought she might connect with Greg and Bobby, then remembered they were driving over to Plymouth, where Greg's parents lived, to spend the day and have dinner. A movie matinee had only killed a few hours. So, mostly, she'd moped. And followed that up with a restless night's sleep.

Now, cursing the fact that she'd spoiled her chance to talk with Derek, Abby turned away from the window and dressed for her three-thirty meeting with Bert Mayo.

The town counsel was a short, round, pleasant man. Being Devon's lawyer was only a part-time job. In addition, Bert conducted a law practice in a square, white-shingled building on Main Street.

He ushered Abby to a worn leather armchair, then sat down behind his scarred oak desk. "Crummy day," he commented, glancing out the window.

"That, it is."

"What can I do for you, Abby?"

She leaned forward. "I need advice, Bert. It looks like Clara Gould's property is going to be sold, without Clara's knowledge, before the town gets a chance to buy it."

"Without Clara's knowledge? How could that be?"

"Gordon Ryder," Abby said bleakly. She sat back and unfolded the whole story to Bert. She left out Derek's unexpected morning phone call. But she did say that accurate information probably could be obtained from a man named Tom Channing, who headed Van Heusen Inc.'s Boston office.

Bert Mayo scrawled a note on a scratch pad and promised, "I'll get in touch with Channing later today."

"Bert..." Abby strove to get her thoughts in order, her words straight. Her mind kept straying to the memory of Derek's voice on the phone, and how it had changed from warm to cold.

She began again. "Bert, I was wondering... what about zoning restrictions? Aren't there bylaws that would prevent a resort complex being built out on the bluffs?"

"Unfortunately, no," Bert said. "If the land were within the National Seashore boundaries, there'd be no chance of a resort complex or anything else going up. But Clara Gould's property is within a commercially zoned area, I'm sorry to say."

Seeing Abby sag, Bert went on, "Devon, like too many other Cape towns, has been lax in its zoning restrictions. Things are finally tightening up, but it's like locking the barn door too late. In the case of Clara's land—that part of town—I see no way there could be new zoning legislation enacted in time to prevent legal development."

"What about conservation laws?"

"Well, that's a possibility. But again, Devon has been unbelievably lax. Too little, too late. In any case, Clara's land is all upland, is it not?"

"Yes, I suppose it is."

"If it were marsh or a bog...if altering the vegetation would affect the ground water supply, then you might have a case. The state and federal laws are quite protective of certain types of terrain, even when they fall within private property."

"So you're telling me there's no way to stop Van Heusen from building a Voyager, if in fact they own the land?"

"Well, assuming the sales contract between Ryder and Van Heusen hasn't been finalized, there's a little time left. But very little, Abby. Our one chance would be to get Clara Gould to turn the deed to her property over to the town before Ryder and Van Heusen sign the contract."

Abby frowned and admitted, "I'm not sure I understand what you're getting at, Bert. Clara could turn her deed over to Devon before the voters vote to buy her property?"

"She could, but she would have to act on faith. If the article didn't go through, it might jeopardize her sale to a third party, such as Van Heusen. In other words, say the town turns her down, and in the interim, Van Heusen decided to buy property elsewhere."

"Can't you, or one of the selectmen, assure Clara that the article's going to pass?"

"No," Bert said. "It *looks* like the article will pass, Abby. But to say for certain that it will pass would be risky, insofar as acting responsibly for the town is concerned. Those kinds of statements can backfire, with expensive consequences. There was a case just recently where a town in western Mass. was sued successfully because their finance committee wouldn't go for a deal after the selectmen made it."

"What about Gordon Ryder?" Abby asked. "Could he sue the town if the sale to Van Heusen was stopped?"

Bert looked solemn. "Not if Clara has revoked his power of attorney, no. Based on what you've told me, Abby, getting Clara to do that, then getting her to surrender the deed to her property, is about your only chance of saving the mill."

"That's asking a lot of her," Abby mused. "I'm not sure she's up to it."

"She's a spunky old lady. Don't underestimate her."

Abby didn't underestimate Clara Gould. But she was disturbed at the thought of presenting her with these new problems. Especially since, in the process, Clara's faith in her nephew was certain to be destroyed.

She was deeply troubled as she drove out to Devon Manor. She hated involving Clara in her bitter battle, but kept trying to assure herself that Clara would be even more upset if the windmill weren't saved than if she learned unpleasant truths about her nephew's motivations for involving himself in her affairs.

In the course of ninety years, Clara must have faced a lot of unpleasant truths. And, Bert was right. Clara *was* a spunky woman.

When she reached Devon Manor, however, Abby quickly realized there was no way she could present the issue to Clara today.

"Her heart's been kicking up a bit," a nurse told Abby. "Nothing terribly serious, but we sedated her to keep her calm. Expect her to be fuzzy."

Clara seemed pleased to see Abby, but she was vague, not at all up to talking. After only a minute or two, she closed her eyes and dozed off.

Abby was heavy-hearted when she left the nursing home. The week, she thought dismally, was starting out on a bad note. The pace, as it happened, did not improve.

Monday night, Abby's Conservation Commission meeting ran too long. People seemed inclined to argue over the most ridiculous trivialities. Bobby came down with a bug Tuesday, which he'd evidently caught from Melanie Doane's kids. Abby suggested she go to Greg's house to take care of Bobby, and for once Greg agreed.

By Thursday, Bobby was fine, but then it was Captain's turn to develop a problem—an ear infection that required a trip to the vet. And so the week went.

Greg had been talking for a while about riding out on the "Outer Beach" some sunny Sunday. His pickup was a four-wheel drive with a requisite sticker permit for beach travel, so he and Abby and Bobby could get far away from the crowds, spend the day in the sun and surf, and—relatively speaking—pretty much have nature to themselves.

"This'll be the last chance till fall, though," Greg warned Abby when he called her Saturday. "Next weekend is the Fourth. From then till Labor Day, forget it. Too many people get the same idea. Anyway, the weather is supposed to be great tomorrow, eighty degrees and not a cloud in the sky."

Abby grabbed at the chance to escape. "What can I bring?" she asked.

"Just yourself. You're always bringing something. No need, this time."

"I'll bake brownies," Abby decided.

"Fine," Greg agreed, knowing she'd do it even if he protested.

She was ready and waiting when Greg and Bobby pulled into her yard the next morning. Greg climbed out of his pickup and asked, "You have a portable grill, don't you?"

"Back in the shed, yes."

"I would have brought ours, but I haven't used it since last summer and it rusted out," Greg said disgustedly. "I'd rather not waste time stopping to get a new one, if we can take yours."

"What about charcoal and lighter fluid?"

"I got that yesterday. Plus—" Greg broke off, seeing the sleek black Mercedes coming slowly up Abby's lane. "You expecting someone?" he asked.

"No, I wasn't. Maybe it's lost tourists."

Captain and Bobby had been romping in the yard. When the luxury sedan came to a stop beside Greg's truck and Derek Van Heusen climbed out, Captain rushed over and jumped up on him, frantically wagging his tail.

Abby glared at her dog, muttering, "Traitor," under her breath. She tried to slip on a mask of indifference as Derek sauntered in her direction. It was the toughest acting job she'd ever faced. Derek's sudden appearance was the last thing on earth she would have expected.

Greg spoke first, saying easily, "I thought you'd headed cross-country a week ago."

"I did, Greg. And now I'm back."

"Hi, Derek," Bobby shouted as he wrestled Captain to the ground.

"Hi, there, Bobby. Been catching any fish lately?"

"Lots," Bobby answered. "The lighter sinker works great!"

"Good," Derek said. Then he added, "Hello, Abby. How have you been?"

Abby heard a foreign quality in Derek's voice. He sounded strained, subdued.

"I've been okay," she said. "And you?"

"Pretty good."

The more
you love romance . . .
the more
you'll love this offer

FREE!

Mail this heart today! (See inside)

Join us on a Silhouette® Honeymoon
and we'll give you
4 free books
A free Victorian picture frame
And a free mystery gift

IT'S A
SILHOUETTE HONEYMOON—
A SWEETHEART OF A FREE OFFER!
HERE'S WHAT YOU GET:

1. Four New Silhouette Special Edition® Novels— FREE!

Take a Silhouette Honeymoon with your four exciting romances—yours FREE from Silhouette Reader Service™. Each of these hot-off-the-press novels brings you the passion and tenderness of today's greatest love stories . . . your free passports to bright new worlds of love and foreign adventure.

2. Lovely Victorian Picture Frame— FREE!

This lovely Victorian pewter-finish miniature is perfect for displaying a treasured photograph. And it's yours FREE as added thanks for giving our Reader Service a try!

3. An Exciting Mystery Bonus—FREE!

You'll be thrilled with this surprise gift. It is useful as well as practical.

4. Free Home Delivery!

Join the Silhouette Reader Service™ and enjoy the convenience of pre-viewing 6 new books every month delivered right to your home. Each book is yours for only $2.74* each—a saving of 21¢ off the cover price. And there is no extra charge for postage and handling. It's a sweetheart of a deal for you! If you're not completely satisfied, you may cancel at anytime, for any reason, simply by sending us a note or shipping statement marked "cancel" or by returning any shipment to us at our cost.

5. Free Insiders' Newsletter!

You'll get our monthly newsletter, packed with news about your favorite writers, upcoming books, even recipes from your favorite authors.

6. More Surprise Gifts!

Because our home subscribers are our most valued readers, when you join the Silhouette Reader Service™, we'll be sending you additional free gifts from time to time—as a token of our appreciation.

START YOUR SILHOUETTE HONEYMOON TODAY—JUST COMPLETE, DETACH AND MAIL YOUR FREE-OFFER CARD

*Terms and prices subject to change without notice. Sales tax applicable in NY.

© 1991 HARLEQUIN ENTERPRISES LIMITED

Get your fabulous gifts ABSOLUTELY FREE!

MAIL THIS CARD TODAY.

GIVE YOUR HEART TO SILHOUETTE

Yes! Please send me my four Silhouette Special Edition® novels FREE, along with my free Victorian picture frame and free mystery gift. I wish to receive all the benefits of the Silhouette Reader Service™ as explained on the opposite page.

PLACE
HEART STICKER
HERE

NAME _____
(PLEASE PRINT)

ADDRESS _____ APT. _____

CITY _____ STATE _____

ZIP CODE _____

235 CIS ACEV
(U-SIL-SE-01/91)

SILHOUETTE READER SERVICE™ "NO-RISK" GUARANTEE

—There's no obligation to buy—and the free gifts remain yours to keep.

—You pay the low subscribers'-only price and receive books before they appear in stores.

—You may end your subscription anytime by sending us a note or shipping statement marked "cancel" or by returning any shipment to us at our cost.

OFFER LIMITED TO ONE PER HOUSEHOLD AND NOT VALID TO CURRENT SILHOUETTE SPECIAL EDITION® SUBSCRIBERS.

© 1991 HARLEQUIN ENTERPRISES LIMITED

START YOUR
SILHOUETTE HONEYMOON TODAY.
JUST COMPLETE, DETACH AND MAIL YOUR
FREE-OFFER CARD.

If offer card below is missing write to:
Silhouette Reader Service, 3010 Walden Ave.,
P.O. Box 1867, Buffalo, NY 14269-1867.

DETACH AND MAIL TODAY!

BUSINESS REPLY MAIL
FIRST CLASS MAIL   PERMIT NO. 717   BUFFALO, NY

POSTAGE WILL BE PAID BY ADDRESSEE

SILHOUETTE READER SERVICE
3010 WALDEN AVE
PO BOX 1867
BUFFALO NY 14240-9952

NO POSTAGE
NECESSARY
IF MAILED
IN THE
UNITED STATES

Reluctantly she met his eyes and felt like she was being seared by a deep blue blaze. God, what a color! His shirt was stark white in contrast, and his jeans, to her surprise, were almost as faded as Greg's jeans. They fit his long, powerful legs like a glove, and made him look sexier than ever.

"Looks like I've interrupted something," he observed.

Greg spoke up. "We're heading to the Outer Beach for a cookout."

Before Derek could respond, Bobby rushed up with Captain on his heels. "Hey!" he suggested, his enthusiasm brimming over, "Dad brought his surf rod. Why don't you come along, Derek?"

Derek looked stunned. "Thanks, Bobby, but I don't think so," he said. "The reason I stopped by was to go over something with Abby. It can wait till another time...."

"Why not come along?" Greg cut in, and Abby could have throttled him. "We have plenty of food, and there's plenty of room in the truck, if you don't mind sharing the back with Bobby and Captain, that is. The cab is full of junk. Abby's going to have to squeeze in as it is."

Derek glanced at Abby, then turned to Greg. "I'd love to come along," he said. "I even have a bathing suit in the car."

Abby, still reeling from the jolt of seeing him, felt a hot-cold aftershock hearing Derek agree to Greg's invitation. How could he sound so nonchalant, when she was feeling like every nerve in her body had been set on fire? She wasn't even ready to see him, let alone spend a whole day with him on the beach.

She needed distance from Derek, needed to maintain perspective. When he was near, it was too easy to become distracted, to forget the things she needed to remember. Such as the fact that Bert Mayo had called Tom Channing during the week, and determined that Derek's signature was all that was needed to finalize the sale of Clara's property... and thus assure the destruction of Devon Mill.

Had Derek signed that contract? Was he just now coming from Boston to tell her the news himself? Was this a company car or another rental?

The questions tumbled, and abruptly Abby asked, "When did you get back from California?"

Derek held her gaze. "I got into Logan late last night, picked up this rental car and drove directly down here. It was after midnight when I checked in at the Oceanside."

He turned to Greg. "Look," he said, "on second thought, I don't think I can join you, but thanks for the invitation. I'll get in touch with you later, Abby."

"Hey, come on," Greg protested. "It's settled. Bobby, get Abby's grill, would you please? And Abby, did you remember to bring suntan stuff so you won't burn to a crisp?"

"Yes," she managed.

"Got a ball for Captain?"

"Yes."

"Then let's get going."

Derek held the cab door open for Abby, and she climbed in, awash with a mix of feelings that were so complex she couldn't even begin to straighten them out. She let the emotional brew simmer as Greg got the rest of the act together. She heard Derek laugh at something Greg said, and knew, from what they were saying, that Derek was helping Greg rearrange things in the back of the truck to make extra room.

Finally they started out. And, as they reached Nauset Beach in Orleans and continued south on the sand, Abby had to admit that—despite Derek's presence—the day could not have been more perfect. The air was warm and clear, the sky was a study in infinite blue, the dunes were a soft gol-

den beige, the spiky beach grass was sun-bleached green—
and the vast North Atlantic was the color of Derek's eyes.

Slowly Abby began to relax. She couldn't deny the heady
excitement of knowing Derek was just a few feet behind her
in the back of Greg's pickup. She couldn't refute the sensation of undiluted joy that shot through her, despite herself, because he was so near. Those feelings overshadowed
the things that had gone on between them, as well as the
negative things that were certain to happen.

She told herself that she was living *now* and *now* became
overwhelmingly important. No matter what tomorrow
might bring, she would make the most of what was being
offered to her today, Abby promised herself. Time with
Derek, in one of the most beautiful, and relaxing, settings
she could imagine.

"Care to try some fishing, Derek?" Greg asked.

They'd driven along the well-marked sandy trails, found
an isolated stretch of beach to claim as their own private
picnic site and parked facing the pounding surf.

Derek shook his head. "Thanks, but I've never done any
surf casting."

"Dad can show you," Bobby said quickly. "Dad's great
at casting."

Abby saw Greg's thin face flush at this praise from his son
and felt good for him. She knew Greg didn't always realize
how much Bobby adored him, and it was nice to see this
outward evidence.

"Maybe after we eat," Greg said. "Anyone hungry?"

"Yeah!" Bobby shouted.

Bobby played ball with Captain while Greg set up the grill
and got a fire going. When he started broiling hot dogs and
hamburgers, Abby set out rolls, pickles and condiments on

their blanket table cloth, shaking her head negatively when
Derek asked if he could help.

Greg had brought along a couple of folding beach chairs.
Derek, returning from behind the dunes where he'd changed
into black and green swim trunks, opened a can of beer,
then stretched out in one of the chairs, turning his face up
to the sun.

Abby stopped what she was doing and caught her breath
at the sight of him. His eyes were closed, and the gentle
breeze ruffled his dark hair. The bruise on his forehead—
evidence of the collision that had rocked them both in more
ways than one—had faded. But the memory of trying to
tend to his wound, then dripping ice water all over his chest,
was as vivid as yesterday.

Abby surveyed him. His profile didn't look nearly so
square and uncompromising. And, relaxed, his handsome
face was void of the sternness and aloofness that usually
characterized it.

Her gaze traveled down the full length of his body, and
the more she studied Derek, the more she became conscious of an inner twisting deep within her. It was a coil of
desire, slowly unwinding, yet at the same time stretching
tighter and tighter....

Derek's chest was rising and falling to the slow, easy
rhythm of his breathing. Abby remembered how it had felt
to press her head against that chest, to get close to his
heartbeat, and the inner twisting combined with a sweet,
sensuous ache.

Her eyes traced the flatness of his stomach, the tautness
of his thighs... to the private areas concealed beneath his
sharp-looking bathing suit. She imagined the transformation that would happen to his body—if he were aroused. She
remembered feeling the beginning of that transformation
when they'd embraced on Mill Beach under the full moon.

The late morning sun was hot enough, but the rush of heat that surged into Abby's body more than rivaled it. Suddenly she realized what she was doing, realized where she was, and cut her fantasy short. Bobby and Captain were close by, and if Greg, tending the grill, had any idea...

"What do you need, Greg?" she called over. "Plates?"

"I'll just put everything on a platter," he told her, "and everyone can help themselves."

At that, Derek stirred. "Boy," he said drowsily, "I was drifting off fast. Do me a favor, Abby. Don't let me slip off like that again. I'm not used to this sun."

"You look like a tanner, not a burner."

"I am, but I still have to go slow."

Abby tried to visualize Derek with a deep tan and soon decided to give up—he was handsome enough as he was. If she allowed herself to again wander off on tangents, she'd lose the urge to eat. She'd be thinking of something else entirely.

They feasted to the sound of rolling breakers crashing against the shoreline, and no one uttered much more than a word until just about everything was devoured.

"Delicious," Derek finally said.

"Yeah," Greg agreed. He stood and smothered a yawn. "I think I'll stretch out for a while."

"I think I'll build a sand castle," Bobby decided. He looked up at Abby and Derek. "Want to help?"

"Maybe later," Derek cut in, before Abby could answer. "I was thinking about a walk down the beach. Would you join me, Abby?"

She shrugged. "I suppose the exercise would be good."

She was tempted to suggest that Bobby give up building his sand castle and come with them. But she didn't. Soon, she and Derek were walking along the edge of the water, alone.

They were out of earshot of Greg and Bobby when Derek observed quietly, "You didn't want me to come, did you?"

She didn't know what to say.

"You don't have to deny it, Abby. I should have waited until I contacted you on the phone before barging in at your place. I was anxious to see you, that's all. I have something I want to show you. Also, there are things we should talk about."

Abby's laugh was short, bitter. "I wouldn't say we have much to talk about."

"Abby, I'm not out to wreck your town."

"Not the town as a whole, Derek. Just one of its most irreplaceable assets. Not to mention twelve beautiful, unspoiled acres."

Derek let that slip by. He knew they had to talk, but he wished it didn't have to be now. It would be better later, as they were bound to argue. For the moment, he just wanted to be with Abby, enjoy her company, share this glorious summer day.

He watched her pick up a shell, study it briefly, then toss it back on the sand, and her beauty and grace struck him full force. She really *was* like no other woman he'd ever seen, ever known. But then she turned, her expression so bleak, it jolted him.

"You really don't give a damn, do you?" she asked, sounding more defeated than angry.

Derek stared at her, baffled by this change in attitude, as she went on, "You see life only in terms of dollars and cents, don't you, Derek?"

Her question shocked him...and also hurt. He kept walking, trying hard to let the cold ocean water splashing at his feet distract him from retaliating to this personal attack.

It was a minute before he glanced down at her and answered, in a thick voice, "I hope not." But the echo of

Abby's question continued to assault his senses like the waves pounding just a few yards offshore.

The memory of Hugh Faulkner sprang to mind. Faulkner, Derek was beginning to understand, had been the loneliest man he'd ever known. True, the loneliness had been skillfully concealed both from his two sons, and from Derek as well. True also...Faulkner had definitely seen life only in terms of dollars and cents.

Was he following that closely in Faulkner's footsteps?

Abby said, "Derek, I'm sorry. That was cruel of me."

He stopped and face her. "Why be sorry, Abby? Maybe what you say is true."

"No, Derek, it's not. I didn't mean it. It's just . . ."

"It's just what?"

"It's just that I've never cared much about money and power. I don't think I ever could. To me, other things are far more precious." She reached down by her feet and plucked a glistening rock from the sand. "Like this," she told him.

Derek took the stone from her, felt its smoothness, examined its charcoal-gray colors. "I wonder how many years it's taken for the sea to polish this so perfectly?"

Abby felt her heart swell. For once, Derek was seeing something the way she saw it.

"Hundreds, maybe thousands," she guessed. "And there's not another stone like it in the entire world."

"No?"

"See that band of lighter rock going around the middle?"

"Yes."

"According to Cape Cod legend, that makes this a lucky stone. When you fine a lucky stone—or if you're given one—it means you'll have a year of good luck. The wider the band, the luckier you'll be."

Derek regarded the stone more closely, then heard Abby say, "I want you to have it, Derek, as a special gift from me."

They were far down the beach from Greg and Bobby. But even if they hadn't been, Derek would have done exactly what he did next. He reached out and touched Abby's cheek. Then he bent slightly and kissed her gently on the mouth.

"I'll keep your lucky stone with me always and forever," he promised.

Chapter Nine

The doorbell rang, and Captain barked. Abby, about to switch off her reading lamp, glanced at the bedside clock. It was a quarter past ten. Not that late, but too late for Greg to be returning unless she'd forgotten something, left something in the pickup he thought she might want.

But she hadn't left anything. She was sure of that.

Just as she was sure she knew who was at her front door.

She slipped out of bed, tugged her terrycloth robe over her white cotton nightgown and wished she had some sexy, alluring lingerie. Something that would make her look as provocative as she suddenly wanted to feel.

Was she out of her mind?

Derek, standing on her threshold, looked sheepish. "I've done it again," he confessed. "Showed up on your doorstep without calling first. I didn't wake you, did I?"

"No."

"I was afraid you'd say no if I invited myself over."

Would she have said no? Abby couldn't give herself an honest answer. If she had any *sense* she would have said no. But where Derek was concerned...

She saw he wasn't moving an inch.

"*Are* you going to ask me in?" he prompted.

"Well, since you're here..." She didn't finish.

Derek was holding a brown paper bag in one hand, a long cardboard tube in the other. He held out the paper bag. "Scotch," he said. "I was hoping you'd join me for a drink?"

"Where did you get that? The liquor stores are closed on Sundays."

"I know," he said with a faint smile. "I found that out when I tried to buy you a bottle of wine. I brought the Scotch from the Coast. I hope it'll do."

"Yes."

He followed Abby out to the kitchen and watched her take two glasses out of her cupboard.

"You pour," she suggested. "Want ice?"

"Please."

"Derek, why are you here?"

He didn't hesitate. "I have something I must show you, Abby, and I didn't want to hang around when we got back from the beach. Frankly, I didn't know how Greg would take it."

"Didn't know how he'd take what?"

"I thought he might feel I'd overstayed my welcome. I felt like he wanted to spend some time alone with you. It seems as if you and Greg are very close."

"I certainly don't deny that."

"Are you in love with him, Abby?" Derek couldn't believe he was asking her that. Her relationship with Greg Nickerson was *her* business. Yet...he had to know.

"I love Greg," Abby said. "But I am not in love with him. If you've been hearing things around town—"

"It's not that. It's just clear to me that Greg's very fond of you."

Abby pulled out a chair and sat down at the kitchen table. "You've talked with Gordon Ryder, I take it?"

"Before I went back to California, yes."

"Well, that should have been enough."

Her face was grim. Derek saw a muscle twitch in her jaw and fancied he saw hurt shadowing her beautiful eyes. Again, he wondered how any man could ever have left her.

She went on, "I'm sure Gordon filled you in on Greg and me . . . and Ken and Sally. Right?"

"Abby, please. I didn't come here to talk about that."

She ignored him and said tightly, "So our marriage partners walked out on us? So what? That was a long time ago. Greg and I have gone on with our lives. People still talk, I guess. I can't stop that. But whatever Gordon told you probably is no more true than most of the things he says. He's always been a great one for distorting the facts."

Derek saw Abby's chest heave as she drew in a breath and expelled it. "Greg and I are friends, and that's *all,*" she emphasized. "Neither of us wants it any other way. The kind of friendship we have is special and wonderful. It wouldn't be the way it is if we were lovers. Does that answer your questions?"

Derek said very softly, "Abby, there's no need for you to be so defensive. I wasn't questioning you, not in the way you think. I simply got the impression that Greg was waiting for me to leave before he and Bobby did. Maybe I was overreacting."

She didn't answer.

Derek waited a moment, then said, "Anyway. . ."

He sat down across from her, and put the long cardboard tube next to his drink.

"Before we get into this," he said, "I want you to know I thought today was terrific. Having the chance to relax on the Outer Beach with you and Bobby and Greg was like being in another world."

"It is another world out there," Abby said. "And it always will be, thanks to the National Seashore."

Derek reached for his Scotch, determined not to let her provoke him. On the beach today, there had been no intrusive overtones about Devon Mill, or conservation, or environmental protection, or historic preservation. He and Abby had helped Bobby build a sand castle. Greg had given him a casting lesson and had insisted he'd done well, though he didn't catch anything. Abby had challenged him to a swim in the icy Atlantic. He'd body-surfed in the breakers. The day had passed too fast.

Already, now, Abby was edging toward their private obstacle course. Latching on to the issues that kept them apart. *Thanks to the National Seashore.*

He got the message.

He looked at her sitting across from him...so near and yet so far. He'd never seen a woman who could be so sexy with her hair mussed and no makeup on. Her baggy terry robe would have looked like a sack on anyone else, but satin and lace couldn't have made Abby more desirable than she was right now.

Derek wrested his eyes away from her, picked up the cardboard tube and slid out a roll of large paper sheets. "I want to show you something," he said, unfurling them.

Abby saw sketches and knew what they represented without being told. "If those are the plans for your Voyager, I don't want to see them."

"Wait, Abby...give me a chance."

"A chance to what? Look, Derek, I don't appreciate your coming to my house in the middle of the night to...to show me something...like that." Abby stammered over those words, but added defiantly, "I was right all along, wasn't I?"

"What do you mean?"

"Life is all dollars and cents to you." She stood and clutched the edge of the kitchen table. "Tell me that isn't true."

Derek's eyes glinted dangerously.

"The hell life's all dollars and cents to me," he grated. He stood, too, and circled the table. Glaring down at her, he raged, "Your problem is, you refuse to see anyone's point of view but your own."

He grabbed her shoulders, determined to make her listen. "You accuse me of seeing life only in terms of dollars and cents. But you...you run away from life. You chase after lost causes that keep you from facing yourself, your loneliness. You look for things you can escape into. Sometimes, Abby, there is no escape."

Derek ground out the words, but his anger was mixed with a desire so sharp he felt like his guts were being torn apart. Abby tried to push his hands away. Instead of yielding, Derek meshed his fingers over hers and clung tighter.

"You think I came here just to show you the plans for my resort? Well, lady...you're wrong."

Abby struggled against his grip, her face stubborn and rebellious. But the glimmer of tears in her green eyes got to Derek, washed away his logic and his restraint. Seeing the moisture in Abby's expressive green eyes, he forgot about the point he so desperately wanted to get across. All he could do was groan—and sweep her closer.

She made one last stab at resistance and tried to pull away. But the demands of Derek's smoldering eyes, his persistent hands and finally his mouth, were more than she could deal with.

He freed her fingers, let his palms slide off her shoulders, trail the length of her arms and mold her hips. And suddenly she was clutching him, pressing her fingers into his flesh as they started to kiss. Hungry kisses that nibbled, then devoured.

Derek's tongue began a voyage. Abby, welcoming the exploration, knew this was only the first invasion, the first penetration of an inner part of her. A sample. But she knew, too, that this was the turning point. She could no longer deny herself. She wanted all of him. She wanted him to have all of her.

He started to slip her robe off her shoulders. She restrained him, but only to whisper, "Not here. Not here."

Derek's arm was around her waist as they climbed the stairs. In her bedroom, he tossed her robe on a chair, then guided the straps of her nightgown over her shoulders. Abby felt the thin cloth slither down her legs and pool around her ankles. She watched him pull off his shirt. Then she could watch no longer without helping.

She reached down for his belt buckle and undid it...then found the zipper and released the hard male core that was straining against the denim.

"Derek," she whispered. "Derek, I need you."

"Not nearly as much as I need you."

He lifted her onto her bed. She lay against sheets already crumpled and raised her arms to pull him next to her. She touched those tendrils of curly hair on his chest, felt his warmth and tested the theory that as her fingers roamed lower there would be heat, undeniable evidence of his desire....

Derek moaned, his hands cupping her breasts as his tongue blazed a trail of temptation from the hollow of her throat across first one upthrust nipple, then the other...and then followed a path to the center of her personal, private universe. Abby, set afire, tugged him even closer, arching herself against him as he sent her off on a delirious solo journey. But then, when she thought she'd reached the summit of the world, he came to join her in that ultimate voyage that has to be taken by two.

He filled her with molten bliss, rocked her into dimensions she'd never known existed. Moons and comets and stars shattered the darkness. The universe exploded in sparkling fragments of light. Abby shuddered convulsively, her breathing coming in uncontrolled gasps. Derek groaned, called her name. Called it again and again. Then, spent, he lay beside her, gently folding her into his arms.

Outside her open windows, the night was cool and still. Derek tugged a blanket over them. Abby snuggled, her head on his shoulder. And, in this aftermath of lovemaking, she was saturated with a feeling she'd never expected to experience with Derek.

Total peace.

Abby felt a kiss on her forehead, and heard her name being called softly. "Abby?"

She stirred, but didn't open her eyes.

"I have to go. I'll call you tomorrow."

"Okay," she murmured sleepily.

A minute later, she was sitting straight up, staring into the darkness. She heard a car door thud, heard a motor rev and knew Derek was gone.

She switched on her bedside lamp and, for a moment, wondered if she'd dreamed...everything. Then she saw the dent his head had made in the pillows, smelled the fragrance of his hair on the sheets. The clock told her that it was five-fifteen in the morning.

Quickly she slipped out of bed, pattered down the stairs, opened the front door and peered outside at the spot where Derek's car had been parked. Gone. Not even the sight of taillights disappearing up the lane.

Why had he left? It was almost morning. He could have stayed. She wanted him to come back. She wanted to make love with him again, and again. She needed...reaffirmation.

Why did he leave?

Abby went out to the kitchen, switched on the light and put the kettle on to boil. Maybe a cup of something hot— herbal tea, even coffee—would help settle her down. In a while, dawn would come, the sun would rise. It would be impossible to go back to sleep.

She saw Derek's Scotch bottle on the counter by the sink. Their glasses were still on the kitchen table, virtually untouched. Also untouched were the sketches he'd brought to show her. The plans for his resort.

Slowly, reluctantly—but unable to stop—Abby picked up the top sketch and looked at it. It was an artist's aerial rendition of the entire site. And...the face of Clara Doane's twelve acres, as she knew them, had been altered completely.

There was no more windmill, no homestead.

Abby saw a long, three-story motor inn fronting Mill Bluff Road. Saw Mill Lane divided. One way, it led to a number of smaller two-story motel units, all placed at angles to afford each room with a view of the bay. The other way, it ended in a semicircle by what appeared to be an auditorium or conference center, located precisely atop the mill site. There were also a large, angular restaurant-lounge overlooking the water, two free-form swimming pools, plus tennis courts and ample parking.

The buildings were attractive, she couldn't deny that. The architecture harmonized with the land and the environment, she couldn't deny that, either. Obviously the renderings had been done by an architect with imagination . . . an architect who appreciated the rule that this Voyager, like all the others, be unique.

Abby glanced at the other sketches—a street-level view of the complex from Mill Bluff Road, a view from the bay and more detailed drawings of the restaurant and the conference center.

She hated them all, each and every one.

"Damn him!" she cursed. "Damn him and his Voyager!"

Furious, she snatched the drawings off the table and threw them across the room. She briefly considered tearing each sketch to shreds, before the label on the cardboard tube caught her eye. Casey & Martin, New England Concepts & Design. It was, no doubt, the firm Derek had hired to design this particular project.

She forced herself to calm down, then bent and picked up the sketches and laid them on the table one by one. For the first time, she noticed the signature "Sheila Casey" in the corner of each. Only then did it strike her that she'd come close to destroying someone else's property.

The sketches were crumpled, but not too badly. Carefully Abby rolled the sheets together and inserted them back in the tube. Even so, the evidence of her sabotage was still there. Too bad, she thought defiantly. Derek had it coming. What could he possibly have thought he'd accomplish by showing her the sketches?

The kettle hissed, spewing forth steam. Abby fixed a cup of tea, stirred in sugar and saw that it was beginning to get light outside. She'd been half asleep when Derek had left. Now she remembered the gentleness of his goodbye kiss, the softness of his voice. What, exactly, had he said to her?

I'll call you tomorrow.

Tomorrow, not today.

Why not today? What was he doing today?

The calendar by the refrigerator caught Abby's eyes. She'd forgotten to turn the page. Now it hit her full force that June was over. Today was the first of July. Tomorrow night she'd be getting up on the floor at the special town meeting to present her article to the voters.

Suddenly she knew what Derek was up to. He was going to Boston to sign the sales contract that would make Van Heusen Inc. the owners of Clara's property.

This was her last chance to stop him.

She put aside the teacup, her mind working furiously. If she could get the deed to the property from Clara before Derek could sign the contract, nothing either Derek or Gordon Ryder did would matter.

Abby had known Marjorie Higgins, the receptionist at Devon Manor, for years. But when she told Marge that she had to see Clara Gould on a matter of urgent importance, the receptionist looked troubled.

"It's only eight o'clock, Abby," she protested. "Normal visiting hours don't start until eleven."

"I realize that, Marjorie. But this is an unusual circumstance. An emergency. Believe me, eleven would be too late."

"Something to do with the mill?"

"Yes."

"You really need to see Mrs. Gould about it?"

Abby tried to restrain her impatience. "I wouldn't be here if I didn't."

"Let me check with Mrs. Fulcher, the nursing supervisor. I'm not even sure Mrs. Gould's awake yet. Even if she is, she might not be in any shape for visitors...."

Please, Clara, Abby prayed. *Let this be one of your good days.*

A minute passed. Then two. Then three. Abby was a bundle of nerves by the time Mrs. Fulcher preceded Marjorie Higgins back into the lobby.

"Good morning, Abby," she said pleasantly. "Clara's been up for an hour, she's had her breakfast, and she'd doing just fine. You know where her room is."

The old lady was sitting in an armchair by the window, crocheting a strip of yellow wool. "Hello, Abby," she said, smiling. "What a nice surprise."

Abby hated the thought of how soon Clara would be disillusioned. She took a chair, positioned it close to Clara and sat down. "What are you making?" she asked.

"A crib blanket for Roscoe Chase's granddaughter. She's expecting in September."

Abby noticed that Clara's crocheting was as exquisite as it had always been. "It will be lovely," she said sincerely.

"I hope so."

"Clara...."

Clara looked up, and her faded brown eyes sparkled. "Tomorrow's the big day, isn't it?" she queried.

Abby was surprised. She hadn't expected Clara's memory to be so acute. It occurred to her that maybe Clara's "bad days" were due more to medication for her heart problem rather than to any kind of mental failure.

She said, "Yes, tomorrow's the day, Clara. But...I need something from you to make sure everything goes through without a hitch."

Clara set aside her crocheting. "What would that be, dear?"

"The deed to your property, Clara. Bert Mayo told me the sale to the town would be guaranteed if we could turn the deed over to the selectmen now."

"Now?"

"Yes, today." Abby felt time's sudden pressure and wished she could add, *Right this minute. Right this second.*

"Oh my," Clara said, looking worried. "I'm not sure that will be possible. Gordon has the deed...."

"Gordon has it?" Abby felt like the bottom of the world had dropped off into space.

"Yes, dear. I turned over my valuable papers to Gordon when I decided to live here. I believe he put them in his safe deposit box for safekeeping. He's been such a help to me these past few months. He looks after everything, takes so much off my hands. I don't know what I'd do without him."

"Clara, you're absolutely sure he has the deed?"

"Yes. But we can get it from him. Though not today, I'm afraid."

Not ever, Abby knew.

"Gordon was in to see me yesterday," Clara volunteered. "He said he was going over to Martha's Vineyard today on the early ferry. He's been out there quite a bit, recently. He's handling some property in Edgartown."

"I see." Abby faked a small smile and asked—even though she was sure it didn't matter—"When's he getting back?"

"Well, he was staying over tonight and thought he might have to stay over tomorrow night, too. He said he didn't want to miss the meeting, but he might have to. I reminded him it isn't necessary that he attends the meeting. He's not a resident of Devon any longer, so he couldn't vote even if he did go."

Abby nodded, trying not to let her distress show. But Clara, this morning, was a hard person to fool.

"What is it, dear?" she asked. "You seem so troubled."

"I . . . I suppose I just hope everything goes well tomorrow night," Abby hedged. She was realizing she couldn't bring herself to spoil Clara's illusions about Gordon. Unfortunately the outcome of his actions would soon enough speak for itself.

"Everything will go just fine," Clara assured her. "Everyone who visits me tells me what a magnificent job you've done with the mill campaign."

Except I've lost, Abby thought dismally. *I've lost.*

Derek met Sheila Casey for lunch in a chic Back Bay restaurant Tom Channing had recommended.

They ordered, then Derek said, "I hope you don't need those sketches you sent over to the office, Sheila. At least, not immediately. I took them down to the Cape with me and inadvertently left them there."

"They were only copies," Sheila assured him. "I keep the originals under lock and key."

"Maybe Tom told you this," Derek said. "Before you do any more with the plans, I'd like you to spend time with me at the site."

"Suppose I drive down to the Cape one day later this week?"

"This will take more than a day, Sheila," Derek stated. He tested the wine the sommelier had brought and nodded approval. "Frankly I have reason to believe I'll be facing considerable opposition to the construction of the Voyager in Devon."

"Because you'll be demolishing a historic site?"

"Ouch," Derek said, and smiled wryly. "I wish there were a word other than *demolish*, but . . . yes, that's what's going to happen. People might not have been so concerned, except there's been a campaign to preserve the old Devon Mill that has everyone stirred up."

A campaign spearheaded by the most unforgettable woman in my life.

Derek tried—not too successfully—to blot out yet another of the mental images of Abby that kept infiltrating at the most inopportune of moments. The intermittent visions of her were like subliminal messages . . . except he was very much aware of them.

It was difficult to concentrate on the issues at hand when he kept remembering making love to Abby. One of the hardest things he'd ever done in his life was climb out of her bed and walk away from her in the predawn hours of a summer morning.

God knew he'd been thinking of Abby, not of himself. If he'd followed instinct, he would have gently awakened her with soft kisses and gentle, provocative touches guaranteed to lead them both in the same direction all over again. As it was, he'd stood at the side of the bed staring down at her, watching her sleep, watching Abigail Eldredge with all her defenses down. And he'd loved her vulnerability, loved her.

He'd also left her . . . then. Because he'd learned enough about Devon in a very small space of time to appreciate how tongues would wag if—by some crazy mishap—someone encountered him at Abby's place. She was on so many committees, involved in so many causes, there was no telling who might appear on her doorstep for one reason or another. And Derek knew he was the last person anyone would expect to find there, and gossip would flare.

So he'd walked out, and his arms had been feeling empty ever since.

Sheila said something. Derek caught the word "campaign" and nodded, forcing himself to pick up the threads of their conversation.

"Yes," he said, "as a result of a campaign, the town planned to buy the Gould property and preserve the old mill, make a park around it. Obviously that's not going to happen. In time, people will come around to our side. But for a while, Van Heusen Inc.'s apt to be pretty unpopular.''

"Where do I fit in?"

"I'd like to counter the windmill campaign with a campaign of my own. I want to present the Devon Voyager and what it will mean to the town in the most favorable possible light. I sincerely believe that because of the Voyager there'll be a considerable positive impact on the town. Not only economically, but culturally as well.''

Sheila smiled. "You don't have to sell me."

"But I do need you to help me sell the people of Devon," Derek said. He added, "Don't misunderstand me. I like your initial sketches very much. But I think you'll do even better when you spend more time on location. It's a unique place, Sheila."

"Yes," she nodded. "That's what I felt the day I drove down with Andy Bennett and looked the property over."

"I know. You captured the atmosphere, no doubt about it. I merely think you can capture even more after a second visit. I want the Voyager to harmonize in every possible way with the setting, the environment. I don't want us to miss a single opportunity."

He paused, then went on, "With the Fourth this coming Thursday, many people will be taking a long weekend. Meanwhile, there are certain things in Devon that need to be ironed out." He was thinking of tomorrow night's special town meeting, of how he had to prevent Abby from getting up to propose an article that no longer had any validity.

"Suppose you plan to come to the Cape next Monday? Would that fit in with your schedule?"

"Yes, it would be fine."

Derek and Sheila parted outside the restaurant, going in different directions. Derek, though he'd intended to take a cab directly back to Van Heusen's offices overlooking Boston Harbor, strolled first toward the Public Gardens, and he spent a little time watching the famous swanboats sailing around their small lake.

Again, he was thinking about Abby. This time, about the fact that he hadn't managed to get her to really look at Sheila's sketches, and he wondered if she'd subsequently done so when she was by herself?

He'd intended to put the sketches to her in the manner that ad agencies put presentations to him. He'd intended to try his damnedest to sell Abby on his point of view. But one quick glance had been enough for her. Anger had flared . . . then led to the most intense lovemaking he'd ever experienced.

Again, memory surged, and he wanted Abby with a desperation that was as new to him as most of the feelings she aroused in him. Again, he pictured the two of them together and imagined that he could actually smell her special fragrance, feel her softness—and, at the same time, share the fire of her passion.

There was no doubt in his mind about her response to him. But their having shared an unforgettable experience didn't change the problem between them. Thinking again of Sheila's sketches, Derek was suddenly sure Abby wouldn't have approved of what she was seeing even if Sheila had drawn the Taj Mahal, or a magnificent castle on the Rhine, or any other of the world's architectural gems. Abby would still be unyielding.

What could he do to make her look beyond her own immediate concerns?

Derek wasn't sure he could do anything, but he still intended to try. Eventually he hoped to convert many of Abby's supporters over to his side. Meanwhile—and of prime urgency—he had to convince Abby to withdraw her article. She'd only make a fool of herself if she got up and presented it on the floor of the town hall. He didn't want that.

Now, frowning, he walked over to Arlington Street and hailed a cab to take him to the company offices, where he found Tom Channing waiting for him.

Channing said immediately, "I've taken the liberty of chartering a plane."

"A plane?" Derek frowned again. "Why?"

"Russ Phelps called from Lenox an hour ago. That tract of land he found us out near Tanglewood has a serious bid from a major developer."

"Oh?"

"Russ says if we don't act, we'll almost certainly lose out. Frankly Mr. Van Heusen, this is another instance—like the Devon Mill tract—where there couldn't be a more perfect piece of property for a Voyager. The price is high, however . . . and, in view of the competition, Russ feels you and I should take a look at the site before we make an offer."

Phelps had made a favorable impression on Derek at their meeting shortly after Derek's first arrival in Boston. The field rep, he felt sure, would not be suggesting that he and Channing make this quick flight to western Massachusetts without good reason.

"How long will this take?" he asked.

"I didn't know exactly when you'd be back, so I scheduled the flight for four o'clock out of Logan. It's less than an hour by air, several hours by car. Phelps has reserved rooms at the Berkshire Hilton in Pittsfield for us, for tonight."

"It will be necessary to stay over?"

"Yes, I'd certainly say so. We'll have time to take a quick look at the property before dark, and this evening we can go over the detailed plans of the land, the costs involved, taxes, etc. First thing in the morning, we can go back and have a closer look. Once you've made your decision, Phelps can take it from there.''

Derek made some mental calculations. He would have to be back in Boston by early tomorrow afternoon if he wanted to make Devon in time for the town meeting.

''The plane you chartered, Tom . . . is that just a one-way deal?''

Channing nodded. ''I thought we'd either rent a car and drive back when we're finished, or charter a flight from Pittsfield Airport, whichever you prefer.''

''Charter a plane for the return flight,'' Derek decided. ''But first, may I use your office for a couple of minutes? I need to make an important call.''

This time, Derek dialed Abby's number himself. But there was no answer at the other end of the line.

The phone rang and rang, into an empty stillness.

Chapter Ten

Where the hell was Abby?

Derek slammed the phone down. He had tried to call her twice last night, and twice so far this morning. He'd meant to explain that he'd been unavoidably delayed in the Berkshires, but would be back in Devon in time for tonight's meeting.

He desperately wanted to convince her to back off on the windmill article. He didn't want her to go through the experience of presenting the article to Devon's voters, only to be told on the floor that its whole premise was null and void because the property was no longer for sale.

Derek swore softly as he left his room to join Tom Channing and Russ Phelps in the Berkshire Hilton lobby. There, he exerted discipline in the effort to put Abigail Eldredge out of his mind until he'd attended to the business at hand.

It wasn't easy. But the long years of concentrating on immediate matters, of learning to focus, paid off. With considerable effort, he got himself in gear.

Yesterday there'd been time for only a swift survey of the 22-acre property Phelps had discovered a few miles southwest of Pittsfield, but Derek had liked what he had seen. That impression was confirmed, now, as he, Phelps and Channing walked over the site with Phil Jorgenson, the realtor representing the owner.

"There used to be a private girls school here," Jorgenson explained. "The academic hall burned to the ground several years ago, but three dormitories still remain. Quite a bit of potential in them, I might add. Fieldstone buildings with slate roofs and lots of rooms, all on the way to the lake."

"Why is the present owner selling?" Derek asked.

"He bought the property as a land investment with no real thought of developing it himself, or of using the dorms. He's decided it would be financially advantageous to sell at this time."

Derek paused by a towering stone fireplace covered by ivy. "This was part of the school?"

"Of the main building, yes," Jorgenson told him.

The acreage adjacent to the fireplace had long ago been cleared and looked like a park populated with oaks, elms and maple trees. A rich green lawn swept to the two-lane country highway that fronted the property. Behind them, the grass soon met with pine woodland.

"There are trails through the woods going up to Shaker Mountain," the realtor said. "Excellent for hiking, horseback riding or cross-country skiing. Over here is the main drive, which heads past the dorms to Lake Sharon. Swimming, sailing and canoeing are your options there. And fishing, of course. The lake is full of trout."

Fishing made Derek think of Bobby Nickerson. Thinking of Bobby Nickerson made him think of Abby.

He glanced at his watch. God, it was nearly eleven. This was taking forever.

"The lake's within walking distance," the realtor was saying, already starting to lead the way across the grass to the paved drive.

"You've seen the dorms and the lake, Phelps?" Derek asked abruptly.

Russ Phelps looked surprised. "Yes."

"Then I think we'll bypass that part of the tour. Thank you, Mr. Jorgenson, but unfortunately I'll have to cut this short."

For a moment, the realtor was speechless and unable to camouflage his disappointment. That gave Derek the clue that maybe the developer who was allegedly interested in the tract wasn't quite as avid as he'd been presented to be.

"Frankly I'd hoped to show you more," Jorgenson finally said. "But if you've got other, more pressing matters...."

"I do," Derek said.

On the return trip to Pittsfield, the realtor talked about the attractions of the area, including Tanglewood, the summer home of the Boston Symphony Orchestra. He made a few passing references to the property he'd tried to show, but didn't push. Derek, only half listening, was struck by the intense green of the grass, shrubs and trees of the Berkshires. The colors reminded him of Abby's eyes.

As they neared the hotel, Jorgenson could no longer contain himself. "I take it the property we saw doesn't suit you, Mr. Van Heusen?" He looked at Derek in the rearview mirror. "I wish I had something else even half as good to show you. Unfortunately I don't. If I may say so, the site really would be perfect for one of your resorts."

Derek smiled. "I quite agree, Mr. Jorgenson. I'll talk the matter over with my associates, and Mr. Phelps will get back to you with our offer. Not what your client is asking, but a serious offer, nonetheless."

"Now, Tom," he said to Channing, "you and I need to get to the airport."

The phone was ringing as Abby walked into the house after a quick trip to the store to get milk and a box of dog biscuits for Captain. She ran across the living room, but when she picked up the receiver, she heard only a dial tone.

This was the second time today she'd missed reaching the phone in time. Earlier, when she'd come back from a morning walk with Captain on the beach, the phone had been ringing. Whoever was calling hung up just as she answered it.

These small frustrations added to the list that was beginning to build up. One damned thing after the next was complicating her life. But the thought of facing the crowd that was sure to cram the town hall tonight was most unnerving of all. Abby wished she could take a sleeping potion that would knock her out until around noon tomorrow.

This morning, she'd tried to reach George Cobb at the town hall soon after it opened. The selectman's secretary had reported that her boss was with the tree warden at the library, discussing taking down two huge locusts that threatened to fall on the roof.

"It could take awhile," the secretary had said, "or Mr. Cobb could walk in any second. There's no telling."

Now Abby dialed the selectman's number again, and this time caught George as he was about to leave for an early lunch. She wasted no time on pleasantries, but came right to the point.

"George, I need to see you."

"The days should be forty-eight hours long," George complained. "Between now and the meeting tonight I have so much to do there's no way I can get it all in. If what you've got on your mind could possibly wait..."

"It can't wait, George."

"Well, I'm taking time out for a quick bite at Nonnie's. After that, I have an appointment I can't miss."

"I'll be at Nonnie's in ten minutes."

The home-style restaurant was a favorite with Devon locals, though it attracted its share of tourist business, too. Abby and George were served quickly by Nonnie's daughter, Chris.

As he munched a ham-and-cheese sandwich, George asked, "What's this all about, Abby?"

Abby glanced around the room, saw a dozen familiar faces. Her voice low, she said, "I want you to withdraw the windmill article from tonight's warrant."

George stared at her. "You want me to *what*?"

"I want you to withdraw the windmill article."

"Withdraw it? Why, for heaven's sake?"

Abby waited while three older ladies—one, she knew, a friend of Clara Gould's—walked past. Then she continued, "Clara gave Gordon Ryder her power of attorney when she went into Devon Manor, and he's sold her property to Van Heusen Inc."

"Abby, you can't mean that."

"Oh, but I do. Gordon made a deal without Clara's knowledge. A very lucrative deal that unfortunately appears to be legal."

Amazing, Abby thought as she spoke, how succinctly you could put a whole saga of wasted effort, defeat and bitterness into a few sentences.

"Why haven't the selectmen been told anything about this?" George demanded.

"Because no one knew. It was all done very quietly. By the time I found out, it was already too late. I guess I hoped till the last minute something would happen so this *wouldn't* happen. I did talk to Bert Mayo yesterday...."

"He hasn't said anything to us."

"I think he was waiting to see if I could get the deed to Clara's property from her. That was the last slim chance we had to avert Gordon's sale."

"Who did you say he sold to?"

"A company called Van Heusen Inc. They own the Voyager Resorts out on the West Coast and in the Caribbean. Now they intend to build a resort here. And the hell with Devon Mill. They're planning to tear it down."

"Van Heusen was at your rally a couple of weeks ago, wasn't he?" George guessed. "He was the fellow you thought I might recognize. I heard rumors, afterward, that he was in town. We all should have known what he was up to."

"Don't blame Derek Van Heusen," Abby said, to her own surprise. "Gordon is the culprit in this. I talked with him the other night out at the homestead. The next morning, I went to see Clara, hoping she would revoke the power of attorney she'd given him."

"And?"

"She was having a mild heart problem, so they'd sedated her. I went back yesterday and came right out and asked her for the deed. Gordon has it locked up somewhere."

"What did Clara say when you told her the mill was going to be lost?"

"I didn't tell her, George. I didn't have the heart to disillusion her about Gordon. Clara started talking about how great he's been, how he's looked after her interests since she's been in Devon Manor. She cares a lot for him ... and he *is* the only relative she has left in the world. She's put her total faith and confidence in him. I just couldn't undermine that, no matter how wrong it is."

George nodded thoughtfully. "I can understand that, Abby. But when Clara finds out what Gordon's done...well, it's going to be quite a shock."

"Gordon said he planned to break the news to her very carefully. I hope to God that's what he does. As of yesterday, she was bright and happy, and thanked me for my work to save the mill. When she finds out what's really going to happen..."

George Cobb's big hand closed over Abby's much smaller one. "Stop blaming yourself," he told her. "You've fought like hell for Devon Mill. No one can fault you if Gordon Ryder cut the rug out from under you. There's just one thing...."

"What?"

"I can't withdraw the windmill article from tonight's warrant. The warrant's already been printed and published in the papers—and put on display at the post office and the library."

"Then what do we do?"

George sighed. "Well, you'll have to get up on the floor of the meeting and ask that the article be retracted because the issue's no longer valid." His face and tone expressed his sympathy when he added, "I hate to see you in that position, Abby. But there's no other way."

Abby thought about that as she drove home.

This wasn't the first time she'd lost the battle for a cause she'd espoused. She'd been strongly against the construction of the Devon Mall, but the mall had been built. She even patronized it once in a while.

But she'd be damned, she thought bitterly, if she'd ever patronize Derek Van Heusen's Voyager.

* * *

Derek parked his car as close to the town hall as he could get, which was several blocks away. Once again, Abby Eldredge was drawing a packed house. But tonight, he reflected, walking toward the Victorian building, her speech was going to suffer defeat, rather than victory. Tonight would drive a wedge between them that the largest bulldozer in the world would be unable to dislodge.

The irony of a bulldozer coming between him and Abby Eldredge suddenly struck Derek full force, and again time went in reverse.

It was early fall, and Derek was almost eleven, hurrying from school to do his paper route before heading over to the pier to fish. Sometimes, Faulk would be there. Sometimes not.

Sam Van Heusen had been fired from his job at a convenience store, and Derek knew it was just a matter of time before the landlord would tell them he needed their room. Mario was generous, and patient about the rent that was always overdue. But one night he came to the door after Derek was in bed, and Derek heard him say to Sam, "Look, man, I can give you till Monday, but things aren't that great. Maria and I have to get our money for this place."

Sunday at sunset, Sam fell down the back stairs and was knocked unconscious. The rescue squad came and, suspecting Sam might have a concussion, took him to the hospital.

Derek sat on a hard bench in a corridor until a doctor came out of the emergency room. "You're Mr. Van Heusen's son?" the doctor asked.

"Yes."

"Where's your mother?"

Derek had heard that tone before, and knew trouble could result if he gave an honest answer. If the authorities found out he had no one but Sam, he might be put in a children's home, or someplace equally terrible. And that was the last thing he wanted, despite Sam's shortcomings.

"My mother's in the bathroom," he lied. "Is my father okay?"

"He's banged up a bit, but he'll be all right." The doctor was about to say more when he was paged over the PA. "Tell your mother we're keeping him overnight for observation," he advised Derek. "I'm pretty sure he can go home tomorrow."

Moments before he'd fallen down the stairs, Sam had told Derek that he shouldn't go to school in the morning, that they'd sneak out of their room while Mario was off buying groceries for the restaurant. They'd leave, then hitch along the coast toward San Diego.

"I'll mail Mario the rent we owe him once I get another job," Sam had said.

Late Sunday night, Derek had to tell Mario what had happened, and Mario patted him on the shoulder. "No problem, kid. You and your old man can stay a couple more days. You come down to the cantina in the morning for your breakfast. Then you go to school, and we take it from there."

Derek nodded, went up to the room, but had a bad night's sleep. It was the first time he'd ever been completely alone—somehow, Sam had always made it home to crash. In the morning, he deliberately skipped school—another first—and got his pole and tackle box. He needed desperately to speak to Faulk. Not to ask for money, but to ask for advice. Sam had lost jobs because of his drinking, but he'd never fallen down a flight of stairs.

There must be help for people like Sam. Trouble was, help probably cost money. Derek couldn't quit school and start working full-time, could he? Not when he was only eleven years old. These questions, and a thousand others, tumbled inside his head.

Faulk would know the answers.

Derek cut across vacant lots and alleys, then looked ahead toward the pier, hoping to see Faulk out at the end, fishing. Instead, he saw trucks and men and machinery all over the beach. A couple of the abandoned shacks already had been knocked down. But it was the sight of the monster bulldozer moving toward the pier that stopped Derek cold.

He dropped his fishing gear and ran across the sand, his heart pounding hard. "What do you think you're doing?" he shouted up to the bulldozer driver. "Stop! Stop!"

"Get back, kid!" the man yelled. Then he spit out a stream of tobacco juice and put the big machine in gear.

Derek was stunned as the whole world filled with the noise of the bulldozer rumbling into the pier. Tears of rage and frustration filled his eyes as he watched the machine slowly and methodically start to crush the pier into heaps of rotted lumber.

He staggered backward, devastated because there was nothing he could do to halt what was happening. Then he felt a hand grasp his shoulder, and turned to see Faulk.

It was Faulk, wasn't it?

Derek recognized the familiar face, but the morning sunlight fell on a figure clad in an impeccably tailored business suit, not old fishing clothes. Glancing beyond this man, he saw a stretch limo parked up on the road, and a cluster of other men in business suits standing next to the limo.

"Faulk?" Derek stammered, confused.

He clutched a dark blue sleeve, pointed frantically at the bulldozer driver. "Faulk! You're just in time. Stop him! He's going to take down the pier."

"Come walk with me, Derek," Faulk said.

"Now?"

Derek tried to shake the arm that was guiding him away from the pier. "There's no time," he protested. "You've got to stop him!"

"No," Faulk said. He let Derek break free, but remained where he was.

Derek stared at him, his breathing ragged. He followed when Faulk moved along the beach away from the noise, then demanded brokenly, "Faulk, what's going on?"

Faulk stopped and looked squarely into Derek's eyes. "I should have told you about this sooner," he said. "I can see that now, and I'm sorry."

"Told me about *what*?"

"We're getting rid of the pier and the shacks," Faulk said. "There were a few legal hassles over the summer, but finally everything's been settled. The first step is to clear all this away."

"What first step?"

"Derek, I'm going to build a resort hotel here that will be the biggest and best in the whole damned state."

There was no mistaking the pride in Faulk's voice. Which made the realization of what was happening all the more terrible.

"You mean . . . *you're* doing this?"

"I own this part of the beach, Derek," Faulk said, "including the pier. Thought I might as well take advantage of the quiet and do a little fishing while the lawyers were handling their jobs." The deep-set eyes actually twinkled. "You're a helluva lot better fisherman than you were the first time we met. But more than that, Derek, I enjoyed your company, really enjoyed it."

Derek was too shocked, too confused, to recognize the compliment. The deep hurt cut through him like a cold, sharp knife. It was all he could do to choke out the question.

"How could you tear down the pier?"

The twinkle faded from Faulk's eyes. He was silent for a moment. Then he said, "Derek, the truth is... all things must come to an end. That's what happened with this old pier. It was built long ago, and it lasted many years. But now it's standing in the way of progress—and nothing is more important than progress."

Derek felt the tears running down his cheeks and wiped them away, still too hurt to talk.

Faulk placed a gentle hand on his shoulder. "Remember this, Derek," he said. "The world has to move on. If you ever hope to get ahead, you have to move with it. You can't let sentiment stand in your way."

"What's... sentiment?"

"Feelings, Derek. That's what sentiment is. And this is a lesson you're not too young to learn. Never mix sentiment with business, or you'll never get anywhere. If there's a choice, always put business first. You can trust business, Derek, provided you keep a clear head. You can't trust sentiment. It's as shifting as this sand under our feet."

Faulk stood back. "Good luck, Derek," he said. Then he turned and walked up to where the men were standing by the limo.

Derek didn't wait to see what happened next. He bolted back to the room above Mario's as fast as his legs would carry him, flung himself on the sagging cot that was his bed, and cried until he had no more tears to shed.

That afternoon, when the papers for his route were dropped off, he saw Faulk's picture on the front page. The caption spoke about Hugh Faulkner, president of the Faulkner hotel chain, launching a resort project in Jacaranda that was sure to get the town's economy back on its feet.

Derek couldn't have cared less about the economy, about Jacaranda, about anything. At that moment, he only wished he could pile up his papers and set them on fire.

He did the route in a daze. When he returned to the room, Sam was back from the hospital, wobbly but in one piece. He told Sam that Mario had said they could stay on a couple of days. The response was, "That's good of him, but I think we'll go now."

The sun was low over the Pacific when, up on the highway, Sam and Derek lucked out and caught a ride all the way to La Jolla. The next day, they went on to San Diego where Sam got a job in a bakery, which he held for three weeks. Then he was fired, and the cycle started all over again.

Six months later, Sam Van Heusen was dead.

Derek shook himself mentally as he entered the lobby of the town hall. With each step he forced himself away from the past and back into the present—a present that held more than its share of problems.

He'd tried to get Abby on the phone a couple more times, and failed. He'd also hoped to get back to Devon before the town office closed, but that hadn't happened. Now he needed to find someone who could tell him how to go about getting permission to speak at tonight's meeting.

Again, there were tables set up by the stairs that led to the auditorium. Officials were checking off names from the list of registered voters. When Derek said he wasn't a voter in Devon, he was politely but firmly told he would have to sit in the balcony above the auditorium. Only registered voters were permitted seats on the floor.

That was fine with him. He didn't give a damn about where he sat. All he cared about was getting the chance to speak to the crowd—before Abby did.

He spotted Will Jenkins, the manager of the Oceanside Motel, and it was like finding a long-lost friend. He explained his problem to Jenkins, as much of it as Jenkins needed to know, anyway. Jenkins took him to Henry Cahoon, the town moderator... the man he needed to see. Cahoon quickly introduced him to the intricacies of the town meeting procedures.

"What you have to do is find a registered voter who'll stand up, when the time comes, and tell me there's a non-resident present who has vital information concerning the article about to be taken under consideration," Cahoon explained.

Jenkins, standing nearby, said quickly, "I'd be glad to do that, Mr. Van Heusen."

"Good," Cahoon approved. "Now, Mr. Van Heusen, after Will's spoken his piece, I'll have to ask the voters to vote on whether they will allow you to speak. Usually, a voice vote will suffice. But if the Ayes and Nays sound close, I'll call for a show of hands. I doubt that'll happen. I think people will want to hear what you have to say."

"Thank you," Derek said.

The stairs to the balcony were narrow and twisting, and the seats there were nearly full. Derek eased past people to an empty place near the top row and, from this high vantage point, searched for Abby down below. At first, he couldn't find her. Then he spotted her in a front row aisle seat, with Greg Nickerson sitting next to her.

She was wearing pink—possibly that same pink dress she'd worn the night of her campaign meeting, Derek imagined, and immediately remembered the way the fabric had hugged her sexy figure. Her chestnut hair was highlighted by the auditorium's ceiling lights, and she looked beautiful, even from a distance.

As Derek watched, she turned to say something to Greg. And suddenly he envied Greg in a way he'd never before envied anyone. He would have given almost anything to be sitting next to Abby himself—even under these circumstances, as adverse as they promised to be.

Finally the meeting was called to order. Henry Cahoon, standing at the lectern, got down to business quickly, and Articles One through Four on the warrant were soon dispensed with. Then the moment came to present Article Five, the proposed purchase of Clara Gould's land, including the Devon Mill.

Will Jenkins, the manager of the Oceanside Motel, immediately got to his feet. "Mr. Moderator?" he called out.

"Yes, Mr. Jenkins," Cahoon said.

"It has been brought to my attention that Mr. Derek Van Heusen, a nonresident of Devon, has vital information concerning Article Five. I ask your permission to allow Mr. Van Heusen to address the voters."

"Do I hear a motion to that effect?" Cahoon asked the assembly.

The motion was made and seconded, and Cahoon called for the vote. At least, Derek thought gratefully, there was no doubt about the result. The Ayes clearly outdecibeled the Nays.

Derek quickly made his way down the balcony stairs, then strode up the aisle to the front of the auditorium. Then an unexpected case of the jitters began to take over. He'd spoken before all sorts of groups, in all sorts of places. He was a practiced professional...who now wondered if he'd be able to utter a solid syllable.

He tried hard not to look at Abby as he mounted the stage steps and stood before the microphone reserved for speakers. But he couldn't resist glancing toward her, and saw that her green eyes were filled with accusation and scorn. It was a moment Derek knew he would never forget.

He forced control, made himself say evenly, "Mr. Moderator, ladies and gentlemen...my name is Derek Van Heusen, and I am a resident of San Francisco, California. I am president of Van Heusen Inc., a San Francisco-based company that owns and operates resort hotels. I asked to address you tonight because my firm has purchased the twelve-acre tract of land belonging to Mrs. Clara Gould."

Sound waves rustled through the auditorium, as he added, "I know many of you will be disappointed by this news. But...our purchase of Mrs. Gould's property renders Article Five null and void."

Derek was sure he heard a few four-letter words muttered in disgust. He turned toward the moderator. "May I amplify that statement, Mr. Cahoon?" he asked.

The moderator nodded. "Quiet, please," he told the assembly.

Voices subsided as Derek turned back to the mike. He concentrated on speaking slowly and levelly, and continued, "My company's purpose in acquiring the mill tract is to construct a Voyager Resort there."

Now audible protests swept through the crowd, and Cahoon rapped for silence. "Kindly allow Mr. Van Heusen to speak," he ordered.

"What's there to say?" a man near the rear shouted. He got to his feet and moved to the door. "The windmill's going to be destroyed, so what difference does it make what he says?"

Variations of that sentiment were voiced here and there, and Cahoon rapped for silence yet again. All the while, Derek waited patiently.

"Mr. Van Heusen?" the moderator prompted.

Derek took in the hundreds of pairs of eyes focusing on him, but avoided the pair that meant more to him than anything else in the world. "I hope what I say will make a great deal of difference... to all of you," he said. "I realize Devon Mill is an integral part of this town's history. And...I appreciate the efforts Miss Abigail Eldredge made to save the mill, with the intention that it be restored."

Briefly Derek glanced down at Abby. She looked colder than an iceberg, and every bit as lethal.

"But, I do not plan to save the mill."

More protests arose, which Derek silenced himself.

"My plan," he said, in a voice that commanded attention, "was—and is—to build a major resort complex in your town. Mrs. Gould's property was on the market, and Van Heusen Inc. was fortunate to acquire it." He held up a hand, staving off objections, and went on, "I could go into great detail about how the Voyager will be designed fully in harmony with the environment, about how many permanent jobs will be created, about how many millions of dollars in taxes and other revenues this will mean for Devon. But...I won't. Rather, I'd like to speak briefly about the mill itself."

Quickly the big room was still.

Into that stillness, Derek said, "Devon Mill, as many of you know, is in very poor condition. Just a few days ago, I sought the opinion of a highly regarded local carpenter about the feasibility of moving the mill to another site. This would be possible, provided another site were obtained.

"However, as I understand it, much of Devon Mill's significance is connected with the site where it stands—the site where it was built, where for decades it performed its task, and where—for ten years now—it has been allowed to deteriorate.''

He paused, remembering the words of Hugh Faulkner, and finished, ''Unfortunately all things must come to an end. And that end has come for Devon Mill, insofar as the physical structure is concerned. Devon Mill, however, will always be part of this town's history and—as I hardly need point out to you—will be cherished and remembered in many ways. Please be assured that my company—and the Devon Voyager—will be committed to doing its utmost toward preserving the spirit of the mill, and everything it has stood for.

''Thank you,'' he finished, ''for giving me this opportunity to speak to you.''

Derek relinquished the floor to Henry Cahoon and turned away from the microphone. He certainly had not expected a round of applause, but the icy silence that enveloped him as he stepped down from the stage was daunting, at the least.

He strode up the aisle to the exit doors knowing every eye in the place was upon him. Then felt a cold chill sweep over him as he hurried down the stairs and outside.

A large part of his conscious reasoning urged, ''Go back to the Oceanside and belt down some Scotch.'' Instead, he drove out to Mill Bluff Road, turned onto Mill Lane, and parked at the end of the loop.

There, Derek stared through the moonless night at the structure that was his nemesis.

Chapter Eleven

Abby watched Derek leave the auditorium and fought the impulse to run after him. She wished she had the strength to battle him physically. She wanted to pound him with her fists and slash at him with words.

What an idiot she had been!

Until the very last minute, until Derek actually stood in front of the microphone and spoke his piece, she'd had hope, subconscious hope her mind dared not let come to the forefront. But she knew, now, that it was too late. She knew what a fool's paradise she'd been living in.

Deep down she'd been clinging to the belief that Derek, because of the intensely special moments they'd shared, because of the feelings that had run so strongly between them from the first moment they'd set eyes on each other, wouldn't sign the sales contract with Gordon Ryder. That he'd withdraw his offer to Gordon, and let Devon buy the mill.

Abby wanted to laugh. She wanted to scream. She wanted to rant and tear her hair out. How could she have believed—subconsciously or otherwise—that *she'd* had enough effect on Derek Van Heusen to alter his main motivations in life—to cause him to consider such an immense sacrifice? He, whose gods were money and power.

Had she really thought he would turn his back on a major business deal because they'd been to bed together? Because they'd found a soaring, sensual joy in each other such as she, at least, had never experienced before?

Had she really thought he would forget about his profit motives because she'd fallen in love with him? She had been stupid enough to think he returned that love, at least a little bit.

Abby bit back a sob. Right now, she was close to hating Derek. Yet, if he were to take her in his arms . . .

What a weak-willed imbecile she had become!

Henry Cahoon said, "Would someone make a motion to nullify Article Five?"

Abby stiffened her spine, stiffened her resolve, and stood. "Mr. Moderator," she said, "before a motion is made, I would like to be heard."

Henry Cahoon nodded and said formally, "Miss Eldredge." He moved aside to let Abby take his place at the lectern.

Abby looked out at the people cramming the auditorium. She'd heard comments that this was possibly the largest crowd to ever attend a special town meeting in Devon. She didn't doubt that was true. She and her Save Our Mill campaign were the reason most were here.

A deep sense of failure threatened. Abby knew if she let its darkness engulf her, it would be like being swallowed up by a tidal wave. She wouldn't even be able to speak.

Instead, she made one of the biggest efforts of her life as she forced herself to stay calm and say, "I wish to make a motion that Article Five be withdrawn from the warrant. But before the vote is taken, I want to speak to you. What I have to say is meant for each and every one of you.

"As you were just informed, Devon Mill has been purchased by outside interests. The mill will be demolished, and the Gould property converted into a resort complex. Those, I regret to say, are facts.

"There are more facts with which you should be acquainted. Negotiations for the sale have been underway for several months. Those negotiations were conducted discreetly, however, and it is only recently that anyone in Devon learned of them.

"Until the last hour—until the last minute, before this meeting—there was hope that by some means this sale could be averted, and the town permitted to acquire Devon Mill. However, the sale is bona fide, and will not be rescinded.

"Many of you know Clara Gould, the owner of the property in question. For those of you who do not know her, Mrs. Gould is ninety years old and, for the past eight months, has been a resident of Devon Manor. She's lived in this town all her life and wanted to see the mill restored as a memorial to her late husband. That is why she was willing to sell her property to the town at a price far below its market value.

"What I want you to know is that Mrs. Gould did not participate personally in the sale to Van Heusen Inc. The sale was undertaken by a relative of hers to whom she had given her power of attorney.

"Mrs. Gould does not know that this action has taken place. Therefore, I trust that any of you who may have occasion to visit her in the near future will be gentle—either in imparting this news to her, or in discussing what has happened. The sale, legal though it is, is certain to shock her.''

Abby fought for steadiness as she continued, "What I wish to say to you personally is that I appreciate, more than I can ever tell you either individually or collectively, the time, effort and energy so many of you put into our attempt to save Devon Mill for our town. I bitterly regret that our work was fruitless. However, even if we had known sooner that this sale was in the works, there is nothing we could have done to stop it—no more than there is anything we can do now."

She turned to Henry Cahoon. "Mr. Moderator," she said, "I move that Article Five be withdrawn from the warrant as the issue it involves is null and void."

Abby walked back to her seat as Henry Cahoon asked, "Do I hear a second?"

She sat down, staring straight ahead. After a minute, she felt Greg's hand close over hers.

"Are you okay?" he asked quietly.

She nodded.

"Would you like to leave?"

"Yes," she said, "but I'm not going to. I'll stick it out."

The remaining articles in the warrant were dispensed with quickly, and the meeting was adjourned.

Abby started up the aisle, Greg virtually propelling her, but the going wasn't easy. She was badly shaken. Also, people stopped her all along the way to express their sympathy, which made it even harder to maintain a surface composure.

Downstairs in the lobby, members of the local press corps converged on her. Abby was besieged with questions and tried to field them by making her answers as objective as possible. But the strain she was under made it difficult to camouflage the churning emotions that were tearing up her insides.

A TV reporter asked, "What impact do you feel a Van Heusen Voyager will have on Devon, Miss Eldredge?"

"I suppose we can expect a boost in the tourist trade," Abby said tersely. "Not that Devon isn't already over-crowded in the summer."

"Do you feel it would have been preferable for Van Heusen Inc. to have chosen a town other than Devon for the new Voyager?"

"Of course I wish they'd chosen another town," Abby snapped. "I wish Van Heusen Inc. had never heard of Devon...and that Devon had never heard of Van Heusen Inc."

The reporter persisted, "Do you think, in view of the town's sentiment about Devon Mill, that perhaps the company might change its plans about not restoring the windmill—maybe preserve it as a tourist attraction?"

"No." Abby snarled the negative, heedless of what she was saying at this point. "The company won't preserve Devon Mill. It wouldn't be profitable. As a matter of fact, there will be a conference center exactly where the mill now stands."

"You've seen plans for the proposed Voyager?" The question came from a reporter on one of the Cape's weekly papers.

"Yes, I've seen them," Abby said coldly. "Devon's due for a big, glitzy resort complex—and history be damned."

Abby became aware that the TV camera was zeroing in on her face as she said that. The strain became too much.

"Please," she said, "that's enough."

Greg gripped her arm. "Let us by," he ordered quietly, then shepherded Abby through the crowd that had gathered to watch her press interview.

They had driven to the meeting together in Abby's car. Now, as Greg hurried her across the parking lot, he said, "Give me the keys, Abby. You're in no shape to drive."

She wasn't about to argue.

She slumped down in the front seat and pressed her hands against her temples. Her fingers were icy.

"That was terrible," she said. "Like an inquisition."

"Well, you worked up a lot of interest in the mill with your campaign," Greg pointed out. "And the Fourth of July's coming up, so patriotism and history are the big deals of the day. Otherwise, maybe the Cape TV stations wouldn't have bothered to cover the meeting." He added slowly, "We should have realized the mill would make good holiday copy."

"What good would it have done?"

"You could have been better prepared."

Abby frowned. "Better prepared?"

He nodded. "You could have written a statement you could have read to the media people."

"Do you think I would have said anything different in a statement?"

"You might have toned down what you did say."

"I doubt it. I said what I felt."

Greg waited until he'd driven out of the town hall parking lot and was turning onto Main Street. Then he said carefully, "In all fairness, I doubt Derek Van Heusen intends to build a glitzy resort. I take it you've seen the plans. Is that the way they came across to you?"

"The Devon Voyager won't be a simple little motor inn," Abby said tightly. "It'll be a great big complex—lots of buildings, parking lots, a conference center, swimming pools..." She broke off, then demanded, "Just how the hell do you think plans for such a place *would* strike me?"

Greg didn't say anything.

"Well?" Abby persisted.

"Look, Abby... you're bushed," Greg murmured sympathetically. "But at least this is over. Now..."

She waited. "Now *what*?"

"I hope you'll put this behind you. Find something else to interest you."

"Get myself another cause?" she suggested nastily. "Something else to get involved in, so I can shoot off my mouth and work up public sentiment?" She scowled. "That's not about to happen, Greg. I've had it. I'm not a total fool. I know you've always felt I push my way in where angels fear to tread. But no more, let me tell you."

"Hey, wait a minute," Greg protested. "I've never criticized what you do. So, you're always into something. I admire you for that. The town needs people like you."

"You can say that after tonight?"

Greg didn't answer, and after a minute, Abby simmered down.

"I'm sorry," she said. "I didn't mean to take it out on you. You're right. I *am* bushed. And... so damned disappointed."

"I know. I also know you're too hard on yourself. Actually right now you're a local heroine, though you don't seem to realize that."

"I feel like a local idiot."

"On the contrary, you had solid support and—regardless of what has happened—people are still behind you. You'll find that out for yourself on the Fourth, when you ride on the float. I'll bet you get more cheers than everyone else put together."

Abby stared at him. "The float?"

"The windmill float," Greg explained. "Don't tell me you've forgotten about it?"

"Of course I haven't forgotten about it. But the Devon Mill float was supposed to represent victory, not defeat. Talk about something being null and void! Greg, there's no way I'd consider putting that float in the parade after what happened tonight."

Greg pulled into his driveway, brought the car to a stop, then sat back. "You," he reminded Abby, "are not the only person involved in that float. George Cobb's riding on it, so is Helen Rogers, so are a lot of other people I can think of. Also, I have a vested interest in it, myself. I've been working on the replica of Devon Mill in my spare time for the past three months, remember?"

"Yes, I remember," Abby admitted wearily.

"I'm not about to let all that work go to waste."

Abby wished they were at her place instead of his, so she could stalk out of the car, go in the house and slam the door. He was being both unreasonable and inconsiderate. Didn't he have any respect for her feelings?

"Mrs. Baker is sitting with Bobby, and I want to take her home," Greg said. "Otherwise I'd suggest you come in so we could talk more."

"I can drive Mrs. Baker home," Abby volunteered.

"No. You need to get home yourself and go straight to bed. I suggest you dip into that brandy you usually save for special occasions. It might help you sleep."

Greg went on, "I'll take care of Mrs. Baker, but I want to do it now, so I can come back here and go to bed myself. I need to get an early start. Lots to do tomorrow... I have to finish putting the float together with the members of your committee. We're to meet back of my shop at six o'clock, if I remember correctly."

Abby wanted to shake him. How could Greg, usually the most understanding person in the world, be like this?

"I intend to call the committee members first thing in the morning and tell them we've cancelled the float," she informed him.

"Don't do it."

Greg climbed out of the car, came around to her side and leaned down, peering through the open window. "That would be a real admission of defeat," he pointed out. "A big mistake. You'd be doing Devon Mill an injustice. Nothing's changed about the mill's *history,* and that's what the float's commemorating. Think about that."

Abby thought about what Greg had said as she drove home and had to admit he was right. But the idea of riding through town on the mill float was downright traumatic. George Cobb was to play the role of miller. She was to be the miller's wife, and Melanie Doane had made her a red, white and blue colonial costume to wear.

Abby shuddered, and couldn't wait for the Fourth to be over.

Derek turned on the TV in his room at the Oceanside and switched the channels around till he found a local Cape station. Then he sat back and waited for the eleven o'clock news.

He'd seen a mobile television unit outside the town hall as he was leaving. Maybe it wasn't the mill sale they were covering—he didn't know what other issues had been slated for the meeting—but he wanted to make sure.

He didn't have long to wait. Abby's face filled the screen, and his first thought was that she looked exhausted. Then he heard her say, "I wish Van Heusen Inc. had never heard of Devon . . . and that Devon had never heard of Van Heusen Inc."

Derek flinched, then stiffened as he heard her add that Devon was about to have a "glitzy" resort on the old mill site. She'd just admitted she'd seen Sheila Casey's preliminary sketches. Had she judged them without even *looking* at them, for God's sake? How could she possibly call Sheila's designs "glitzy?"

Derek registered the scathing way in which she stated that Devon Mill wouldn't be preserved, because it wouldn't be "profitable." And that remark, "...and history be damned," stung. He wouldn't have expected Abby to be so unfair.

A slow anger began to seethe as he watched her face twist with resentment, and listened to her bitter voice. Damn it, he didn't deserve this.

He certainly wasn't the sentimentalist Abby was when it came to preserving old things, nor would he want to be. But he had a healthy respect for history. In his opinion, however, the past belonged to the past. Its lessons should be utilized, not wallowed in.

Derek watched Abby break away from the reporters, saw Greg Nickerson grip her arm and steer her through the crowd, and his resentment boiled over.

Abby had been bitchy tonight, damned bitchy. He'd done nothing that merited those kinds of comments. If he had needed anything to bolster his conviction that he should stay in Devon and see the Voyager project through personally, this was it.

She'd deliberately prejudiced people against him with her speech before the TV cameras tonight. He was sure the local newspapers wouldn't be any kinder.

They weren't.

The weekly Devon *Herald* literally had stopped their presses so the front page could be devoted to a story headlined "Devon Mill to be Demolished by Developer."

The Cape *Daily Wave* had also given the mill sale a banner headline. They had put their story on the wire, so there was even a short front-page story in the Boston *Globe*.

Derek read the newspaper accounts as he ate an early breakfast in the Oceanside's coffee shop. There were pictures of Abby accompanying the stories, and she looked belligerent and defiant in every one. But to his eyes, she also looked beautiful.

He put the papers aside, finished a second cup of coffee and knew that he needed to sit down and map out a course of action. But there was no immediate chance for that. Derek found media representatives waiting to interview him outside the coffee shop. Once they'd discovered Derek Van Heusen was in town, it hadn't been that hard to track him down.

He referred the reporters to Tom Channing for details about the sale and smoothly got off the hook himself by fielding questions with an expertise born of long practice. He refused to comment on Abigail Eldredge's remarks. No matter how he felt about what she'd said, he didn't want this to become a prominent-local-citizen versus big-time-entrepreneur battle.

Not that he wasn't going to battle with Abby. But their war would be fought in private. He would not give her the satisfaction of making a public statement about her or her ill-fated campaign. But it would be a long time, he thought grimly—if ever—before he would forget her saying coldly, "I wish Van Heusen Inc. had never heard of Devon . . . and that Devon had never heard of Van Heusen Inc."

Abby hadn't been speaking merely of his company, she'd been speaking of *him*.

She wished she'd never heard of *Derek* Van Heusen.

"Well, lady," Derek muttered as he went back to his room, "it's late in the day for that. Damned late in the day."

Derek dialed Tom Channing in Boston and asked crisply, "What's the deal on the Gould homestead?"

"What do you mean, Mr. Van Heusen?"

"Did we buy the place furnished or unfurnished?"

"Unfurnished. Mr. Ryder mentioned there are a lot of valuable antiques in the house. Under the terms of the sales contract, he has a month to move everything. He said he started packing things up, but didn't get very far."

"Make him an offer for the house contents," Derek instructed. "If I know Ryder, he'll be glad to sell the whole package as a unit. Send Andy Bennett down to Falmouth to deal with him. Have Bennett get an appraiser and come out here if he questions Ryder's price. What I'd like is everything but personal photographs and papers. And Tom..."

"Yes?"

"I'd like to move into the house by the end of the week."

"*You'd* like to move into the house?" Channing didn't attempt to hid his astonishment.

"Yes."

"You plan to stay there?"

"For a number of reasons, yes. I want to be on the scene, Tom, until everything's well under way. Sheila Casey will be spending some time in Devon next week. She can stay at the house, too. I may also want Bennett to stick around."

"Anything special you want me to do?"

"Not yet. But I do want you to get the staff started on putting out bids for a general contractor for the job. I may opt for a Cape contractor, I may not. Depends."

Derek terminated the conversation with Channing and sat back knowing that he should call Sheila Casey and set up a precise schedule with her. He also should have talked to Channing about the Berkshire property, and whether or not it looked like the owner was going to accept a satisfactory price. He'd have to call Boston back after a while.

As soon as it was nine in San Francisco, he would touch bases with Grace Duncan and Bill Engalls to determine what important matters required his consideration.

But for the moment . . .

He closed his eyes and could see Abby as she'd appeared on TV. He felt like a video tape of her bitter, angry face had been imprinted into his mind. He wished he could push an erase button, and knew he couldn't.

The decision to move into Clara Gould's old house—and to buy its contents from Gordon Ryder—had been spur of the moment. Now Derek tried to tell himself that his rationale was sound. He needed a headquarters while the project was being planned, and what better place than on the site itself? Also, the house needed to be occupied when there was such sentiment in town against the Voyager project. He couldn't imagine vandals in Devon, but still . . .

Did Abby Eldredge have anything to do with any of his decisions?

"No," Derek said aloud, then branded himself a liar as he put on his sweats and started jogging across town, heading in a direction he'd never gone before.

Chapter Twelve

Somewhere, in a teacher's handbook, perhaps, Abby had read it was best to tackle difficult work first—get the unpleasant tasks over with. Then, with the burden lifted, everything else would be that much easier.

She had intended to follow that precept today. She would force herself to visit the nursing home early and break the bad news to Clara Gould.

But that didn't happen, because her telephone began ringing before she'd even had breakfast.

Friends of Abby's, supporters of her efforts to save the mill, called one after the next to commiserate about last night's happenings—and extol her for the great job she'd done. In addition, the people who were involved in the windmill float wanted to be sure tonight's six o'clock meeting was still on.

Her answer, but for Greg, would have been, "No!"

Now it was a begrudged, "Yes, we'll meet at Greg's shop at six."

It was late morning before Abby left her house. She arrived at Devon Manor clutching a bunch of bright blue hydrangeas for Clara, which she'd clipped from the bushes in her front yard. Her nerves were on edge. She dreaded facing Clara, who almost certainly must have heard about the sorry results of last night's meeting.

Many of Devon Manor's residents were outside on this beautiful early July day. Some were sitting in wheelchairs, others were strolling around the grounds. Abby took a quick survey and saw that Clara wasn't among them. That only increased her apprehension, and her steps quickened as she hurried toward the wing where Clara had her room.

On the threshold of that room, she stopped short.

Clara was sitting in her armchair by the window. Derek was in a chair facing her. They were deep in conversation.

As Abby watched, Derek smiled. Clara returned the smile, and suddenly looked about twenty years younger. Abby didn't wonder at that. Derek's magnetism, his effect on women—something she knew about all too well—could be irresistible. It was a force he seemed able to turn on and off at will. She didn't trust it. She didn't trust him.

What the *hell* was he doing here?

It was Clara who glanced up and saw her. "Abby," she exclaimed, "I'm so glad you've come."

Abby slowly crossed the room, then stooped and kissed Clara's cheek. "I intended to get here earlier," she said. "But I got tied up on the phone." She met Derek's eyes as she spoke, and saw his smile fade.

"You know Mr. Van Heusen, don't you?" Clara queried.

"We've met," Abby allowed. Purely to appear civil in front of Clara, she muttered, "Hello, Derek."

"Hello, Abby." Derek stood and offered, "Here, take this chair. I have to be leaving."

Momentarily Clara seemed disappointed. Then she brightened. "It was very kind of you to come, Mr. Van Heusen," she said.

"It was my pleasure, Mrs. Gould. I'll be back to see you again, all right?"

"I'd like that," Clara told him.

Derek took Clara's hand and pressed it gently. Suddenly Abby couldn't stand any more of his byplay. "I'll get a vase to put the flowers in," she said.

"Hydrangeas." Clara was delighted. "I always think of them as Fourth of July flowers. Those are such a gorgeous shade of blue."

Abby nodded and promised, "I'll be right back." She made a hasty exit.

A nurse's aide put the flowers in a vase, and Abby lingered to talk to the girl, wanting to give Derek time to leave. She didn't want to risk an encounter with him, especially the way she was feeling now. For the moment, she'd had all she could take.

But when she started back to Clara's room, vase in hand, she found he hadn't left. He was waiting for her, and there was no trace of a smile on his face. He looked even more forbidding than he had the first time they'd met.

"Take your choice," he invited crisply. "Lunch? Dinner? Or a meeting at either your place or the Oceanside?"

"There's no choice to be made," Abby informed him. "I'm tied up today and tonight."

"Then you'll have to untie yourself."

Abby started to speak, then saw something she'd never seen before in Derek's intense blue eyes. A smoldering anger. A defiance aimed directly at her.

Startled, she asked, "What is it you want?"

Derek's laugh was short and bitter. "Do you really want me to answer that question?"

Abby felt her cheeks grown warm and hated the fact she was flushing. The last thing she wanted was to show him how he affected her.

"Look, Derek," she said, "I need to go. Clara will be wondering what's happened to me."

Instead of backing off and letting her by, Derek came closer...so close that if either of them moved an inch they'd collide. He looked dark and threatening, and despite her resolve, Abby flinched.

At the sight of her reaction, pure fury flickered across Derek's face. "Don't act like that, damn it," he demanded. "I'm not about to strangle you...much as I'd like to."

"*You* want to strangle *me*?"

Abby bristled. "Why did you come here?" she asked. "Couldn't you leave Clara alone? Don't you think she's had enough? Or are you suddenly feeling guilty about what you've done?"

Derek ignored that last jab. "Did Mrs. Gould look like she objected to my presence?"

"Clara's a lady. She'd suffer through your presence no matter how she felt."

"Really?" Derek's eyes were twin studies in derision. "Go talk to Mrs. Gould about my visit. Ask her for yourself."

"I intend to do exactly that."

The tension between them was like a rope pulled tight. Then, as Derek looked down at Abby Eldredge staring up at him, belligerently, his anger and exasperation faded. And he knew he loved her.

"Abby," he said softly, "this is ridiculous. Things don't need to be like this between us."

"How could they be otherwise?"

"I think you know the answer to that as well as I do."

Derek wanted to kiss away the mutiny he saw stamped on Abby's face, kiss away the defiance that tightened her mouth. He wanted to run his hands through her chestnut hair, caress the hollow of her back, move with her into the sensual, sexual spiral that they'd shared only once...that he wanted so badly to share again.

"Look, Abby," he said huskily. "You owe me a few minutes of your time."

"Owe you? How do you figure that?"

"You said some things last night that were just not true. You made false accusations. You were bitchy as hell."

"How did you expect me to be?"

"Fair," Derek said.

"I said what I felt."

"Then you meant it when you said you wished you'd never heard of Van Heusen Inc.?"

"I said I wished Devon had never heard of Van Heusen Inc."

"Don't spar, Abby. I took your remark personally. You would take it personally, too, if you were in my shoes." His heart was in his throat as he posed the next question, but he persisted. "Do you really wish you'd never met me?"

Derek saw the answer in her face. And, but for the vase of flowers she was holding in front of her like a shield, he would have taken her into his arms then and there.

"I'll be at your house at three," he declared.

"I won't be home."

"Then I'll wait till you get there."

"Waste your time if you want to, Derek. I don't care."

Abby Eldredge was the most stubborn woman he'd ever met! And the most desirable. With her cheeks flushed, her eyes sparking and her breasts taut against the sheer white fabric of her blouse, it was all he could do not to knock the vase of flowers to the floor and capture her.

In the middle of Devon Manor?

Derek had to smile at the thought, and the thought of humor helped. His voice, though still insistent, was milder as he said, "I do have to talk to you, Abby."

"You've said that ever since we first met. We didn't have much to talk about then. We have considerably less to discuss now."

"That's not true. I don't expect you to change your opinion, but I do hope you'll listen to what I have to say."

Derek spoke firmly, and Abby knew there was no way she would get rid of him until she'd heard him out. But then ... then she absolutely must thrust this man from her life—for the sake of her sanity, for the sake of her heart.

She compromised. "I'll meet you at the ocean beach. You can walk down and meet me by the administration building."

"How about stopping at the Oceanside and picking me up?"

Abby visualized knocking on the door of Derek's motel room—and knew what might happen once he opened that door. She shook her head. "It would be better if we meet at the beach," she told him.

Derek had to be satisfied with that. "Three o'clock," he confirmed. "By the administration building."

"Right."

Their meeting would be brief, Abby promised herself as she walked back to Clara's room. She had no intention of getting into a discussion with Derek about his Voyager, or anything else. Which meant it would be a one-sided conversation.

She put the hydrangeas near the window in Clara's room, then faced Clara and said, "Sorry I took so long."

Clara smiled knowingly. "Did you run into Mr. Van Heusen on his way out?"

How could anyone suggest that Clara wasn't sharp?

"Yes," Abby admitted. She took a closer look at Clara, and was surprised by how serene she seemed.

"He's a charming young man, Abby."

Abby had no answer to that.

"I thought it was very kind of him to come here personally to discuss his purchase of my land. Gordon had indicated there was a private buyer interested in the property, but frankly I didn't pay too much attention. It didn't occur to me to do anything other than sell my land and the mill to the town. But Mr. Van Heusen has made me see how Gordon has acted in my best interest."

Abby couldn't believe what she was hearing. She'd been expecting to find that Clara either had had a heart attack, or was on the verge of one. Was it medication that was making her so tranquil? No, Clara's eyes were clear, her speech distinct.

Maybe, Abby thought, it was living to be ninety that made one accepting of whatever happened.

Clara said gently, "Roscoe Chase called this morning to be sure I wasn't too upset about the sale. We talked about the wonderful job you did, and we're both so sorry your plan didn't work out. I know how much saving Devon Mill meant to you, Abby. Believe me, I do. But times change, and places change with them."

Clara was consoling *her*. It was too much.

Abby laughed shakily. "You're remarkable."

"I'm not remarkable at all, my dear."

"Ah, but you are. I'm the one who's sorry the campaign failed, because I know how much you wanted Devon Mill to stand as a memorial to your husband."

"There will be a memorial to Randolph," Clara said. "Mr. Van Heusen plans to name his conference center Randolph Gould Hall. And that's not all he plans. He says his architect is coming to Devon next week. He's wants me to meet her and see the sketches she's done."

Abby was finding this hard to accept. Clara, incredibly, was actually *enjoying* the idea of being on the inside track with Derek. No wonder the man had become a millionaire by the time he was thirty! He could sell sand to the Arabs, and get gold back in return.

Derek was waiting at the administration building when Abby arrived at the beach. She spotted him as she drove by looking for a parking space, and tried to blot out her instant impression of a tall, handsome, sexy man—clad in navy swim trunks and an unbuttoned tan shirt—leaning nonchalantly against the building, his arms crossed.

At 3:13 in the afternoon, the lot was still almost full. Abby had to walk a fair distance back to where Derek was waiting, and her heart pounded all the way. She wasn't ready for a session with Derek and was annoyed to think she'd agreed to one so soon. She should have said no to him, should have let time and distance temper her feelings.

If only she could erase the memory of their evening in Provincetown, their moonlit embrace in the shadow of the windmill, their passionate night together in her bed where the ardor between them had exploded in ways she would never forget. If only she could keep a level head and concentrate on his negatives.

Abby knew, as soon as Derek straightened and strolled over to meet her, that she'd made yet another mistake. Spending even seconds in his presence was the most dangerous, the most terribly tempting, thing she could do.

His swim trunks were considerably snugger than they'd appeared from a distance. Derek wasn't flaunting his masculinity, but his bathing attire left little to the imagination. Abby was thankful for the camouflage provided by her oversized sunglasses. She was sure that her eyes were telling a story of yearning and desire she didn't want him to read.

She'd worn a swimsuit, too, under a colorful cotton dress. She'd intended to talk with Derek, maybe sit with him on the beach, then go for a solitary swim at a pond near her house. Derek, it appeared, was ready for a dip in the ocean. He had a towel slung over his shoulders and seemed full of energy.

"Well, Miss Eldredge," he greeted her. "You finally made it. I was beginning to think I'd been stood up."

"Sorry I'm late," she mumbled.

"Shall we swim first, or talk?"

Right now, Abby decided, she could use a plunge into the cold Atlantic to cool down her personal thermostat.

"Let's swim," she told him, hoping she sounded more indifferent than she felt.

She started along the wooden boardwalk that led out to the beach and tried to keep a few steps ahead of Derek. Then she found a smooth stretch of sand above the tide line and fluffed out the blanket she'd brought.

"Is that for both of us?" Derek asked.

"If necessary," Abby said coolly.

She took off her sunglasses and hoped the fire in her eyes had died down. Still, she kept her gaze averted as she headed toward the water. She was determined not to show her vulnerability, or give Derek an opening. But when the edge of a wave rippled over her toes, she drew back. July or not, the water was freezing.

Derek laughed. "And you a native?" he teased.

He plunged past her into the water and was soon up to his waist. Then he dove through a breaker and came up feeling like he'd been thrust into a tub of ice. But he was thankful for the temperature-lowering effect the ocean water was having on his body.

Turning, he saw Abby hovering close to the shoreline, and suddenly he was struck by a temptation too great to resist. He let the waves push him toward her until he was close enough to fill his cupped hands with frigid water. Then he splashed the water all over her.

Abby screamed. Then she lunged toward Derek, everything but revenge temporarily forgotten. *Two can play this game,* she was thinking, when an incoming breaker spun her off balance and she staggered into his arms.

Derek wasn't ready for her. He sprawled backward, and Abby took advantage of the opportunity. She put both hands on top of his head and dunked him.

He came up sputtering, his eyes glinting with mischief as he reached for her. His intention was to do to her what she'd just done to him, but as his hands touched her shoulders that intention changed. Restraint went out with the tide as Derek clutched Abby close, battling the waves as he tasted the salt on her lips, then plundered her mouth with his.

They clung, the waves pushing them forward one moment, the undertow tugging them backward the next. And their kiss deepened, like the far reaches of the ocean, as Derek put into it something he'd never before given a woman.

Caring. Caring, mixed with a passion so intense he felt like he was on fire, in the middle of a cold, cold sea.

Abby leaned on his strength as they rode the swell of the waves. She could not have withstood the tug of the undertow on her own, but she felt the power in Derek's arms, the power in his legs...and a different kind of power in the way he was captivating her.

She was no match for him right now—because she wanted him so much. Pride and common sense told her she should push away from him and strike for shore, but she couldn't. Rather, she could only give back what he was giving her, and let her love show in the process, as it fused with passion.

Finally Mother Nature took the upper hand. The sea delivered a wave that surpassed all the others, towering as it crested then crashed toward shore, taking Derek and Abby with it. There, they escaped from its grasp, then sprawled together on the sand, breathless.

"Had enough?" Derek challenged.

How did he mean that? Abby wondered. She'd not had nearly enough. Nor, she was sure, had he. Yet she'd already gone considerably further than it was safe to go. Now was the time to stop.

She trudged up the slope to the blanket, aware that the fabric of her pale green swimsuit was clinging to her flesh, molding her breasts and emphasizing her swollen nipples. Their hardness was not due to the cold seawater alone. Derek was equally responsible, and she was sure he knew it.

She lowered herself to the blanket and reached for her sunglasses before starting to towel herself dry. Derek stretched out next to her, heedless of the water beading his hair and glistening on his skin. As she watched, he procured a pair of dark glasses from under his shirt and slipped them on.

Was he as much in need of camouflage as she was?

"I can't stay too long," Abby said. "I have a meeting at six I can't miss. So...what did you want to talk to me about?"

"Monday, and again yesterday, I tried calling you several times," Derek told her. "From Pittsfield, and from Boston. I wanted you to know that."

"You were in Pittsfield?"

He nodded. "We're buying land near Lenox for a Berkshires Voyager. I'd planned to get back here Monday night so I could talk to you, but that became impossible. Then, I wanted you to know I'd be back in time for the meeting. I wanted to tell you I intended to speak. I didn't want it to be a complete surprise."

Abby didn't comment, and Derek imagined he could actually feel the wall of her resistance. "Abby," he reminded her, determined to break through that wall, "I've been aboveboard with you from day one."

She shook her head in denial. "How can you say that, Derek? You've been planning your move for months."

"From San Francisco, and from Boston, Abby. Not from Devon. Remember, we met at the mill the morning after your rally. And later that same day, I came to your house and told you exactly what I was going to do."

"Yes, I know that." The words came slowly. "I just didn't think you had a chance of succeeding. Anyway, you kept the full truth from me."

"What are you talking about?"

"You said Sunday, when we went to the Outer Beach with Greg and Bobby, that you hadn't gotten back in Boston till late the night before."

"That was true."

"How can it have been? Unless you had someone meet you at the airport with the sales contract. Or did you actually wait to sign it till just before you came back here yesterday? If so, that was taking a risk, wasn't it? There might have been a chance the town counsel and I could have found a way to circumvent you."

"What are you getting at, Abby?"

"On the beach Sunday, I didn't think that you and Gordon Ryder had concluded your deal."

Puzzled, Derek said, "I must be missing the point."

"Until the last minute," Abby admitted, "I thought you might change your mind."

"About buying Mrs. Gould's property?"

"Yes."

Derek sighed heavily. "I signed the contract while I was still on the West Coast," he said. "The Boston office finalized the deal with Ryder, then expressed the contract to my office in San Francisco. I signed it and sent it back."

"I should have known."

"What you should have known was...we didn't make this move lightly. We've been planning this venture into New England for three years. It wasn't dreamed up on the spur of the moment, nor will it be accomplished overnight."

When Abby didn't comment, he added irritably, "I can't imagine why you'd think I might have considered reneging."

"I suppose," she said, "I expected too much."

Derek had been lying on his stomach. Now he turned on his side, propped up on an elbow, and faced her. "Exactly what the hell do you mean by that?"

Abby couldn't sit up any longer. She felt wobbly all over. She stretched out on her back, but avoided glancing toward Derek. Staring straight ahead, she said, "I said enough last Sunday about your thinking only in terms of dollars and cents. I apologized, but now I guess I was right in the first place. Making money is the only thing that matters to you, isn't it, Derek?"

He gritted his teeth, then let the words escape. "No, it isn't. You matter to me."

"*I* do? How can you say such a thing?"

"Because it's true."

"Then how can you possibly..."

"How can I possibly build a resort on the Gould property, tear down the windmill you revere, and still care for you?" He answered his questions, "Because business and feelings are two entirely different things."

"That's a strange thing to say."

"It's the way I live."

"So that makes it right?"

"I didn't say that."

Derek paused, and chose his next words carefully. "Look, the way we are is due to many different factors." He hazarded a guess. "I'd say you had a happy, carefree childhood."

Surprised, Abby turned to face him. "Yes, I did." She sensed that he was waiting for her to add to that, and said, "My father worked for the telephone company. We lived in a big old house over near Snow Harbor. There's a lawyer living there now."

"You were an only child?"

"No. I have a brother. He's married, has two kids and lives outside Washington, D.C."

"Are your parents still living?"

"Yes. Mom's had arthritis for years, so Dad took early retirement and they moved to Florida—Vero Beach, on the east coast."

"You visit them?"

"I usually go down for Christmas. They usually come up in August."

"They were always around when you were growing up, weren't they?"

"Yes, Derek. Why do you ask?"

He stretched out on his back, close to Abby, then took off the dark glasses and closed his eyes, black lashes sweeping his cheeks. His hair had dried into an unruly mess of waves. Right now, he looked very vulnerable.

"Derek?" Abby murmured.

"Yes?"

"Why did you ask about my parents?"

"Because I want to know more about you. I'd also like you to know more about me."

"Tell me," she said softly.

He started slowly, carefully, because it had been many years since he'd volunteered his life story to anyone. Now, he didn't want to make it into a tear-jerker, because that would only evoke pity from Abby. He didn't want her pity. He wanted her love.

Still, he had to make a stab at gaining her understanding. Then, perhaps, she'd see that the hardness of his philosophy wasn't all wrong. In today's business world, no one could be soft and succeed.

He spoke first about Sam, then about Faulk. He tried to stick to the highlights, tried to leave out the feelings he'd experienced then, and those he was dealing with now. But Abby, listening intently, began to fill in the gaps. By the time he reached the part where he'd discovered the pier was going to be demolished, she was aching.

She wanted to shed hot, scalding tears for him, wanted to console him with kisses, and fought off the urge to do both. She knew if she showed too much emotion, Derek would close up and shut her out.

When he told her, flatly, that Sam had suffered a fatal coronary at the age of forty-two, it was all she could do not to reach out and tug him toward her, murmuring soft words of love and assurance in his ear.

Instead, she asked, "What did you do after that?" striving, as she spoke, to keep the quaver out of her voice.

"Sam had an older brother, Marcus, who lived in Sacramento," Derek said tonelessly. "He and his wife took me in."

"They had no children of their own?"

Derek shook his head. "It must have been extremely difficult for them to have an eleven-year-old kid suddenly thrust upon them. My uncle was a very religious man, very strict...."

Abby waited for him to go on.

"I lived with Uncle Marc and Aunt Louise till I was sixteen," he said. "Then I cut out, went to San Francisco and moved into an apartment with some friends. I went to high school, and I worked a couple of nights a week and on the weekends."

"What kind of work?"

"Different jobs. The last one... I was a desk clerk in a hotel that, as it turned out, belonged to Faulk."

"You saw Faulk again?"

"Oh, yes, I saw Faulk again. One Sunday, he walked into the hotel lobby and we nearly bumped into each other. I recognized him right away. After a minute, he recognized me, too. That was the beginning of a whole new era."

"What happened?"

Derek opened his eyes, turned his head, and looked at her. "Haven't you heard enough, Abby?" he said. "Can't you see why I feel about things as I do?"

"What about Faulk?" she persisted.

A brief, bitter smile appeared, then vanished. "Faulk was an amazing man," Derek said. "Sometimes, I've thought maybe he had a guilt complex about the way I found out about the pier. Then again, I doubt it. In any event, he offered to put me through college with the proviso that I work for him for five years after graduation.

"So I went to college, then on to graduate school. Faulk realized that with the added education I would be even more valuable to him. He had two sons of his own who were already in his business. Each, incidentally, was the product of a marriage that ended in divorce. But he wanted me in his business, too. He said I was the most strongly motivated person he'd known—except for himself.''

"How long did you work for him?"

"Only three years, as it turned out. Faulk was killed in a car crash on an L.A. freeway. Bang, gone . . . just like that. A man who'd worked his way up from nothing to head a huge corporation—a real American success story."

Again, the bitter smile crossed Derek's face.

"Believe it or not, Abby, it had never occurred to me that I might be included in Faulk's will. His two sons were the major beneficiaries, and rightly so. But Faulk left me a hundred thousand dollars...which I put to very good use."

"You followed Faulk's golden rule?"

"Yes." Derek was quiet for a minute, then went on, "Basically Faulk was right. Business is something you can count on, if you give it all you've got. Whereas sentiment had already let me down. Witness what happened to the pier in Jacaranda, the place I loved most in the world, and —" his voice fell to a lower note "—to Sam."

Abby felt so choked by the emotions Derek was evoking that she was afraid she'd give way and break down in front of him. That was the last thing she wanted to do. It took all her strength to hang on and ask, "You never regretted what you might have lost along the way?"

"There was never anything to lose along the way."

"You really feel that way?"

"Yes."

"Then I suppose you're right. You followed Faulk's rule, and you have what you want."

Derek put on his glasses again, so Abby met only opaque darkness as she looked at him.

"Do I?" he asked. Then he stood and stretched, effectively ending the conversation before she could answer.

Chapter Thirteen

The parade route was roughly two miles long. It started at the Grange Hall near Snow Harbor and ended at the athletic field in back of the high school, where the floats were judged.

Abby, sitting in front of Greg's ten-foot-high replica of Devon Mill, with George Cobb at her side, wished she'd followed her intention of withdrawing her entry from the parade. But when the windmill float moved onto Main Street and she heard the cheers of the crowd jamming the curbs, she knew Greg was right.

Devon Mill deserved this homage.

Then she saw Derek, standing between a balloon vender and a cluster of tourists.

As the float came slowly abreast of him, he seemed so close Abby felt she could reach out and touch him. Their eyes met, and blue fire merged with emerald fire. Then the float moved on, but the memory lingered.

Abby had been troubled about Derek since they'd parted at the beach yesterday afternoon. She'd offered to drop him off at the Oceanside, but he'd opted to walk, saying he needed the exercise, which she doubted. She'd never known a man who looked more fit.

She'd gone home to dress, then kept her date with Greg and the people involved in putting the windmill float together. Outside Greg's shop, she'd spent the next couple of hours tacking red, white, and blue paper rosettes to the sides of the big trailer they'd been loaned for the float's base, while Greg and the men on the committee hoisted the replica windmill out of the shop and anchored it into place.

All the while, she'd reviewed the story Derek had told her. She wondered if maybe he'd suddenly become so withdrawn because of the sadness over the memories—or because he regretted the revelations he'd made.

Abby knew, from what she'd read about Derek, that he deliberately kept a low profile. Until now, though, she hadn't realized what an extremely private person he was.

Once again, there were unresolved issues between them. This time, the issues had nothing to do with tangible matters like the mill. They were considerably more personal. She understood Derek better. At least, she thought she did. Still, she couldn't accept his philosophy. And she detested the late Hugh Faulkner for having branded a ten-year-old boy with such a bitter view of life.

She heard shouts of "Atta girl, Abby," and forced herself to smile and wave, but her heart wasn't in this performance. Her heart was with that lonely man standing back along the curb, looking after her. Again, he had surprised her. She wouldn't have expected him to come to the parade.

Derek hadn't intended to go to the parade. He'd wanted the latest issue of *Business Week,* so he drove up to Bassett's Pharmacy on Main Street where he'd discovered a good magazine selection. He parked behind the pharmacy and was getting out of the car when he heard band music.

Curiosity prompted him to investigate, and he reached the curb just as the Devon High School Band was marching by. At that point he lingered, knowing there was no way he could drive back to the Oceanside as long as Devon's Fourth of July parade was usurping the main road.

A Cub Scout unit passed by, and he spotted Bobby Nickerson strutting along in his blue and gold uniform. Then he saw the windmill float approaching. And . . . Abby, standing in front of the replica, smiling and waving at the crowd.

Her unexpected appearance rocked Derek. She'd said nothing yesterday about participating in a Fourth of July parade.

She was dressed in a patriotic costume, and she looked just as gorgeous, as desirable as always. Then her eyes locked with his in a brief, intense encounter before the float moved on.

Derek, following the progress of the float, was clutched by a deep depression. The Devon Mill replica seemed symbolic of the friction that constantly put the brakes on their attraction to each other. One way or another, the damned mill would always come between them.

Derek reached into his pocket and closed his fingers over the lucky stone Abby had given him. He caressed its smoothness, remembering that moment on the beach when she'd plucked it from the sand. He'd kept the stone with him ever since.

His mind was in a haze as he watched the rest of the parade. Finally fire engines from several communities joined forces to form a strident rear guard. With horns blowing and sirens wailing, they created an ear-splitting din. In their wake

Derek heard his name called and turned to see Greg Nickerson making his way through the crowd.

"I spotted Bobby," Derek volunteered when Greg got close. "He looked great. Incidentally, did you build that model of the windmill?"

"'Fraid so," Greg replied.

"Well, you did a terrific job. The weathered shingles really give it character."

"Thanks," Greg smiled. "The shingles came off a garage I refurbished."

"The sails were an authentic touch, too. The wind wasn't turning the arms, was it?"

"No, an electric motor was. Now I guess I'm stuck with the damn thing. I'll probably keep it in a shed back of my shop in case Abby wants to use it in next year's parade."

And the year after that. And the year after *that,* Derek thought dismally. Devon Mill, whether standing or demolished, real or replica, would live forever.

Greg said, "I'm on my way to the athletic field. After the floats are judged, there'll be games and contests for the kids. Naturally Bobby won't want to miss any of them. Care to come along?"

"Thanks, but I'll have to pass," Derek said.

Despite the friendliness of Greg's invitation, he suddenly felt very much a stranger. He didn't belong here on Abby's terrain. A fresh awareness of that swept over him. With it came a terrible sense of desolation.

Back at the Oceanside, he thumbed through *Business Week* and noticed the paragraph on Van Heusen Inc.'s acquisition of Yamasaki Properties U.S.A. He put the magazine aside and reached for his briefcase. He'd brought a stack of important papers to the Cape that had been faxed to Boston from the San Francisco headquarters and needed his attention. But he soon discovered he was too restless to concentrate.

Once again, he turned to physical action as a kind of sedative and went for a long run. With so many people out on the beaches or participating in Fourth of July activities up in the center of town, the residential areas were relatively deserted. Derek narrowed his focus to running, his mind and body working in unity, and the dual exertion helped.

When he got back the phone was jangling as he opened the door to his room. He closed it quickly and immediately was on edge again. It was a holiday. Who else would be calling him but Abby?

"Mr. Van Heusen? It's Tom Channing," he heard.

Derek's disappointment was profound.

He sat down on the edge of the bed. "You're working on the Fourth of July, Tom?"

"Not really. I'm home. But I just had a call from Andy Bennett and I thought I should pass on his information to you."

"Oh?"

"Andy wasn't able to touch base with Gordon Ryder until last night. Mr. Ryder's been in Martha's Vineyard the past few days. Andy told him you want to move into the house and are interested in buying the contents. Furniture, antiques, everything. You were right. Mr. Ryder's more than willing to sell everything his aunt owns as a single package. Evidently he started to pack up some of the stuff, but nothing had been moved."

"Did he suggest a price?"

"A hundred and fifty thousand," Channing reported. "He had a rough inventory Andy went over with him, and Andy thinks the price is about right. There are a couple of original oil paintings with considerable value, a lot of old

glass and china, a vintage piano, all sorts of antique furniture...."

"I'll go for it," Derek decided.

"I'll tell Andy. He can wind things up with Mr. Ryder
tomorrow. Meantime, Mr. Ryder has no problem at all with
your moving into the house right away. There's bed linen,
towels, blankets... everything but food, he said. And both
the phone and electricity are on."

"Thanks, Tom," Derek said.

"I think Andy's still annoyed at himself for screwing up
on his initial report about Miss Eldredge," Tom reported.
"Though, as you know, there wasn't much subsequent information. Anyway, he doesn't want to goof where Ryder's
concerned. He's still in Falmouth. I have his number if you
want it."

"You call Bennett, Tom. Tell him to deal with Ryder
ASAP tomorrow morning, then to knock off for the weekend. He's done a good job. So have you."

"Thanks, Mr. Van Heusen. Oh, there's one more thing."

"Yes?"

"I had a call from Pittsfield. Our offer for the Berkshires property is acceptable."

"That's great, Tom. Tell Bennett Monday afternoon will
be time enough for him to get down here. In fact, you might
touch base with Sheila Casey. Maybe she and Bennett can
come down together."

"Will do," Channing agreed. "You'll be at the Gould
house from now on?"

"Just as soon as I can check out here."

Ordinarily Abby would have been feeling great. The
windmill float had won first prize this morning. Bobby had
triumphed in several of the races and contests for the kids.
She'd spent the afternoon sailing on George Cobb's ketch

with George, his wife and a number of friends. Soon it would be time to go to the beach with Greg and Bobby to watch the fireworks.

But there was absolutely no savor to any of these things she usually loved to do.

She fed Captain, showered, then decided to wear jeans instead of shorts tonight. Despite the warmth of the day, it would be cool on the beach once the sun was gone.

She tugged a light sweater over the jeans, then felt a bulge in her right hip pocket. Reaching in, she withdrew a crumpled white handkerchief spotted with her blood. A man's handkerchief with the monogram DVH embroidered in one corner.

Abby hadn't worn this pair of jeans since that morning when she and Derek met by accident at Devon Mill. Now the memory came back, so vivid she would have sworn she could smell the scent of the wild roses and hear the bee buzzing as it searched for pollen.

Was that when she'd fallen in love with Derek?

She'd never put much stock in love at first sight, but *something* had definitely happened to her that warm June morning by Devon Mill. Certainly she had neither felt nor acted normal ever since.

Where was Derek now? she wondered. He was a stranger in Devon, a stranger who had quickly generated notoriety for himself—and stirred up a fair measure of antagonism as well—by getting up in front of the whole town and wiping out, in a terse statement or two, the efforts and hopes of people who had lived here all their lives.

At the athletic field, even as her float was being awarded first prize, Abby had kept scanning the crowd, looking for a man who would be taller than most people and whose dark hair would gleam like black satin in the sunlight. But he hadn't appeared.

Now, in the early evening, she yielded to an impulse too strong to resist. She picked up the phone, dialed the Ocean-side Motel and asked for Derek. She'd invite him to watch the fireworks with her, Greg and Bobby at the beach. The worst he could say was no.

The clerk at the Oceanside said politely, "Sorry, ma'am, but Mr. Van Heusen checked out earlier today."

"Checked out? He couldn't have!"

"Sorry, but he did."

"When?"

"I don't know exactly, ma'am. I just came on. If you'll wait a minute, I'll check...."

Abby's pulse started throbbing. She'd seen the look on Derek's face when their eyes met this morning. There'd been no time for either of them to mask their emotions. And, for a single, blinding second...those emotions had triumphed. She'd *felt* that moment of revelation. Certainly he must have felt it, too.

How could he leave town without even saying goodbye?

The clerk came back on the phone. "Mr. Van Heusen checked out about one o'clock," he reported.

"Did he say where he was going?"

There was a pause. Then, "No, he did not."

Abby placed the receiver back in the cradle and, for a long moment, sat very still, staring into space. Captain nudged her knee, and she patted him absently. He sensed her mood and cuddled closer, whimpering. She hugged his head.

"Why, Captain?" she asked aloud. "Why?"

The doorbell rang. And rang again. Hope couldn't be submerged, but it quickly turned to dejection when Abby opened the door and saw Bobby Nickerson grinning up at her.

"Ready?" Bobby urged. "We want to get a good place."

Abby loved fireworks, but tonight she couldn't wait for the grand finale. Even the cascades of colorful rocket showers that filled the dark sky, the explosive bangs that reverberated through the air, and the cheers of the crowd didn't lift her spirits.

Maybe Derek had driven up to Boston for business reasons. Maybe he'd taken off somewhere to visit friends for the holiday weekend. Or...maybe he was already flying back to San Francisco, leaving Devon once and for all.

But . . . he'd told Clara he would be back to see her.

Abby remembered him saying that, and began to breathe again.

Derek unlocked the front door of the Gould house and fought back the feeling that he was an intruder. With all the windows closed, it was not only hot inside, but the air smelled musty. He put his suitcase and briefcase in a corner and walked around the living room, noting, as he pulled up shades and opened windows, that the glass in many of the small panes was wavy, imperfect.

Old, he suspected. Probably very old.

Looking around the room, he saw cardboard cartons and newspapers, the evidence of Gordon Ryder's packing efforts. Some were already filled with items wrapped in newsprint. Derek carefully uncovered one item, a miniature glass vase in an incredible shade of cobalt.

One of Clara's treasures, he could imagine.

He wished he knew something about antiques. He'd never been interested in old things—except for the Jacaranda Beach pier, which fell into a different category of oldness. His concentration, for as long as he could remember, had been geared toward the future, not the past.

Maybe his lack of interest in old things was because there'd been no heirlooms in his family. Sam had sold everything long before they'd arrived in Jacaranda. Then, and after, there'd only been a few meager possessions . . . nothing they couldn't quickly pack and carry.

Derek walked around the living room, touched the mirrored finish of the rosewood piano, admired the subdued texture and color of the oil painting, a harbor scene misted with fog, that hung over the mantel.

A vision of his San Francisco condo flashed through his mind as he moved into the dining room and saw the corner cupboard filled with old glass and china. He had wanted everything strictly contemporary in his condo and had hired a top Bay Area decorator to follow his wishes. The result was as avant-garde as tomorrow, extremely expensive and equally impersonal.

The cabin up in the Sierras was different, though—as rustic as the condo was sleekly modern. It had been minimally furnished when Derek purchased it, and he'd left it that way. Again, it reflected nothing as personal as these items that Clara Gould had collected over a lifetime, or the things he'd seen in Abby's house.

He could imagine the fun Abby would have fixing up the cabin, giving it character, making it a place not just to escape to, but a retreat unlike any other. Not for the first time, Derek pictured her in that Sierras setting. Then he pictured her, even more vividly, in *this* setting. And he wished she were with him now.

She would know about many of Clara Gould's beautiful antiques, about the past. She would make the past come alive for him—something he had never experienced.

In the kitchen, he spotted the rocks glass in the sink and the empty Bourbon bottle on the counter. Ryder's leftovers, he supposed. There was a carton of milk gone sour in the fridge. A couple of cans of soup sat on a cupboard shelf. But not much else, as Tom Channing had mentioned.

A trip to the store was in order, but first Derek stepped out the kitchen door—and immediately found himself confronting Devon Mill, five hundred feet away.

For the first time, despite its rundown condition, the mill commanded his respect, and he began to appreciate some of the things Abby had said about it. The significance of a two-hundred-year-old structure that had withstood freezing winters and raging hurricanes, while providing a crucial service to the people of the town, was not to be negated.

Derek started along the miller's path, gripped by a fascination that surprised him. The front of the mill, facing Cape Cod Bay, was bathed in golden light. Derek had the impression of a giant sentinel guarding the bluff and beach below it. And, as he neared the mill yard, he remembered Abby saying that the miller had spotted British boats approaching Snow Harbor during the War of 1812. And his warning had saved the town.

Abby had spoken, too, of how man's use of the wind to harness power dated back to the most obscure reaches of history. Derek looked curiously at the big wooden structure looming above him, thought about its purpose and significance...and began to understand what both it, and history, meant to Abby.

She spoke of history as if it were a living entity. To her, he could see, it was. A continuation, like a chain linking past to present, with new links extending to capture the future.

But then, she had roots. He didn't. His Uncle Marcus had been his only relative. Both Marcus and Louise were dead now, and actually had been out of his life since he'd left their house when he was sixteen. He had never gone back.

Later, much later, guilt had unexpectedly touched him one day as he passed a church in downtown San Francisco. The church reminded him of his deeply religious uncle, a man who had never missed a Sunday mass in his whole life.

After that, Derek had hired a private investigator to track down Marcus and Louise. He'd found they were no longer living and had felt a sense of loss even though he'd never loved them. They had taken him in, after all, when Sam died. Looking back now, he had no doubt they'd done their best to raise a headstrong and bitter young boy. He only wished he'd shown them a little gratitude.

He knew nothing of his mother's background, nor had Marcus been able to enlighten him about her. She and Sam had fallen in love, married. That's all Marcus knew.

Now Derek thought about how different his background was from Abby's. Hers was steeped in history and tradition. Her family had come to New England long ago...had once owned this land upon which he was now standing. And the homestead. And the mill.

Derek opened the gate cautiously, then traversed the overgrown yard and tugged the mill door open. It creaked as he stepped past it into the gloomy interior. Peer though he might, Derek could make out only vague shapes, and a flight of open, wooden steps leading to an upper level.

He promised himself he would buy a flashlight, one with a powerful beam, when he went shopping. In the morning he would return to the mill and explore every corner.

Derek fixed a cheese sandwich for his supper and washed it down with a cold beer as he watched the glorious sunset over Cape Cod Bay. Then, with darkness, he discovered that his vantage point high on the bluff gave him a good view of the fireworks display across town.

Again he wished Abby were with him. He wished they could have shared a simple supper, then watched the fireworks together. Probably she was there at the beach with Greg and Bobby Nickerson, and hundreds of other people.

The fireworks over, Derek went inside, tuned in some music on the radio in the kitchen and started to unpack the cartons Gordon Ryder had filled. Again he wished he knew more about antiques. Each object he unwrapped was unique. Delicate or durable, exquisite or plain, every item had its own special beauty.

He worked slowly, setting things out on the tables in the kitchen and dining room, and the hours went by unnoticed. When at last he glanced at the clock, it was after midnight. Time to call it quits, he decided. He made up the four-poster bed in the downstairs bedroom, and soon was asleep.

In the morning, after cooking a hearty breakfast of eggs and sausage and home-fried potatoes, Derek set out for the mill, anxious to explore. But halfway along the miller's path, he came to a halt. Abby's yellow car was parked in the loop at the end of Mill Lane.

He moved ahead slowly, and at first didn't see her. Then she emerged around the side of the mill, studying it intently. Derek saw the camera in Abby's hand, saw her step back, focus and shoot. This she continued to do, unaware of his presence.

Why, he wondered, was she doing this? Surely, Devon Mill had been preserved for posterity in the form of photographs. He remembered the blowups hung in the town hall lobby the night of her rally, and the postcards he'd seen in the pharmacy and coffee shop.

Finally Abby straightened, turned and saw him. "Derek." She stared as if she were seeing a ghost. "What are you doing here?"

He deliberately kept his tone light. "Might I not ask the same question?"

"Oh, I see. It's *me* who's trespassing now. Is that it?"

He had to smile. "Aren't you?" he teased.

"I suppose I am."

There it was—that defiance again. Why, he wondered, did she always have to get her back up so quickly?

She held her camera as if she felt he might confiscate it. "I wanted to take a few pictures of the mill," she said. "For myself. The light is just right at this time of morning. . . ."

"You don't have to explain," he told her.

Abby held her ground as Derek moved closer. "What's that for?" she asked, noticing the flashlight he was holding.

"I want to take a look inside the mill."

Her brow creased in a perplexed frown. "I thought you'd left Devon. I tried to reach you at the Oceanside last night and they said you'd checked out."

"You called me?"

"Yes, I called you." She sounded defensive as she added, "I wanted to invite you to watch the fireworks with Greg and Bobby and me."

"I should have invited the three of you to come up here," Derek said. "The view was spectacular."

"You were *here* last night?"

He nodded.

"Why?" Abby asked. "Where?"

"I've moved into the house."

"Moved into the house? I didn't see your car."

"I'm parked back of the kitchen."

Abby still looked perplexed. "Why have you moved into Clara's house?" she asked, then quickly corrected herself. "I should say, why have you moved into *your* house?"

"I decided I might as well use the house as a headquarters while final plans for developing the site are worked out."

"I see. And why do you want to poke around the mill?"

"Curiosity."

"That's rather sudden, isn't it?"

"Yes," Derek admitted. "Though you made quite a case for windmills that first night I heard you speak. Frankly I'm interested to see how this one works."

Abby hesitated, then decided, "All right. Years ago, Randolph Gould showed me how to operate this mill. I never actually did it, but I can probably show you all you'd want to know, if you'd like me to."

Derek could not have dreamed up a more improbable scenario than being escorted through Devon Mill by Abby Eldredge, and initiated into its working. Old Randolph Gould had taught her well, he realized, as Abby carefully guided him up the broken steps and began explaining the function and operation of the many moving parts.

For more than an hour, she talked about the cap, the arms, the sails and tailpiece . . . the windshaft, brakewheel, spindle, hopper and grinding stones. She lectured Derek on the skill of milling and answered his questions with an expertise that astonished him. Every minute, he was held spellbound both by her knowledge . . . and her beauty.

Finally they emerged into the sunlight. Suddenly the confidence Abby had displayed while she was telling him about the mill seemed to dissipate. Derek sensed that in another moment she would be leaving—and he wanted to keep her here.

"Abby," he said, "I have a favor to ask."

"What kind of favor?"

"Would you come back to the house with me? There are some things I'd like to ask you about."

"What things?"

"Antiques."

"You mean . . . there are antiques left in the house?"

"Didn't you think there would be?"

"The last I knew, Gordon Ryder was packing things up. I assumed he'd have moved them out by now."

"He started the job," Derek said. "But he didn't finish."

"What do you mean, he didn't finish?"

"He sold me the contents of the house." Derek waited for an explosion.

To his surprise, Abby looked curious instead. "You?" she queried. "Why on earth would you want Clara's old things?"

Perhaps she mean didn't mean to be derogatory, but that was the way she sounded.

Derek restrained a quick retort. "I saw no point in furnishing the place when it was already furnished," he said. That, he imagined, was just about what she'd expect him to say. And he knew that until her viewpoint changed considerably, there was no way he was going to tell her that he'd bought the Gould antiques so that—in due course—he could give them to her.

Chapter Fourteen

Derek repeated his earlier invitation. "Will you come back to the house with me, Abby?"

Abby sidestepped a direct answer. "What is it you want to ask me about antiques?"

"I need a quick education in the whole subject. Gordon Ryder packed up half a dozen cartons of stuff before I arranged to buy everything. Last night I started unpacking, and I'm intrigued by what I've found—I'm intrigued by everything, actually. The paintings, the piano, the whole works."

"Intrigued by their value. Is that it?"

Derek stiffened. "No," he said tightly, "that's not it. Right now, I'm not interested in the dollar worth of these things. What I'd like is information . . . such as you gave me about the windmill. I thought you'd probably know quite a lot about antiques. Maybe I was wrong."

Abby frowned. "Gordon told me he intended to set aside anything Clara wanted. Do you know if he did that?"

"No. I doubt he had time. But naturally Mrs. Gould can have anything she wants. I'll take it up with her. Unless you'd like to?"

"Ah, no," Abby said, not sparing the sarcasm. "You talk to Clara, by all means. She seems delighted that you've bought her house and Devon Mill as well. I'm sure she'll be thrilled when she hears you also own her treasures."

Derek's eyes narrowed. "You know, Abby," he said, "bitterness really doesn't become you." He sighed, a sigh of pure frustration. "I have this feeling I'm damned if I do and damned if I don't," he complained. "What is it with you? I know you had some preconceived notions about me when we first met. But hasn't anything that's happened between us since made any difference?"

Abby glanced away from Derek and focused on a sea gull swooping down to the beach below the bluff. The gull circled out over the water, then landed on a rowboat anchored offshore.

"Abby?" Derek asked. "Did you hear me?"

"I heard you," she murmured. She looked at the mill, looked at the split-rail fence surrounding the mill yard, then said, her voice very low, "I don't know what it is with me, Derek. I've always had a tendency to blurt things out, then wish I could take them back. But...I'm worse with you than I've ever been with anyone else."

"I have that bad an effect on you?"

She turned and faced him. "Bad isn't the right word. Sometimes you surprise me, that's all. You do something, or you say something, and it rubs me the wrong way."

"And you want to strike back?"

"Yes, I want to strike back. And I don't stop to think about how I'm coming across till it's too late."

Derek surveyed her gravely. "What did I do to surprise you just now?"

"Seeing you here surprised me. I thought you were in Boston, or maybe you'd gone back to California." She shrugged uncomfortably. "I don't know. This was the last place I expected to see you."

"Anything else?" Derek queried. "There is more, isn't there?"

"Well, I didn't expect you to suggest that Clara could have anything she wanted from the house."

His eyebrows arched. "Why the hell not?"

"Because...oh, I don't know."

For a few seconds, Abby looked helpless. Then she pulled herself together and said, "Yes, I do know. But no matter how I put this, it's going to sound terrible."

"Say it anyway."

"Okay. It isn't that I doubt your generosity. I'm sure you're an extremely generous person. It's easy to visualize you making big gestures. For instance, I can picture you donating huge sums to charities."

"But?"

"Well...it's hard to think of you bothering with the small things, like going to Devon Manor to tell Clara about buying her property—which was very kind of you, incidentally. Or suggesting that Bobby use a lighter sinker. Or playing ball with Captain like you did on the Outer Beach the other day. Or helping with Bobby's sand castle. Or—"

"I believe I get the point."

Abby looked up, saw the rigid set of his jaw and knew she'd done it again. "Dammit!" she exploded, "I told you that everything I try to say to you comes out wrong."

He surveyed her thoughtfully. Then he said, "Maybe that's my fault more than yours. Just remember...this image that's been created of me isn't set in stone. I'd hoped maybe you'd already found that out, but it seems we still have a way to go."

His sudden smile was as warm as the morning sunshine. "For the third time, will you come back to the house?"

"For a few minutes," Abby decided. "But I can't stay long."

Derek let Abby proceed him along the path to the homestead. He held the kitchen door for her, then led her to the dining room table first. "I've tried to keep similar things together," he told her.

"Good idea," Abby agreed. After a cursory inspection, she commented, "I noticed these were missing the night Gordon was here." She picked up a squat glass container with a pewter lid. "This is called a Christmas salt," she told Derek. "They were made by the famous Sandwich Glass Company and are quite rare. Clara has a collection . . . yes, I'd say they're all here."

"Do you think she'd like to have them?"

"Possibly. She didn't take many personal things with her when she went to live in Devon Manor. The move was difficult enough, emotionally as well as physically, without her having extra decisions to make. I think she just wanted to get it over with. But maybe now..." Abby shrugged. "We'll talk to her and see."

We'll talk to her and see. Not I. Or you. But . . . *we*.

Derek felt a faint ray of hope. He gestured at the sugar bowl she was holding. "What kind of glass is that?"

"Milk glass."

Abby looked down at the sugar bowl and was swamped in memories of those long-ago times when she and her grandmother had visited Clara for tea. Then, on the heels of the memories, came the dread of what was bound to happen to this house she loved so much.

She swung around and confronted Derek. "How long are you going to stay here?"

Derek was watching the careful, loving way in which Abby handled the antiques. Her question startled him. "As long as it takes," he said vaguely. "I want to be certain the Cape Voyager gets off to a good start. Why do you ask?"

"Because I imagine once you leave the house, it'll be torn down, won't it? And I suppose the mill may be torn down even sooner than that. If you've made any definite plans, I wish you'd tell me."

"You're talking about demolition plans?"

She nodded. "I'd rather not be around when the house and mill go. If I could know in advance when that's to happen, I'll arrange to visit my parents or go see my brother and his family."

Abby was looking at him as if he were a hostile stranger. Derek felt a heaviness in his chest and diagnosed it as defeat.

The hope of a moment ago faded. He'd never win with Abby.

He said, "No dates have been set yet for beginning the actual work here. The plans aren't even finished, for one thing. Aside from that, there are all sorts of building permits we'll need to get, contractors to hire...." He broke off, then added, his voice laced with irony, "We won't bring in the bulldozers for at least a month or two. But when that's about to happen, you'll be the first to know."

He added, "This time, you're surprising me, though. I didn't think it would be your style to run away."

"Are you suggesting I should stand out on the bluff and watch while you tear down Devon Mill?"

"While *I* tear down Devon Mill? I don't intend to rip the mill apart with my bare hands."

"Dammit, Derek, you know what I mean."

She scowled at him and moved around the end of the table. In her haste, her elbow nudged a slender Tiffany vase. The vase fell on the hard oak floor with a sickening crash and shattered into shimmering gold shards.

"Oh, no!" Abby cried.

She was on her knees in an instant, searching for pieces, carefully picking up the tiny fragments of glass as if she might magically put them together again.

Derek loomed over her, then, and hauled her to her feet. "You'll cut the hell out of your hands if you're not careful," he said roughly.

"It doesn't matter, Derek. Let go of me!"

Abby broke away from him, so distraught she was almost hysterical. This destruction, by *her,* of a valuable, precious antique was a final straw. Her nerves had been on edge for days, her emotions rubbed raw. Now everything surfaced all at once, and she couldn't hold back the tears.

She turned toward the window, and Derek followed her. He clasped her shoulders, then said gently, "Don't, sweetheart. It was only a piece of glass."

"Only...a piece...of glass?" Abby choked between sobs. "How can you say that?"

"Because that's what it was. Somewhere in the world there must be another vase like it. I'll buy it for you."

She thrust him away, faced him defiantly, tears still streaking her cheeks. "You think you can buy everything, don't you?" she challenged. "Well, you're wrong. That vase was irreplaceable. It was a wedding present to Clara and Randolph Gould, seventy years ago."

"Suppose Randolph or Clara had broken it?"

"They didn't break it. I did."

"If Clara or Randolph had broken the vase, they would have felt very bad, I'm sure," Derek persisted. "But do you

NOW
4 titles
every
month!

See
45¢ Coupon
on Back

Even if you've never read a historical
romance before, you will discover the same
great stories and favorite authors you've
come to expect from Harlequin and
Silhouette like Patricia Potter, Lucy Elliott,
Ruth Langan and Heather Graham
Pozzessere.

Enter the world of Harlequin and share the
adventure.

Journey with Harlequin into the past and discover stories of cowboys and captains, pirates and princes in the romantic tradition of Harlequin.

45¢

45¢

SAVE 45¢
ON ANY
HARLEQUIN HISTORICAL®
NOVEL

TO THE DEALER: Harlequin/Silhouette Books will pay 45¢ plus 8¢ handling upon presentation of this coupon by your customer toward the purchase of the products specified. Any other use constitutes fraud. Proof of sufficient stock (in the previous 90 days) to cover coupon redemption must be presented upon request. Coupon is non-assignable, void if taxed, prohibited or restricted by law. Consumer must pay any sales tax. Coupons submitted become the property of Harlequin/Silhouette Books. Reimbursement made only to retail distributor who redeems coupon. Coupon valid in the United States and Canada. Reimbursement paid only in country where product purchased. LIMIT ONE COUPON PER PURCHASE. VALID ONLY ON HARLEQUIN HISTORICAL® BOOKS IN THE U.S.A. AND CANADA.

IN U.S.A., MAIL TO:
HARLEQUIN HISTORICAL BOOKS
P.O. BOX 880478
El Paso, TX 88588-0478
U.S.A.
Coupons redeemable at retail outlets only.
OFFER EXPIRES AUGUST 31, 1991.

65373 100356

45¢

Printed in Canada

really think it would have affected their love for each other?"

Abby daubed at her tears. "I don't understand you."

"You just inferred I think money can buy everything. In a way, you're right. I do think money can buy most things."

"Just what are you trying to say, Derek?"

"For one thing, I find it ironic that so many *things* outlast the people who've owned them. People are far more perishable. It's occurring to me that maybe that's why I shut people out of my life. I've been afraid to let them in."

Derek's eyes searched her face. "Do you understand what I'm saying, Abby? I locked myself up inside without even knowing what I was doing. Out of fear, because of Faulk, because of Sam. Does that make sense to you? I didn't want involvement because I was afraid it would hurt too much. And because I knew only too damned well, though I never admitted it, that money can't buy what matters."

"What matters?"

"Love and compassion and understanding," Derek said steadily. "The things I didn't let myself think about because I was sure I'd never have them. Then you came along...and—" he finished, his voice husky "—I don't know what I'm going to do about you."

Abby saw the desperate sadness in Derek's eyes, saw the uncertainty twisting his handsome face, and instinctively she reached out to him. Her palms caressed his cheeks. Her fingers brushed his temples. Then she stood on tiptoe and threw her arms around him, hugging him, drawing him against her.

At first, Derek didn't move. Then, slowly, he reacted. He took Abby in his arms, felt her warm body next to his. He smelled the freshness of her hair, the sweetness of her. And when he bent to kiss her, passion and pain churned together as one.

Abby returned his kiss, her own emotions in turmoil. Then she let nature take command, let instinct lead the way, let her hands rove through Derek's hair as their kiss deepened. She feather-touched his neck, then pulled back, breathing harder. She cupped his shoulders as their kiss deepened again, and pushed her body against his, her message eloquent.

Derek hadn't needed this to arouse him. He'd been aroused ever since Abby had agreed to come to the house. Now, her spontaneous, seductive movements only fueled the fire that had begun to ignite, deep in his loins, from the moment he'd seen her outside the mill. Her protests had kept him cool at first, kept his senses intact, his instincts at bay. But now his wanting became a raging necessity. His senses shattered, like the vase on the floor.

Derek groaned as Abby pressed against him. He groaned again when she returned his hungry kisses as if she, too, were starving. He pulled back long enough to whisper, "Darling, I need you. I need to make love with you. I need you ... now."

The tears glistening in Abby's eyes now were tears of joy, of wanting, of need and desire. "Make love to me, Derek," she wished aloud. "Oh please, make love to me."

Derek swept her up in his arms and carried her to the four-poster bed where he'd slept last night. He intended to go slow, feel slow, move slow, but Abby wouldn't let him. And he found he couldn't wait.

Abby's demands, he quickly discovered, were as insistent as his. There was no question of slipping off clothes garment by garment as part of a tantalizing prologue. Impelled by the same fervent ardor, they carelessly cast aside jeans, and shirts, and underthings ... and tumbled wildly onto the bed.

Abby lost all restraint in the heat of her need. Everything that had been pent up within her was released by the power of her passion. All she wanted was to give herself fully to Derek—and receive him fully in return.

He was everything she had ever imagined in a man, and so much more. So much more. Abby soared with Derek, caressed with him, climbed passion's peak with him... before they exploded together, then collapsed.

They lay panting on top of the sheets, arms entwined, groping for words to convey their feelings as their ragged breathing gradually subsided. And when all was said and done, Abby knew she would never again be whole, without him.

Derek—his body glistening, his hair mussed, his mind and muscles totally relaxed—had never felt more at peace. Fingering the gold heart dangling around Abby's neck, the pendant she'd worn at La Chamarita in Provincetown, he asked, "Who gave you this?"

"My grandmother did," she murmured, "on my sixteenth birthday. It was given to her by her grandmother, when she was sixteen."

"It's beautiful," Derek said, knowing how valuable the gold heart must be to Abby. Far more valuable than a coffer of diamonds and emeralds and sapphires and rubies.

Could *he* ever give her something she'd treasure so much?

Abby's eyes were closed, but Derek knew she was not asleep. Tentatively he touched her breasts...and slowly her eyes opened. Derek saw two deep emerald pools in which desire still flickered. But, much as he wanted to fan that desire into flame, he also wanted to talk. There was so much he needed to make her understand.

"Abby," he began, but she wouldn't let him finish.

Softly she pressed her mouth to his, then harder...and harder. And as Derek's thoughts of talking drifted away, his body drifted toward shore—the shore where Abby waited, wanting and needing him more than ever.

Their tempo this time was slow, languorous, but steadily it increased. And then, before either realized what was happening, they were again melting together, spinning the act of ultimate union into a new dimension all their own.

Afterward, this time, Abby slipped into slumber. As he watched her, Derek wondered if she had any idea how much he loved her.

"I can't believe I fell asleep," Abby mumbled as she tugged on her clothes. "I have to hurry! Greg's working in his shop. I told him I'd pick Bobby up at noon. This is my day to do remedial reading with Bobby." She broke off, searched her purse until she found her hairbrush, then furiously began working out the snarls from her tangled chestnut mane.

Derek, sitting up in bed behind her, watched her in the mirror over the dresser. "It's only 11:40, Abby. You've got plenty of time. Why don't you call Greg, if you're worried?" He grinned. "Think you'll have enough energy to handle Bobby?"

"If I can handle you, Derek, I can handle Bobby."

"*Can* you handle me?"

Abby met his eyes in the mirror, saw him leaning casually back against the pillows. He'd pulled a sheet up to his waist, but the sight of his bare chest, his strong arms and his handsome face were enough to start sexual vibes sparking all over again.

"I hope so," she told him. "Can you handle me?"

"Come back to bed and I'll give it my best shot."

"Derek, that's not what I mean."

"I know, darling. I know."

She sat down next to him and kissed him lightly on the mouth. "I really do have to go," she murmured.

"Will you come back later . . . and stay?"

"Derek, I can't. I made plans with Greg and Bobby to go to the movies tonight. Then tomorrow I'm taking Bobby out to Provincetown to go on a whale watch."

"Oh," Derek said. He waited to see if Abby would invite him to either of those outings. When she didn't, he said reluctantly, "You're still worried about what people will think, aren't you?"

"What does that mean?"

"You're still worried that people might connect Abby Eldredge with Derek Van Heusen, and gossip. For God's sake, Abby . . . people will always think what they want. Besides, it's no one's business but ours if . . ."

"If what, Derek?"

He sat back, exasperated. "Never mind," he told her. "We'll get into it some other time."

He got up, pulled on his pants and followed Abby to the door, suddenly feeling disgruntled, incomplete. "I'll talk to you later, okay?" he suggested.

"Okay," Abby agreed. But already she sounded faraway.

Derek stood in the door and watched her hurry out to her Volks, start the motor and put the bright little car in gear. A moment later, she was gone.

Alone, and feeling a gnawing emptiness begin to eat at his insides, Derek started to explore the homestead more thoroughly. He foraged through the dank, dark cellar, then headed to the second floor, noting the nautical rope that took the place of a handrail beside the steep, narrow steps.

Upstairs, the ceilings were so low he had to duck as he went through doorways from one room to another. The wide pine floorboards probably had been there since the house was built. The bathroom, though the plumbing fixtures were outmoded, was a relatively new addition. Though new, in this instance, Derek thought whimsically, could mean anything added since the turn of the century.

Downstairs again, he examined the wainscoting and the mantels in the living room and dining room with new appreciation. He studied the exposed ceiling beams and corner posts, the metal latches and glass knobs used on all the doors. He fingered the ancient bricks that lined the hearths . . . and realized there was no possible way he could tear this house down.

That conviction grew as the noon hour passed. Though he'd never believed in ghosts—and didn't now—there was a certain *presence* to the old house. Derek thought of all the different people who must have lived here during the course of two centuries, of the births, deaths, marriages, celebrations, arguments and lovemaking that had taken place within these walls.

He wished the walls could talk, imagined the stories they could tell—stories that might have faded into oblivion with the passage of time, though many must be known by Clara Gould, and perhaps had been passed along to Abby.

Derek wanted Abby here. He wanted her to share those stories with him, wanted to learn lessons she could teach him, lessons of specific history, lessons of the past—things that had never been part of his life.

Abby had said Greg was working in his shop. On impulse, Derek found a phone book, turned to Greg's shop number and dialed.

"Hope I'm not interrupting something," Derek apologized, when Greg answered on the fifth ring.

"Nah, I was just outside," Greg said. "What's up?"

"I need to talk with you, Greg, as soon as you can spare some time."

"How about now?" Greg suggested. "I was just about to break for lunch."

"Want to meet somewhere?"

"How about I get us some sandwiches from the deli up the street, and you meet me here?"

"Sounds good. Give me directions."

A short time later in Greg's shop, Derek handed over a six-pack of beer he'd picked up on the way.

Greg grinned. "Just what the doctor ordered." He pulled a wooden stool over to his workbench for Derek, then sat down himself. "So, what's on your mind?" he asked.

"A couple of things. For starters, I've been wondering if it's possible to move an old house without damaging it irreparably in the process?"

Greg shrugged. "That depends. When I was growing up, moving a house was a fairly common practice. You'd be driving down a road and all of a sudden a cop would flag you to a stop, or point the way to a detour. And sure enough, up ahead there'd be this huge house being towed along at a snail's pace, taking up the whole road, while guys moved the power lines out of the way, trimmed tree branches…it was quite a sight," Greg reminisced. "But with all the new building going on, I haven't seen a house moved like that in years."

"Do you think the Gould homestead could be moved?"

"That, I wouldn't know. I'd have to look at it very closely, and probably call in an expert."

"I'd like you to do that, Greg."

"You're thinking of moving the house?"

Derek took a swig of beer, then said, "That's about where the idea is right now—at the thinking stage. Meanwhile, I'm living there."

"Well, that's a surprise. Since when?"

"I moved in after I saw you at the parade."

"Does Abby know?"

"Yes, she does."

Derek quickly added, "Finding out about moving the house is project number one. Number two, I need to see a good local real estate agent. Who would you recommend?"

"Well, I know a woman I think you'd like."

Derek took a notepad and a gold pen out of his pocket. "Got her name and number handy?"

"Her name's Stella Gill—" Greg began, then stopped.

Derek saw Greg's hesitation. Did Greg dislike the idea of his buying any more property in Devon? Or did this have something to do with his loyalty to Abby?

"Hang on a second," Greg said then. "I'll give Stella a buzz." He flipped through the phone book, then dialed a number.

"Stella?" he asked. "Greg Nickerson. Yeah, it has been a long time. How have you been?" He listened for a while, then said, "Good, Stella, I'm really glad to hear that. Now...I have a friend who's interested in looking at some property. If you're going to be in your office, I'd like to bring him over."

There was a pause, then Greg said, "Great. We'll see you in a few minutes." He hung up, looking satisfied. "All set," he reported.

"You don't have to go with me," Derek protested. "I didn't mean to drag you away from work."

"I'm glad of an excuse to take a break," Greg admitted. "Which'll it be, your car or my pickup?"

They drove to the realtors in Greg's pickup. On the way, Greg volunteered, "Stella and her husband came to town about ten years ago. She's about my age, Don was a couple of years older. He died a little over a year ago of leukemia.

I saw Stella at the funeral, and I've meant to call her ever since to see how she's getting along."

Stella Gill was a short, pretty brunette, as effervescent and outgoing as Greg was calm and contained. She greeted Greg with a hug and a kiss on the cheek. Derek was amused when Greg actually flushed.

So Greg's hesitation in contacting the real estate agent had been personal. Derek wondered how long it was since Greg had gone out with a woman on a real date.

Stella's eyes widened when Greg performed introductions and the Van Heusen name registered. But she was professional. "How may I be of help?" she asked Derek.

"I'm interested in finding a few acres of undeveloped land," Derek told her. "Doesn't have to be waterfront."

Stella thought about that and said, "I have several listings you might be interested in. I'd be glad to show them to you whenever you like."

Derek smiled. "Now would be fine."

"Then just let me leave a note for my associate, and we'll be on our way."

Greg excused himself, saying he had to get back to the shop.

For the next two hours, Stella Gill drove Derek around Devon in her white Mercedes. He'd thought he'd seen a fair bit of the town, but the realtor opened up new vistas. Despite condos, the Devon mall and two smaller shopping centers, much of the area was still remarkably undeveloped.

"The minimum lot size is one acre," Stella Gill explained. "That makes land more expensive, but it also keeps Devon from turning into just another congested area with one prefab house on top of the next."

As they drove along, Derek found unexpected glimpses of freshwater ponds and saltwater inlets, as well as views of both the Atlantic Ocean and Cape Cod Bay. Stella showed him several properties that were interesting, but when they came to the right one, Derek knew it immediately.

A sandy lane, flanked by pine woods, wound up and over shallow hills and around curves, and ended at the base of a grassy incline. Stella parked, then led Derek to the top.

He gazed down a gentle slope to a pond that looked like a sapphire in a verdant setting. Woods edged the slope and the pond. Derek felt he'd moved back into another century, this place was so peaceful and unspoiled, a haven for wildlife and birds.

"Beautiful, isn't it?" Stella said. "Each time I come out here, I wish I could buy it for myself."

Derek nodded. "It *is* beautiful."

He could visualize the Gould homestead standing exactly where he now stood.

"How many acres are there?" he asked.

"Seven and a half. But you get a plus, because the far side of the pond is conservation land. It will never be built on."

"I want this," Derek decided.

Stella Gill laughed. "I haven't even told you the price, Mr. Van Heusen."

There were moments when Abby had made him feel brash because he had money. Though he knew he was going to buy this land no matter what the price, Derek didn't want to come across that way to Stella. He'd already made enough enemies in Devon. He didn't need any more.

"Well," he suggested diplomatically, "suppose we go back to your office and talk it over?"

Chapter Fifteen

Derek headed for the Devon Mall after he left Stella Gill's office. The shopping center was not enormous, but it did have a good variety of stores, including an artist's supply shop. There was a project kindling in Derek's mind, and he wanted to get his ideas down on paper. He bought a large sketch pad and a selection of colored drawing pencils.

Wandering around the mall, he remembered that Abby had been in strong opposition to its construction, according to Gordon Ryder. As he glanced into a toy store window, then passed a pet shop where three gray angora kittens were playing with a ball of yarn, Derek wondered how Abby felt about the mall now. On this July Saturday, the place was teeming with shoppers, some obviously tourists, but many looking like locals.

The mall was tastefully designed—clean lines, a well-planned, uncluttered interior with wide corridors, subdued recessed lighting, a patio food court with a fountain surrounded by potted plants and trees, and benches where shoppers could relax and rest. It certainly seemed to fill a need, judging by the number of patrons.

Had Devon Mall's final aesthetic design—and the services, merchandise and jobs it offered the community—changed Abby's mind? Derek wondered about that and decided to ask her when the right moment arose.

In the Sierras, at the country store down the road from his cabin, he was seldom recognized. But in the Devon Mall, he discovered he was not entirely incognito. Now and then, a person or couple would turn when he walked by. Probably they'd either seen him at the town meeting or read about him in the local papers.

He stocked up on food and liquor supplies before heading back to the house, aware of the scrutiny, and disliking it. Yes, Devon *was* a small town. It would take being with someone like Abby to ever insure his acceptance here.

Toward sunset, Derek put on bathing trunks and climbed down the rickety steps to Mill Beach. The No Trespassing signs on the edges of the property were remarkably effective. There were a few stragglers wandering along the tide line, looking for shells, but he virtually had the beach and the bay to himself.

The shallow bay water was much milder than the frigid Atlantic on the other side of town, but was still invigorating. Derek swam for quite a while, then floated on his back as the sun touched the horizon and slowly sank from sight. The aftermath of sunset was a sky filled with colors far more incredible than the work of any artist. Nature's palette triumphed and made man's efforts seem paltry in comparison.

Derek felt refreshed as he climbed the stairs to the top of the bluff. But once he'd showered and dressed, he became restless. There was no joy in eating a solitary supper, even with a fantastic view for company.

He took a drink outside and watched as the sky turned dark blue and the stars came out. He thought of Abby and Greg and Bobby at the movies. Bobby would be gobbling a huge container of popcorn. Abby would be sharing. Derek could imagine her lips tasting of butter and salt, and wished he could sample their flavor.

Inside, he cleared the antiques off the kitchen table and packed the Christmas salts in a shoe box. Then he sat down with the sketch pad and drawing pencils and tried to convey his ideas to paper.

It didn't work. He was still too restless to focus his attention and accomplish what he wanted to do. He needed something more active at the moment and settled for exploring a part of the house he hadn't yet visited.

There was a steep flight of stairs behind one of the second-floor bedrooms. Ascending them, flashlight in hand, Derek emerged into the long, low-ceilinged attic. He made his way to the single light bulb suspended from the rafters, pulled its cord, and a soft yellow glow spread around him.

Derek saw old trunks, furniture and boxes. He opened one of the trunks and found a white satin dress that had yellowed with age. Clara Gould's wedding dress, maybe?

He opened a box and saw photographs, many printed in sepia tones on heavy stock. There were pictures of the homestead. Pictures of Devon Mill. Pictures of a tall, lean man standing in front of the mill. Randolph Gould, perhaps?

There was a studio portrait of a young woman in a bridal gown, and, despite the years that had passed since it was taken, Derek knew at once it was Clara Gould. He suspected that the dress she was wearing was, indeed, the dress in the trunk.

He took an assortment of photographs back downstairs. Finally he felt relaxed enough to sit at the kitchen table and start working with the sketch pad and pencil.

Tomorrow, he would visit Clara—and share his new ideas.

The water was rough, Sunday morning, once the *Rainha* cleared Provincetown Harbor. For a while, Abby was afraid she was going to have a seasick kid on her hands, and felt a little queasy herself. But once the guide started shouting, "Whale off the starboard bow!" she and Bobby forgot about their unsettled stomachs and got caught up in the thrill of the adventure. The humpback whales living in the Atlantic off Race Point were magnificent creatures, truly spectacular.

Back on land, Abby insisted that Bobby have something nutritious for lunch before she let him splurge on ice cream and candy. Later, as they strolled along Commercial Street, she was wishing she'd invited Derek to join them today and didn't know why she hadn't. Bobby would have loved having Derek along, just as Derek—she was beginning to realize—would have loved being along.

The hazy sunshine had given way to clouds by the time she and Bobby headed for McMillan Wharf, where she'd parked the Volks. Rain started spattering down just as they reached the car.

"We lucked out," Bobby observed, once they were moving. "Boy, did you ever see anything as *big* as that one whale that came up close to the boat?"

"Never," she answered absently. They were driving past La Chamarita. Suddenly she wanted to be with Derek so much that the yearning became a physical hurt.

"Bobby," she said, "there's a bookstore in the next block. If I can find a spot to park, I'm going to dash in for a couple of minutes. Just stay in the car, okay?"

"Sure," Bobby nodded. "What kind of book are you going to buy? Something for us to read?"

She smiled. "Not this time, Bobby. I just want to get a present for someone."

"A birthday present?"

"No. Just sort of a special present."

Derek glanced at the kitchen clock. It was a little past one. Clara Gould would have had her lunch—or Sunday dinner, as the case might be—by now. He put the shoe box and a few other things for Clara into a plastic shopping bag and drove to Devon Manor.

Clara was sitting in her chair by the window, crocheting. Derek knocked on the open door, then entered the room.

Clara brightened at once. "I didn't expect to see you again so soon, Mr. Van Heusen. Is your architect with you?"

"Mrs. Casey is coming down from Boston tomorrow. I'll bring her to see you sometime during the week. Today, it's my turn."

He pulled up a chair close to Clara and announced, "I have a couple of surprises for you. Ready?"

"What kind of surprises?"

Derek brought out the picture of Clara in her wedding dress. Clara took it and held it gingerly. "Where did you ever get this?" she asked, astonished.

"From a trunk in your attic, Clara...Mrs. Gould, I mean."

"You can call me Clara, Derek," she said impishly.

Derek smiled, and could imagine what a delightful flirt she must have been back in the days when Randolph Gould was courting her. "Clara, then," he agreed, and went on. "Clara, I don't know whether or not your nephew's been in touch with you—"

"Gordon called yesterday, but I was in the recreation room playing bridge, so the nurse took a message."

Bridge, at ninety! This lady did have her wits about her.

"Well," Derek said, wishing he knew of the best way to lead into this, "I decided to move into your house."

"It's *your* house," she corrected him. "And I'm so glad you're doing that. Houses are meant to be lived in."

"Clara...the thing is, I wanted to keep the house the same. Like it was when you lived there. I asked about acquiring the furnishings, and your nephew agreed that would be a practical way to go."

"I see." Clara was peering at the shopping bag. "What are those other photographs?"

Derek held out the pictures one by one, and Clara identified them. "This is Randolph," she said tenderly, pointing to the tall man standing by the mill. "And look at this one." She held out a photo of several people sitting on a checkered tablecloth on the lawn behind the kitchen. "We were having a Fourth of July picnic. See, right there? That's Abby's grandmother. Long before Abby was born."

Derek looked closely, and felt his throat tighten. Abby bore a strong resemblance to the young woman in the old photo. Uncanny, almost. There was that same beauty...and the same determined expression.

When Clara finished examining the pictures, Derek said, "As you know, there are a lot more where these came from. And letters, which, needless to say, I would never think of opening. Other memorabilia, too. I felt strange, Clara, even handling these photos. Like I was invading your privacy. But I thought you'd want to see them."

"You were absolutely right to look around, Derek," Clara said. She took his hand in hers and went on, "I like to think I'm a good judge of character. At my age, one should be. I knew you were a caring person the first time you walked into this room. It took someone special to come here and tell me he'd bought Devon Mill."

She added, "I'd love to see more of the pictures from time to time. And maybe a few letters once in a while, too. Suppose I appoint you my trustee, when it comes to those things?''

"I was going to pack up the personal photos and papers and give them to your nephew," Derek admitted.

Clara shook her head. "Gordon doesn't care that much about family, Derek. Frankly, Abby cares more about the Gould family history than he does."

Derek let that slide by and said, "Clara, I understand there are other things in your house you'd like to have. If you'll tell me what they are, I'll bring them out to you. Meantime, I did bring your collection of Christmas salts. I thought you might like to have them now."

Derek drew the shoe box out of the shopping bag. "They're in here," he said.

Clara's eyes misted, but her voice was steady. "You didn't have to do that."

"I wanted to."

"I wonder how you came to choose the Christmas salts?" she mused. "If I'd been asked, they're exactly what I would have wanted first."

"Tell me anything else you'd like, and I'll deliver it personally. Everything in the house, if you say so."

Clara laughed. "Even if it were possible, I wouldn't want that. The Christmas salts are special. Randolph gave them to me for our twenty-fifth anniversary, and they were quite a find even then. There may be one or two other things I'll think of I'd like to have. But mostly I wish you'd give a few antiques to Abby."

Derek put the shoe box aside and stared at Clara incredulously. "Are you psychic, Clara Gould?" he asked her, only half teasing. "That's exactly what I would like to do. In fact, I want to give everything to Abby."

Clara didn't seem surprised. "You're in love with each other, aren't you?" she inquired calmly.

Derek's smile was wry. "I'm in love with her. Sometimes I'd swear she feels the same way about me. But other times..."

"Abby's been through a lot, Derek. It's a terrible blow to a woman's pride when her husband walks out on her. Particularly when he runs off with one of her best friends.

"Don't misunderstand me," Clara added swiftly. "I don't think Abby ever truly loved Ken in the first place. They were high school sweethearts. That kind of infatuation seldom lasts."

"You and your husband were high school sweethearts, weren't you?"

Clara's eyes twinkled. "There are exceptions to every rule. But Abby and Ken...they weren't right for each other. When he left her, Abby's pride was hurt more than her heart was. Ken's going off as he did was damaging, nevertheless. It took a while for her to get over it. Sometimes I don't think Greg Nickerson's ever gotten over Sally leaving him. I don't know how many times Abby's told me she wishes Greg would even *start* to look at another woman."

"She may get her wish sooner than she thinks," Derek said. His smile was conspiratorial. "Want to share a little gossip, Clara?"

She chuckled. "Why not?"

"Yesterday, Greg introduced me to a lady named Stella Gill. I think he likes her."

"Stella and Greg. They'd be perfect for each other," Clara decided at once. She looked Derek right in the eye and added, "As you and Abby would be."

Derek couldn't believe what he was hearing. He said huskily, "Clara...Abby and I are very different."

"Surface differences," Clara scoffed. "I know you're rich and famous and she isn't. But with the two of you, I don't think that will matter."

"Neither do I. But whether or not Abby will agree is the big question. You've known Abby all her life, haven't you?"

Clara nodded. "Abby's grandmother was my best friend." She indicated the crocheting she'd set aside. "I made a crib blanket just like this for Abby when she was a baby.

"Abby was a lovely little girl," Clara continued. "And she grew into a beautiful woman. She's high-spirited, stubborn, opinionated—I love her dearly, so I can say those things about her. But she's also a wonderful, wonderful person...loyal and devoted to her friends, caring and considerate. If she ever really loves a man, he'll be lucky."

"I couldn't agree more," Derek murmured huskily.

"Then," Clara advised, "don't give up. Winning Abby won't be easy. But nothing worth having ever is."

A light rain was falling when Derek left Devon Manor. His route was familiar now. He drove up Mill Bluff Road and turned into Mill Lane as if he'd always lived there. Then he saw Abby's yellow car parked in the driveway by the house, and Abby standing at the kitchen door.

Derek pulled up behind her car just as she turned and started toward it. She saw him, stopped, and for a moment stood still, the rain dripping down the hood of her bright pink slicker. She was clutching something under the slicker, protecting it from the weather.

Looking at her, Derek felt a tremendous wistfulness and knew it would be so easy to imagine too much, too soon, where Abby was concerned. To spin a marvelous, happy-ever-after fantasy. But there were hurdles to be cleared before he could even begin to dream those dreams. He glanced toward the windmill. Devon Mill was only one of those hurdles.

The rain, though light, was quickly soaking his thin cotton shirt. He came abreast of Abby and said, "Come in, will you?'' He hoped she'd follow his lead. She'd had a reason for coming here, after all, even though she'd been on the verge of leaving when he drove up. He had to know what her reason was.

To Derek's relief, Abby followed. His wet shirt was clinging to his skin by the time they got to the kitchen. Inevitably he thought of the day when she'd spilled icy water on him as she was tending to the bump on his forehead.

Calendar-wise, it was such a short time ago. Yet it seemed to Derek like eons had passed since then. He'd traveled a lot of emotional roads with Abby, reached some very high peaks. A great deal had happened quickly between them. But that in no way lessened the depth and validity of his feelings for her.

Clara Gould had seen that.

He said, ''Abby, excuse me while I go put on a dry shirt, will you? Take off your slicker and make yourself at home.''

Abby's gaze followed him as he walked out of the room. Then she slipped off the pink slicker and hung it on a hook in the mud room off the kitchen. As she did so, it occurred to her that she was as familiar with this house as she was with her cottage—and loved it so much more.

She took the package she'd been holding under the slicker and set it on the kitchen table. As she did so, her eyes fell on a sketch pad covered with drawings. The drawings looked as if they'd been executed hastily. They had none of the finesse of Sheila Casey's sketches. Yet there was a certain boldness to them, as if the person who'd drawn them knew exactly what he was doing.

Curious, she saw a diagram that looked familiar—to a point. Her eyes widened as she focused on a sketch of the Devon Voyager, but a Voyager with significant differences. The conference center had been moved back from the bluff so that it fronted on Mill Bluff Road. Mill Lane ended not in a loop, but at a rectangle marked ''Mill Parking.'' To the right of the parking lot, slashing lines indicated a rise, and at the top of the rise she saw printed "Mill Park." Beyond that, there was a circle. And in the middle of the circle, the single word "Mill."

Abby heard Derek's footsteps behind her. She turned and faced him. He'd put on a shirt that nearly matched his eyes and combed his hair to gleaming smoothness. No man had a right to be so irresistibly attractive, she thought shakily. Then she saw that he was looking beyond her at the sketch on the table.

"If I'd known you were coming, I'd have put that away," he said frankly.

She was almost afraid to ask the question. "What does it represent?"

Derek's smile was rueful. "I've been thinking of ways to have my cake and eat it, too." He shrugged and admitted, "You've won, Abby. I don't think I can stand to see your mill carted off as scrap lumber."

"I'm not following you."

"The damn thing's grown on me. It fascinates me. Though obviously it will have to be moved."

Abby shook her head wearily. "We've been that route."

"Moved about two hundred feet from where it now stands," Derek cut in, before she could go any further. "I called Greg earlier. He's meeting with me tomorrow morning so we can get down to basics about what can and can't be done. Sheila Casey will be coming down tomorrow afternoon, and she'll be around most of the week. I want her to take those ideas I've sketched there," he pointed to the drawing pad, "and make sense of them.

"Believe," he said softly, when Abby looked skeptical. Then he saw the package, wrapped in blue-and-white paper. "What's that?" he asked.

Abby picked up the package and handed it to him. "Something I picked up for you in P-town."

Derek tore off the wrapping and uncovered a large book with a glossy cover. He read, *A Complete Guide to American Antiques,* and flipped through the pages. They were loaded with full-color illustrations and descriptive paragraphs, everything arranged in alphabetical order.

"Thank you," he said softly, touched not alone by the gift, but by this evidence that even when she'd been out whale-watching with Bobby she was thinking of him.

"I thought it might help," Abby said. She waved a vague hand in a gesture meant to encompass everything. "You can begin looking your things up, one by one."

He closed the book, set it down and decided it was almost time to tell her that Clara's treasures weren't his. They were hers.

Almost, but not quite.

He made a sudden decision and said, "Put your slicker back on, Abby, and come with me. There's something I want to show you."

"Now?"

"Yes." Certainly, Derek thought wryly, the weather wasn't ideal. But it would have to do—because he couldn't wait any longer.

He'd found an old yellow slicker in the mud room that he suspected might have belonged to Randolph Gould. It was far more waterproof than anything he owned. He slipped into it, then held the back door open for Abby.

"Make a run for it," he urged. "The car doors aren't locked."

He watched Abby sprint toward the driveway and wondered what it would be like to make love to her in the rain. The imaginary picture was enough to threaten his composure.

Abby sank into the car's comfortable leather upholstery and asked, "Where are we going?"

"Wait and see."

"I'd like to know, Derek. Where are you taking me?"

"That's a hard question to answer," he said, as he drove out onto Mill Bluff Road. "It depends somewhat on your point of view. And maybe on how you feel about paradise."

"You're talking in riddles."

"Not entirely." He tried to divert her. "How was the whale watch?"

"Wonderful. I wished I'd asked you to go along. Derek, where are we going?"

"I think we may be climbing over the rainbow," Derek said. "But I'm not sure."

Abby thought she'd been on every road in Devon, but the private sandy lane onto which Derek finally turned was new to her. She frowned as they drove up and down hills and around curves, and finally came to a stop before a grassy field flanked by pine woods.

"Why are we stopping here?" she asked suspiciously.

The rain was still falling lightly. The view might not be nearly so beautiful in the rain as it was in the sunlight, Derek feared, as he led her up the incline to the top. Then saw his fears were groundless.

There was mist over the trees on the other side of the pond. The pond was a gray pearl instead of a sapphire. But the scene was still enchanted, and he could imagine how it would be in the autumn, when the oaks and maples among the pines flared with scarlet and yellow and orange. And in winter, when nature painted everything white.

"Isn't this private property, Derek?" He saw Abby was still frowning.

"That depends," he said quietly. "I'd like to think it's where you and I will spend a considerable amount of time together. Years, in fact." He scraped a bit of grass with his foot. "I imagine Clara's living room being right about here. Which would put the dining room to our right, and the kitchen over here. The stairs,'' he said, pointing, ''would be about there. And . . .''

"You're thinking of moving the Gould homestead *here*?"

"Yes."

"I—I can't imagine that."

"Then suppose I help you." Derek moved close to her, put an arm around her and gently tugged her to his side. "What I'm seeing," he said softly, "is a chance to borrow the best from the past and bring it into the present. And then incorporate it in our future. I see us here, Abby, raising our kids. Experiencing the whole gamut of emotions people experience, who live full lives. Most important of all, I see us *together*."

Abby tried to push away from him, but he held her fast. She protested, "You're going too fast for me."

"I can slow down if I have to, sweetheart. Though I don't want to. There's so much I want to say to you, it may take forever as it is."

"Derek?"

He had to bend to hear her.

"I'm getting the impression," she said, "that you're either asking me to live with you, or marry you."

"Your impression is right."

This time she did push away, stared up at him, her eyes wide and actually frightened. "Either living with you or marrying you would be out of the question."

"Why do you say that?"

"Because there's no way we could join our lives, that's why." She faced him squarely, unconsciously pushing the hood just far enough back from her forehead so that raindrops trickled down her cheeks. "Derek, there's no way we could join our lives. And that's what you're talking about, isn't it?"

"Of course it's what I'm talking about. Except, if you've no objection, I would like this particular negotiation to conclude with marriage. I want this to be a forever thing, Abby.''

Abby shook her head. She looked miserable and bewildered. Derek knew he had to be patient with her, but his nerves were fraying, and he felt so choked with emotion he was hoarse.

He watched Abby close her eyes, then open them again. He wondered if maybe action would be effective where words weren't, but knew, right now, that that wasn't the case. Abby had to work her way through this.

She stammered, "This is . . . impossible. We're as different as any two people in the world possibly could be.''

Derek took the liberty of quoting Clara Gould. "I'll admit we're different," he said, his voice sounding like he was about to develop a bad case of laryngitis. "But . . . they're only surface differences.''

"Derek, I live in Devon. I'm a third-grade teacher. I lead a simple, uneventful life.''

She'd *led* a simple, uneventful life, Abby corrected herself. Until, not that long ago, a tall, impossibly handsome man had walked across the town hall lobby, and into her life.

Derek said, "I'll be honest with you, sweetheart. If anyone had told me I'd be proposing to you at this stage in our relationship, I would have said they were crazy. But, you see . . . I didn't choose the time, I didn't choose the weather.''

He glanced up at the sky, then turned to look deep into her eyes. "Abby, dammit, I'll get down on my knees in the rain and beg you, if it'll help.''

She sniffed. "You're being . . . ridiculous.''

"Maybe," he allowed. "Sometimes it's difficult to be logical when you love someone so much, you're sure you'll go crazy if you try to keep on living without them. That's the way I feel about you, Abby." He took a deep breath. "How do you feel about me?''

Abby closed her eyes again. The rain caressed her lids.

Derek fought the impulse to kiss the raindrops away. He thought she was never going to speak.

Then, finally, she said, "I love you. Oh, yes, I love you, Derek. When I'm not with you, it's like God took the stars out of the sky, and everything's dark. But..."

Derek couldn't wait any longer. He took her in his arms, and the rain was like a benediction as he kissed her.

The kiss—he felt, he wished—could go on forever. But after a moment Abby broke away, faced him again.

She struggled with the words she had to say to him. She was determined not to blurt out something she'd later wish she could take back.

"I'm not sure love would be enough," she told him honestly. "Say what you will, but the differences between us are...pretty tremendous. I'm not sure I could keep up with your life-style. I'm not sure I could keep up with *you*. One day you might find me dull and boring. And if that happened, my whole world would end."

Derek's laugh rang out freely. "You—dull and boring?" He shook his head. "Sweetheart, you're going to be a hard act to follow *around,* let alone follow."

Then he sobered. "Abby, I wouldn't want you to give up anything. I know how much your teaching means to you. I'd want you to continue with it. I suppose there are logistics to be worked out, but I'm used to dealing with logistics. I see no reason why I couldn't move Van Heusen Inc.'s headquarters to Boston and put San Francisco in the number two slot. Those are all compromises. Probably we'll both have to make compromises."

The rain began to come down harder. Abby stood mute. Derek didn't know whether to shake her, or test his theory about what it might be like to make love under these weather conditions.

Finally he said, "Thank God these slickers are waterproof. But my feet are sopping. Could we go home and slip into something dry and talk this over?"

Home.

Abby took the word out of context and turned it over in her mind. Derek, she saw, was already thinking of the Gould homestead as "home." The house she'd always loved the most.

The thought of living in the homestead—whether here, on this beautiful land, or on the bluff—was so wonderful that it boggled her mind. But she knew, suddenly that "home" meant a lot more than a house...so very much more.

Home would be where Derek was. Home would be with Derek.

She still couldn't imagine being his wife. But now...it was far more difficult to think of *not* being his wife.

She looked up at him and said, "Derek..."

"What is it, sweetheart?"

"Derek, I'll do my damnedest."

She didn't have to finish. He knew what she meant.

He smiled at her. "You don't have to do your damnedest," he said. "All you have to do is be you."

Abby looked at him, saw the love in his eyes, and suddenly nothing else mattered. This might be crazy, utterly crazy...but it was also right.

She smiled up at him, a smile of infinite tenderness, and held out her hand.

"Come on," Abby said. "Suppose we go home."

*   *   *   *   *

proudly presents
the long-awaited ''prequel'' volume of

★ LOVE AND GLORY ★

by
LINDSAY McKENNA

Dawn of Valor

In the summer of '89, Silhouette Special Edition premiered three novels celebrating America's men and women in uniform: LOVE AND GLORY, by bestselling author Lindsay McKenna. Featured were the proud Trayherns, a military family as bold and patriotic as the American flag—three siblings valiantly battling the threat of dishonor, determined to triumph . . . in love and glory.

Now, discover the roots of the Trayhern brand of courage, as parents Chase and Rachel relive their earliest heartstopping experiences of survival and indomitable love, in

Dawn of Valor, Silhouette Special Edition #649.

This February, experience the thrill of LOVE AND GLORY—from the very beginning!

Silhouette Books

SILHOUETTE·INTIMATE·MOMENTS®

NORA ROBERTS
Night Shadow

People all over the city of Urbana were asking, Who was that masked man?

Assistant district attorney Deborah O'Roarke was the first to learn his secret identity . . . and her life would never be the same.

The stories of the lives and loves of the O'Roarke sisters began in January 1991 with NIGHT SHIFT, Silhouette Intimate Moments #365. And if you want to know more about Deborah and the man behind the mask, look for NIGHT SHADOW, Silhouette Intimate Moments #373, available in March at your favorite retail outlet.

NITE-1

Silhouette Books®

SILHOUETTE·INTIMATE·MOMENTS®

FEBRUARY
FROLICS!

This February, we've got a special treat in store for you: four
terrific books written by four brand-new authors! From
sunny California to North Dakota's frozen plains, they'll
whisk you away to a world of romance and adventure.

Look for

L.A. HEAT (IM #369) by Rebecca Daniels
AN OFFICER AND A GENTLEMAN (IM #370) by Rachel Lee
HUNTER'S WAY (IM #371) by Justine Davis
DANGEROUS BARGAIN (IM #372) by Kathryn Stewart

They're all part of February Frolics, coming to you from
Silhouette Intimate Moments—where life is exciting and
dreams do come true.

FF-1

Take 4 bestselling love stories FREE

Plus get a FREE surprise gift!

Special Limited-time Offer

Silhouette Reader Service®

Mail to

In the U.S.
3010 Walden Avenue
P.O. Box 1867
Buffalo, N.Y. 14269-1867

In Canada
P.O. Box 609
Fort Erie, Ontario
L2A 5X3

YES! Please send me 4 free Silhouette Special Edition® novels and my free surprise gift. Then send me 6 brand-new novels every month, which I will receive months before they appear in bookstores. Bill me at the low price of $2.74* each—a savings of 21¢ apiece off cover prices. There are no shipping, handling or other hidden costs. I understand that accepting the books and gift places me under no obligation ever to buy any books. I can always return a shipment and cancel at any time. Even if I never buy another book from Silhouette, the 4 free books and the surprise gift are mine to keep forever.

*Offer slightly different in Canada—$2.74 per book plus 69¢ per shipment for delivery. Sales tax applicable in N.Y. Canadian residents add applicable federal and provincial sales tax.

235 BPA R1YY (US)   335 BPA 8178 (CAN)

Name _____ (PLEASE PRINT)

Address _____ Apt. No. _____

City _____ State/Prov. _____ Zip/Postal Code _____

This offer is limited to one order per household and not valid to present Silhouette Special Edition® subscribers. Terms and prices are subject to change.

SPED-BPADR   © 1990 Harlequin Enterprises Limited

Silhouette romances are now available in stores at these convenient times each month.

Silhouette Desire
Silhouette Romance

These two series will be in stores on the 4th of every month.

Silhouette Intimate Moments
Silhouette Special Edition

New titles for these series will be in stores on the 16th of every month.

We hope this new schedule is convenient for you. With only two trips each month to your local bookseller, you will always be sure not to miss any of your favorite authors!

Happy reading!

Please note there may be slight variations in on-sale dates in your area due to differences in shipping and handling.

SDATES